Hidden Betrayal

Book 1

O'Connor Girls

RHONDA BREWER

Dedication

This book is dedicated to my granddaughter Emma. She makes me smile every day with her energy and giggles.

Acknowledgements

With so many people in my life to thank for making publishing this book possible, I could almost write another book on that alone. However, a simple thank you never seems like enough to convey my gratitude but I will try to do that the best I can with this acknowledgement.

First thank you belongs to the many authors who have become both friends and mentors to me. Then there are the amazing ladies who help with editing and errors. A very special thank you goes to Michelle Eriksen, Abbie Zanders, and Amabel Daniels for their constant support and keen eye. To my dedicated betas and dear friends, Jackie Dawe Ford, Nancy Arnold-Holloway, and Karie Deegan thank you so much for the support and constant encouragement. To my readers, you are the reason that I can continue to do this.

A very special thank you to my husband, Danny who gives me the inspiration for the romantic heroes I write and encourages me every day. To my two children Laura and Colin, both of you show me everyday how proud you are and how much you love me. To my beautiful granddaughter, Emma. You may not be old enough to read yet, but your smile gives me inspiration to keep going. I love all of you.

Chapter 1

Dean 'Bull' Nash must have been a terrible person in a previous life because it was the only explanation. There was no other reason to torture a man with such a formidable weapon.

Kristy O'Connor was too young or at least it was his excuse to avoid her. The truth was, he was ready to cave but family shit brought that to a grinding halt. It was the number one reason he needed to stay away from the auburn-haired angel who drove him to the brink of insanity.

To further complicate things, the blue-eyed beauty was his best friend and business partner's cousin. Keith O'Connor and his six brothers were protective of all four female cousins. Kristy didn't seem concerned about any of them, and she'd made it very clear she wanted Dean.

He almost throat punched his friend when Keith paired him with Kristy for the wedding. Since Keith's new wife, Emily wanted the bridal party to dance together for some silly song about friendship. Dean was forced to be closer to Kristy then he'd ever allowed himself to get since the first day he met her. She smelled like apples and even eating the damn fruit made him hard because it reminded him of her.

"I know you're not gay." She gazed up at him with a flirty smile and nodded to the photographer behind them.

"Never said I was." Dean forced a happy face for the picture.

"I also have it on good authority you aren't involved with anyone." Kristy pressed her body closer to his.

"And who's authority would that be?" Dean didn't need to ask because he knew the source.

Sandy Churchill O'Connor was married to Ian, another of the O'Connor brothers, and she was one of the best computer analysts in the country. Newfoundland Security Services was damn lucky to have her, but she pissed Dean off when she gave Kristy information about him. Sandy seemed to think it was her duty to get him and Kristy together.

"That's not important. I just wonder why you won't go out with me." Damn the woman was direct and it was one of the things he respected about her.

Kristy didn't play childish games, but it was uncomfortable when she made her thoughts known no matter who was in ear shot.

"Maybe I'm not interested." He glanced down.

Huge mistake. Kristy's beautiful blue gaze met his, and it became hard to breathe. His heart pounded, and his cock had a mind of its own.

Every fucking time.

"I can feel your interest. That's not a gun in your pants, Dean" She swayed her hips against him and smirked when a curse escaped under his breath.

"Don't. Do. That." He growled through clenched teeth.

"Give me a good reason why and not the bullshit about the age difference. That's crap because six years is nothing." She grazed her nails across the back of his neck. His eyes closed involuntarily, as he struggled to control the shiver her touch caused.

"Kitten, you might think I'm interested, but I'm not. You're beautiful, and you've got an incredible body. I'm a red-blooded man. When you press yourself against me, it's gonna affect any man. That doesn't mean I'm looking for anything more than sex." Dean wanted to kick himself in the balls when pain flared in her eyes.

"What makes you think I want more than a good fuck?" Kristy stepped back as the song ended. "But I guess you're too old and probably wouldn't be able to keep up. Maybe I need to check out some of the younger hotties around here." Kristy spun around, took two steps away from him and turned back.

Her eyes glistened with unshed tears, and it was the same as a knife to his chest. No matter how much he wanted to take everything back, He couldn't give in. Not now. It was the way it had to be.

"Thanks for the dance, Bull." For her to call him by his nickname drove the knife deeper. She'd told him once Dean suited him much better. "I guess I'll see you around." Then she was gone.

Dean stomped toward the bar because he needed to drink away the emptiness in his heart. With the pain in Kristy's eyes, he knew he'd finally pushed her away. He almost made it to the bartender when a hand clamped down on his shoulder.

"You look like you need this." Ian held out a shot glass filled with a dark liquid.

"Thanks," Dean took the glass and gulped it down his throat without a second thought.

"You okay, Bull?" Ian glanced toward the dance floor.

"Tired, it's been a long week." It wasn't a lie, but it wasn't the truth either.

"No shit, but I've never seen Keith smile like that." Ian nodded toward the middle of the room where Keith and Emily waltzed around the dance floor as if they were the only two people there.

"It's good to see him happy." Dean and Keith had been friends more than ten years. He met the rest of the family when he and Keith moved their security firm back to their home province of Newfoundland.

4

"Something on your mind, big guy?" Ian had become a good friend as well. All the O'Connor men were like brothers to Dean, but he still wasn't ready to discuss his secrets with Ian. Keith was already concerned, and Dean didn't want the entire O'Connor clan pulled into his drama.

"Lots but nothing I care to talk about." Dean didn't mean to sound rude, but from Ian's grin, the doctor was about to be dragged away by his hot little wife.

"Hey, Chrome Dome, can I steal this sex on a stick for a dance." Sandy sidled up next to Ian and pinched her husband's ass. He didn't mind that Sandy continued to call him by that ridiculous nickname. He was bald after all.

"Good luck with that, Ian." Dean chuckled as the couple walked away.

"You think Sandy's ever gonna drop that shit." James O'Connor chuckled from behind him.

"Which shit are you talking about?" Dean laughed.

"Chrome Dome." James chuckled.

"Probably not. Has that woman ever changed her mind?" Dean leaned against the bar.

"That would be a hell no." James held up two fingers, and the cute little bartender set two bottles of beer in front of them. James handed one to Dean.

"You guys are dropping like flies." Dean glanced around the room. The number of O'Connor brothers who were now married was more than half.

"I think it might be contagious." Marina smiled as she tucked herself under James' arm.

"Jesus, is there a shot I can get." Dean laughed.

"You're not funny, Dean Nash." Marina poked him in the chest. "Why are you here and not dancing with… ummm…. Someone?"

"I'm not a big dancer." He lied because the truth was he loved to dance.

"Liar," Stephanie surprised him from behind. The cute blonde was married to James' twin brother John.

"Hey, I am not." Dean would have poked her back, but she was pregnant, and with his luck, he'd poke the baby instead.

"I seem to remember you not leaving the dance floor at Ian and Sandy's wedding last year." Stephanie narrowed her eyes.

"I must've been drunk." Dean chuckled.

"You were not, but this conversation isn't over. I need to talk to Mike for a minute." Stephanie pointed her finger at his face and waddled away.

"You know you shouldn't piss off a pregnant woman, right?" John nudged him as he joined the small circle of O'Connors that now surrounded him.

"Don't you mean, you shouldn't piss off any woman?" Nick O'Connor ducked when Marina tried to slap the back of his head. He was the second youngest of the brothers and one of the wild ones.

"And Nick just demonstrated how to piss off any woman." Aaron 'A.J.' O'Connor, the youngest of the seven brothers, wrapped his arm around Marina but soon moved when James gave him that 'get your hands off my woman' glare.

It was incredible how well the family got along. Sure, they bickered, joked and teased each other, but the truth was they'd die to protect those they loved.

Then there were their parents, aunts, uncles and their fantastic grandmother. They treated Dean as if he was one of the family. Cora was a little odd and tried her best to convince him he belonged with Kristy. She was supposed to have some freaky gift that told her when couples belonged together. The family called her Cora the Cupid.

Dean didn't believe it or pretended he didn't. He couldn't bring Kristy into his life. Not when she didn't even know his true identity. The deceit could turn her against him, and that was his fear. He couldn't keep it hidden forever, and it was a miracle Sandy hadn't let it slip to anyone. That was probably Keith's influence because when Dean first told them who his family was, and why he had to keep it quiet, they both agreed.

Dean couldn't reveal anything to the rest of his friends now especially with the printed stories about his father and his questionable business associates.

It may cost him a lifetime of happiness with Kristy, but he had to protect his family. He couldn't leave it all up to what was left of his family and bringing Kristy into a media frenzy was the last thing the O'Connor family needed.

He'd spent so much of the last ten years out of the public eye, and technically nobody even knew what happened to Augustus Dean Decker.

Such a fucked up life.

Chapter 2

Kristy O'Connor sat on the front porch of her sister's little house and gazed across the street at Hopedale Beach. She loved to spend time at Isabelle's place; she particularly liked to watch the waves crash onto the rocks. The sound and the smell of the beach soothed her.

Isabelle's house was one of five buildings on Beach Street. Her cousin John, his wife, and two children lived next door to Isabelle. The sailing club and her uncle Sean O'Connor's medical clinic were on the opposite end of the road. The other house centered between the medical office and her sister's place was for sale, but it needed a lot of work. Isabelle now referred to the little house as 'the shack.'

As far as Kristy was concerned the house would be beautiful if someone would take the time to see the beauty of it. The view itself was worth the headache to fix it, but that wasn't what she had on her mind at that moment.

She glanced down at the envelope she'd placed on her lap over an hour before. She'd read it over and over for more than a year. So much so she knew it by heart. The card from Dean congratulated her on her graduation from nursing school more than a year ago.

Dean didn't bother to give it to her himself. Probably because he was busy with what she believed was a woman because he ran off every chance he got. At Keith's wedding, she made sure Dean was aware he didn't have to leave Hopedale to find a woman that wanted him, but he lied and said he wasn't interested.

Kristy wasn't egotistical, but she was aware when a man wanted her, and Dean Nash did. She didn't know why he fought their undeniable chemistry. What bothered her the most was what he said at Keith's wedding. It was the first time in her life that she knew how it felt to have a shattered heart.

She avoided him ever since and went as far as to take a date to Mike's wedding the previous week. Not that the ass even saw her with Todd because after the ceremony Dean disappeared. What a difference a year made.

"Why don't you move here and live on my front porch?" Isabelle shouted from the sidewalk.

Her sister owned one of the two restaurants in Hopedale and finally hired someone to help in the evenings, so she didn't have to work from open to close. Isabelle didn't give up her control easy because it took six months of interviews before she finally hired a guy and it sounded as if things worked out.

"Maybe I'll move into the shack." Kristy hitched her thumb over her shoulder towards the house next door.

"I'm sure Keith could keep it from falling down around your head." Isabelle laughed.

Her cousin Keith owned a construction company and often got hired to complete renovations on the older homes in Hopedale. He also ran a very successful security firm he co-owned with none other than Dean.

"How's business?" Kristy asked her sister when Isabelle stepped up on the porch.

"A little slow today but it's steady." She flopped down on the bench next to Kristy and snatched the envelope from her lap.

"Stop torturing yourself with this. It's Bull's loss. Move on and find someone who knows how great you are. How about that hottie you took to Mike's wedding?" Isabelle shook the envelope in her face.

Todd was a nice guy, and her sister wasn't wrong about him being hot, but there was no zing with him. Not like she got with one look from Dean. Doctor or not, Todd wasn't what she wanted. It was hard to explain especially to her big sister.

"I'm moving on as a matter of fact…." Kristy held up her phone.

"What's that?" Isabelle stared at the email. "Aunt Cora told me about a temporary position in a long-term care home just outside St. John's." Kristy shoved her sister with her shoulder.

"You're going to work in an old age home and move to Tors Cove?" Isabelle's eyes grew so big Kristy thought they might pop out of her head.

"It's only for a month, and it's not all seniors. Some are terminally ill and can't be cared for at home anymore." It wasn't Kristy's ideal position, but it gave her more experience. Plus, the money was decent, and she wouldn't run into Dean as often.

She'd been a nurse for over a year, and the call-in list for the hospitals only gave her a shift or two every couple of weeks. It was difficult to get a full-time nursing position unless you wanted to leave Newfoundland and she wasn't that desperate to get away from Dean. Yet.

If she stayed in Hopedale, she couldn't avoid him. He lived in one of the bunkhouses on Keith's property and thanks to her grandmother he always attended family functions. A month wasn't a long time, but the distance from Dean could help her get over him. Maybe.

"When do you leave?" Isabelle asked.

"In two weeks." Kristy smiled. "But you should know I'll be here until I leave and I'm storing the furniture from my apartment in your shed."

Technically she would have had to stay with Isabelle for a short time even if she hadn't gotten this job. Her landlord had decided to sell his house but before she had a chance to find another place, Cora called her. She was ready to move out of the city anyway.

"Well, isn't that nice of me to offer that to you." Isabelle chuckled.

"I know. You're one of the two best sisters in the world." Kristy wrapped an arm around Isabelle and hugged her.

"Let me guess; Jess is the other?" Isabelle rested her cheek against Kristy's head.

"You're still my favorite." Kristy smiled. "But don't tell Jess."

Jess recently enrolled in the police academy. To the family's surprise, it was something she'd wanted to do, but she hesitated because she was afraid to disappoint her father if she didn't do well. Kurt O'Connor was an incredible dad, but as a highly decorated police officer and the current Chief of Police, she had some pretty big shoes to fill.

"She'd kick your ass." Isabelle grinned.

"I wonder how she's doing with training." Kristy hadn't spoken to the middle sister in a few days. Since Jess started training, the sisters didn't get to talk every day. Kristy never went more than a day without a text or a phone call from Isabelle or Jess, so it was a little bizarre not to hear from Jess.

"She's supposed to Facetime tonight, and she'll be back in Hopedale for the weekend." Isabelle stood up and stretched.

"Maybe we can have a sister's night while she's home. I know St. John's is only ten minutes away, but it's probably the last chance we'll get to do it before I leave for Tors Cove." Kristy followed Isabelle into the house.

"We can get Pam to join us too. I don't know what's up her ass lately, but she's wound up tighter than a drum." Isabelle said.

Pam was Cora's only child and arrived back in Hopedale out of the blue more than a year ago. She'd lived on the mainland since she left at the age of twenty. Pam still hadn't told anyone why she'd come home so abruptly. Even Keith was in the dark and out of all the cousins she was closest to him.

"She needs a good stiff one." Kristy wiggled her eyebrows.

"You're terrible." Isabelle shook her head.

"What? She needs a good stiff drink. Get your mind out of the gutter." Kristy pointed her finger at her sister.

"Yeah, ok sure. I'll get Dominic to take over early Friday." Isabelle pulled her phone from her pocket.

Kristy took the chance to call Cora to thank her for the lead on the job. Her aunt ran a very successful private care and physical

14

therapy business. She had connections with a lot of the hospitals, and homes all over the province.

Cora was another reason Kristy was so torn up over Dean. The family cupid swore Kristy belonged with Dean and she'd never been wrong before. It was hard to believe it when year after year passed, and the only thing she got was an aching heart.

"Hello." Her aunt sounded distracted.

"Hi Aunt Cora, it's Kristy."

"Hi sweetie. I was just finishing up some contracts." Cora was her father's sister. She was kind of quirky but always had a smile.

"I won't keep you. I wanted to thank you for letting me know about Comfort Life Care Center."

"I don't know anyone better suited for the job." Cora chuckled.

"I know it's temporary, but at least it's more experience." Kristy wasn't technically unemployed because along with the few shifts she got from the hospital, Kristy helped at her mother's pub until she got a full-time nursing position.

"I'll keep my eye out for you while you're out there. I'd love to have you work with us, but I'm fully staffed at the moment." Cora said.

"That'd be great. Thanks again Aunt Cora." Kristy loved the thought of a position with, Nightingale's Private Care and Therapy but she didn't care as long as she got to do what she loved.

"Don't worry, Kristy. He'll come around." Cora didn't give Kristy a chance to respond. "I've got to run, but I'll see you Sunday at Sean and Kathleen's place."

Her uncle and aunt held the monthly family dinner at their house for years. Attendance was mandatory unless you were close to death or off the island. It had become so much more than a family thing over the last few years.

Not only did the entire O'Connor family attend, but so did the families of her cousins' wives and the men that worked for Keith and Dean.

According to Nanny Betty, it was okay if the guys were on jobs and couldn't attend but when they weren't, it was mandatory for them as well. If they didn't her grandmother would hunt them down with her text messages and explain why no wasn't acceptable.

It wasn't that Kristy didn't enjoy her family or even everyone else. To see Dean and not show how he'd ripped out her heart was difficult. Not that he'd ever know that. She'd become a pro hiding how she felt about him.

"Did I tell you I love Dominic Cook?" Isabelle slipped her phone into her back pocket.

"Ummm… isn't he married?" Kristy laughed.

16

"Yes, and his wife is fine with me loving him. The fact that she's his sous chef helps." Isabelle laughed.

"You hired his wife too?" Kristy didn't realize her sister had hired more than a new chef.

"Petra applied for a job first and told me about her husband." Isabelle plopped down on the couch.

"Do you want to help me find a cheap apartment in Tors Cove?" Kristy sat next to her and opened her laptop.

"Why it's not that far of a drive from Tors Cove to Hopedale. Fifteen minutes or maybe twenty if the weather is sucky." Isabelle propped her feet up on the coffee table.

"I'll be working twelve-hour shifts. I don't want to have to drive back and forth when I'm working."

"We live such exciting lives." Isabelle sighed.

"Shut up. The male O'Connors can keep all the drama." Kristy shuddered.

Over the last few years, five of her male cousins might have found love and started families, but it wasn't without danger and near-death experiences. They were happy, but Kristy wasn't sure love was worth all the drama.

"No thank you. I want a calm and serene existence." Kristy opened her internet browser.

"Is that even possible in this family?" Isabelle nudged her with her elbow.

God, she certainly hoped it was.

Chapter 3

Dean finally found the perfect place for Peyton. Keith enlisted his aunt Cora to help but as far as she was concerned it was for Mr. Flynn's niece. Technically it wasn't a lie because Dean was the elusive Mr. Flynn, but the sweet, quirky aunt of his best friend didn't know that. Of course, he needed to use the fake last name to keep his niece out of the clutches of her father's brother.

Now instead of Peyton Decker-Humphrey, his niece was now Peyton Flynn. She thought the whole thing was ridiculous because it was hard for her to believe her uncle would hurt her. Dean explained why she needed to stay hidden, but it was hard to make her understand that a man that was her uncle was out to get her.

Comfort Life Care was a beautiful property in Tors Cove. When they called to say there was a spot available, he left Hopedale in the middle of Mike's wedding to move her. Her security was one of Newfoundland Security Services employees but as far as the guy knew Dean was only there to take over.

Joel 'Cannon' Wiseman was new to the team which was why Keith assigned the kid to Peyton. He wouldn't ask a lot of questions when Dean moved her with no notice. As far as Cannon was concerned, Augustus Flynn was a new client who needed security for his sick niece.

"Are you sure you don't need me to help with the transfer?" Cannon asked as he loaded Peyton's suitcase into the truck.

"Nope, Mr. Flynn will meet us there." Dean glanced at Peyton in time to see her roll her eyes from where she sat perched in her wheelchair.

"Okay," Joel nodded. "It was a pleasure to meet you, Ms. Flynn." Joel smiled at Peyton then jumped in his car.

"I don't like the name Flynn," Peyton grumbled as Dean helped her into the front of his truck.

"Don't start, Pey. Besides, Flynn was my mom's maiden name. Don't diss the name." Dean folded her chair and pushed it into the back of the truck.

"I seriously doubt Uncle Eric is going to hunt me down." She fixed her oxygen hose and took a deep breath.

"You don't know Eric as well as you think you do." Dean adjusted his mirrors and let Joel drive away before he pulled onto the road.

"Have you talked to mom?" It seemed his niece didn't want to discuss whether or not her uncle was a nice guy but the sadness in her voice broke his heart.

"I talked to her just before I picked you up." Dean reached over and squeezed Peyton's hand.

"Maybe we can set up a time to call her when I get settled." Peyton sighed.

She missed her mother, and it was the first time Peyton was cared for by someone outside of her mom for more than a day or so.

Hannah was twenty years old when she got pregnant, but Ivan Humphrey stood by her and Dean respected the man for that. Especially, after Peyton got diagnosed with Cystic Fibrosis at three years old and he still didn't run away. When Hannah and Ivan got the news, they did everything in their power to make sure their daughter had as healthy a life as was possible.

Dean was fourteen years younger than his sister. He'd been a surprise when his parents assumed they couldn't have any more children. Dean and Hannah grew up in a small town on the west coast of Newfoundland called Jersey Harbour. His father came from what his mother used to call old money. Whenever Peyton needed anything, Dean's parents made sure the little girl had it.

When Peyton's illness got worse, they had to make more trips to the hospital in St. John's for treatment. Dean's father didn't like the idea of dragging his ailing granddaughter back and forth, so he bought a house in the city to make it easier. Dean was happy with their decision because he was attending university in the city at the time. It meant he could spend more time with his family.

21

Ivan's parents moved to the city as well. Dean's dad gave them the in-law apartment over the garage in the new house. They wanted to be close to Ivan and their granddaughter. It was good for everyone involved

Well, almost everyone. Ivan's older brother still lived with Ivan's parents when they decided to move to St. John's. According to Ivan, Eric was furious that the family house was sold, but Ivan didn't care what Eric thought. Ivan almost seemed relieved Eric was finally forced to grow up.

At first, Eric called Ivan several times. It got so bad the family filed several restraining orders. For several years Eric left them alone and even moved out of the province for a short while. It was why Dean felt comfortable to take off to Yellowknife. He returned three years later when Keith decided to move their security service back to Newfoundland.

By that time, Ivan's parents had passed, and Eric's harassment commenced again. It was stressful for Ivan, but his brother-in-law was able to deal with all of it because of Dean's family's support.

Dean's mother died when he was twenty-six, and as much as he tried to go on, his father couldn't dig his way out of the pit of grief. It was hard since Dean still lived in Yellowknife when it happened and felt as if he'd abandoned his father.

Three years later his dad staggered from a pub and got behind the wheel of his car. He didn't make it two blocks when he ran into a pole and died on impact. Dean still carried guilt over that. It was why he didn't talk about them and managed to sidetrack anyone who asked about his family. Even Keith and Sandy didn't ask questions because they knew it was pointless.

Hannah took the deaths of their parents hard, and Dean had to keep it together for all their sakes. His father owned numerous commercial properties in the province, and although Dean was supposed to take over in his father's place, he had his own business to run and he wasn't a Decker in name.

When he was younger, most people would be fake, and Dean hated that. Dean wanted to make his own way in life, and when he used his given name, people would practically bow at his feet because of his family. It was why he dropped Augustus and started to go by his middle name before he ever left Newfoundland.

After he'd arrived in Yellowknife he decided to change his last name as well as his appearance. He shaved his head and did the one thing he'd always wanted. He got his first tattoo and soon most of his torso and arms were covered with them. A couple of body piercings and he looked nothing like Augustus Decker anymore.

His father wasn't pleased about it back then but understood and to make his father happy; Dean used the last name Nash. It was Dean's maternal grandfather's name. Sandy waved her magic fingers, and Dean Nash became his legal name.

Dean buried Augustus Decker when he left Newfoundland, and it was a good thing because rumors started to swirl over some of the business transactions his father entered after his mother died.

Since Dean kept himself out of the public eye, he wasn't about to put himself in the middle of his father's business. It's why he made Ivan the president of Decker Corporation with Dean basically in the background for any major decisions.

Ivan did ask if he could hire an assistant and called Dean to help with interviews and weeding through resumes. Dean told his brother-in-law to hire the person that was the most qualified for what he needed. It wasn't some sort of critical issue with the company.

"Are we going to be passing by a Dairy Queen, I'd love to have an ice cream cone." Peyton dragged him from his thoughts.

She was so much like her mother and more like a sister than a niece to him. Hannah always joked that Peyton was the little sister Dean never wanted. Peyton was six years younger than him and the same age as Kristy.

"You have an addiction." Dean chuckled.

"The first step is admitting it, and I don't deny it." Peyton shrugged her shoulders and adjusted her oxygen.

Dean would do anything for her because he was the only family she had at her disposal. With her father dead, and her mother in jail for his murder, Peyton had nobody left. Dean didn't believe for a minute Hannah would kill Ivan. His sister wasn't that type of

24

person, but she was found in the bed next to him with the gun in her hand.

Hannah told the police Ivan wasn't supposed to be home until the next day. He'd sent a text that afternoon to let her know his flight got delayed and he probably wouldn't make it home until the next day. That evening she received a package from her husband with chocolates and a note that said he loved her. She didn't think anything weird about it because he did it every time he would get delayed overnight.

Hannah ate a couple of the chocolates while she watched a movie on the couch and couldn't remember when Ivan arrived home or how she got to bed. She was confident she didn't shoot the gun because she was terrified of the things. His sister didn't know where the gun came from and the chocolates with the note had vanished.

Hannah could never hurt anyone, but the evidence disagreed. She was charged with first-degree murder and sat in jail until her trial. That was over four months ago, and Dean juggled his life ever since. Luckily Ivan's assistant didn't hesitate when Dean asked him to step in for Ivan. Vince Day took over duties for Decker Corp, and he called Dean if he was unsure of anything.

Keith offered to help several times, but Dean turned him down. Worry over involving the O'Connor family or his pride prevented him from accepting any help from his friend. Guilt gnawed at him for shutting out his friends, but Keith's family went through enough shit over the last few years. They didn't need his drama too.

It's why he was glad to get Peyton into the Comfort Life Care Center. He'd moved her to a house in Gander with round the clock nursing care and security from N.S.S short for Newfoundland Security Services, but the three-hour drive back and forth was about to kill him. Cora warned him to tell Mr. Flynn it would be expensive, but he assured her it wasn't an issue. It was probably one of the first times he was glad to come from money.

Tors Cove was only fifteen minutes from Hopedale which made it a lot easier for him to keep Peyton close and be able to visit his sister in jail.

"Pey, we're here," Dean spoke softly as he opened her door.

"Isn't ice cream supposed to make you hyper?" Peyton stretched her arms overhead.

"It does, but then you crash." Dean helped her from the truck, and she stood on her own for a moment. It wasn't that she couldn't walk, she got winded quickly.

"This is beautiful. It doesn't look like a hospital." She seemed absorbed in the green lawns covered with flowers and trees. People were seated in wheelchairs and on benches enjoying the warm late August weather.

"It's not a hospital, remember?" Dean pulled back the chair once she finally sat in it.

"I still think it's stupid not to use my real last name," Peyton complained.

"Pey, I told you, Eric wants money, and he will not give up until he gets what you inherited from my parents, your dad and your mom signed everything over to you as well before she was formally charged. Plus, if the reporters get wind of you being here, they'll swarm this place." Dean crouched so he could meet her eyes.

"You truly believe Eric would hurt me for money?" Peyton's eyes filled with tears.

"Pey, your dad had major concerns about him before he died. He said Eric threatened him, your mom and you." Dean promised Hannah to be completely honest about everything with Peyton, and he was. He didn't hide things from Peyton.

"Okay, so I'm Peyton Flynn." She sat back in the chair and rested her hands on her lap.

Dean was almost at the entrance to meet with the director of the facility when his phone vibrated in his pocket. He pulled it out and cursed. Keith again. Dean couldn't ignore the man much longer because his friend would get Sandy to track the phone and then he'd come find him.

"Hang on a sec, Pey." Dean stepped back enough to where she wouldn't hear him. "Hello."

"It's about fucking time, asshole," Keith growled.

"Sorry, service is in and out." He lied.

"Yeah, right. Are you out fishing?" Keith chuckled

Dean rolled his eyes but laughed. Fishing was a term he and Keith used when they were out to pick up women. Keith was married now which meant his fishing days were over. Dean was in a bit of a dry spell, but it wasn't because he couldn't find someone to have a quick fuck. It was because of how he felt about Kristy.

"Nah, getting to old for that shit." Dean turned to see Peyton staring at him. "One sec." He mouthed the words.

"Anyway, why didn't you tell me you were moving her today?" Leave it to Keith not to beat around the bush.

"I got this under control." Lie again.

"You're hiding something, Bull. It's pissing me off, but I won't push it for now. You do know I'm here if you need anything?" Dean didn't doubt it for a second.

"I know, but I got this. I'm not hiding anything, but I probably won't be back for a week or so. Need to make sure she's settled" Dean had to ensure Peyton was comfortable in her surroundings and meet the staff that cared for her.

"Kristy is leaving Hopedale," Keith spoke so fast that Dean wasn't sure he heard him correctly at first.

"For good?" He needed to know.

"Could be. Do you want to know where she's going and what she's doing?" Keith baited him.

"None of my business. Listen I gotta run. I'll give you a shout in a day or so." Dean ended the call before Keith could say another word.

"Was that you're girlfriend?" Peyton wiggled her eyebrows.

"I don't have one of those. It was my business partner." Dean shook his head.

"Is he really your business partner or your life partner because mom said you weren't but I'm starting to wonder because I don't remember you ever having a serious girlfriend." Peyton tilted her head and stared up at him.

"Keith's my business partner and happily married. I'm not gay." Dean laughed. "Not that there is anything wrong with that, but I'm most definitely straight."

"Hmm, what's that Shakespeare line… oh yeah, Thou doth protest too much." Peyton laughed when he glared at her.

"You're pushing it, little girl." Dean got to the top of the ramp and pushed the automatic door button.

The Directors office was easy enough to find since it was inside the front entrance. Dean rapped on the door and waited for someone to answer. He was about to knock again when a high-pitched voice echoed across the lobby from the other side. A tall, slim woman hurried toward them almost toppling over a couple of times on her stilettos.

"I'm so sorry; I meant to be here when you arrived. You must be Mr. Flynn." The woman held out her hand, and Dean glanced at her name tag perfectly placed on the lapel of her jacket.

"I was supposed to meet with Sophia Frost." Dean gazed down at Peyton.

"I'm her assistant, Gemma Grimes." Gemma dropped her hand. "Mrs. Frost will be here shortly. Can I offer you coffee or tea?" She flicked her long blonde hair back over her shoulder and gave him a look that told him he could have her on her back with a flirty wink.

Sorry, Sweetheart, not a chance.

Gemma opened the door and motioned for them to go ahead of her. She followed and gave him a flirty smile, but Dean wasn't about to encourage her.

"I'd love tea, Gemma." Peyton smiled as she slapped her hand against his. "Rude much."

"I'll take a coffee please, Ms. Grimes." Dean winked at Peyton.

"I'm sure you and your wife must be…" Gemma had her back to them.

"D's my uncle." Peyton interrupted Gemma, and Dean wanted to groan when the woman slowly turned with a very seductive smile.

"I'm sorry for the misunderstanding." She fluttered her eyelashes as she bent over to hand him the cup.

"D's wife couldn't come because she's taking care of their four children." Peyton sipped her tea and didn't show a hint of a smile.

"Four children?" Gemma gasped.

"Yes, she can't travel now because she's ready to give birth to number five." Peyton smiled when Dean almost choked on his coffee.

"Goodness, that's a big family." Gemma's flirtation stopped cold.

"Yes, it is, and would you believe they want more." Peyton feigned a sigh. "I tell her she's out of her mind."

"If you're finished discussing my life can we start discussing yours." Ms. Flirty wasn't about to find out Peyton's story was far from the truth.

"I'll run and let Mrs. Frost know you're here." Gemma hurried out of the room twisting over on her thin heeled shoes as she closed the door.

"How long do you think it will take her to break her ankle?" Peyton laughed

"Have no idea, but really? Five kids." Dean chuckled.

"I thought six would be a little far-fetched." Peyton grinned. "She had that, I want to lick him from his head to his toe, look and being your wife was too gross."

"Thanks a lot." Dean laughed.

"I didn't realize how quickly I could make up a story like that. Maybe I should be a novelist." Peyton glided her hand over her head as if she wrote it in the air. "Peyton Decker would be a great pen name."

"Not Humphrey?" Dean liked the idea of dropping the Humphrey name but then again it was Ivan's last name, and Peyton's father did nothing wrong.

"Maybe I should use Flynn." Peyton ignored or didn't hear his comment.

"Whatever you want, Pey." Dean stood when the door to the office opened, and an elegant gray-haired woman glided through the door.

"My sincere apologies, Mr. Flynn." The woman held out her hand. "I'm Sophia Frost the Director of Comfort Life Care."

Dean shook her hand and nodded. Sophia was tall, slim and dressed very professionally in a black pencil skirt and matching jacket. Her voice was soft but confident.

"It's a pleasure to meet you, Mrs. Frost." Peyton shook her hand as well.

"You as well, Ms. Flynn. Your uncle says you're looking forward to enjoying a little more relaxed atmosphere that we offer our residents." Sophia smiled as she sat behind her desk.

Dean liked her and hoped the medical staff had the same professionalism.

"I'm looking forward to not feeling like I'm in a hospital." Peyton smiled shyly, and Dean's heart broke.

His niece spent most of her life in and out of hospitals and instead of taking her back to Hopedale, he needed to have her somewhere she felt comfortable. Bringing her home would raise too many questions and Eric would expect him to do that.

This care facility was not anywhere Eric would think to look, because it was out of the city. With Peyton safe, he could figure out who killed Ivan because it sure as hell wasn't his sister.

Hannah took care of Peyton's finances and made sure Peyton had everything she needed medically. Peyton was a wealthy young woman, but it didn't do her any good. No matter how much money she had, the only thing that could save her life was a lung transplant. Her health was deteriorating, and even if a lung became available, Peyton's body could reject the organ or she wouldn't survive the surgery.

With Hannah's arrest, Peyton transferred power of attorney to Dean. Then things got bad. Eric started to send letters to Hannah through her lawyer with threats to reveal her deep dark secret.

Hannah swore she had no idea what the threats were about, but she begged Dean to keep her daughter away from him. She also convinced Peyton to update her will to make sure her daughter sent the money where she wanted it to go.

"Mr. Flynn, did you want to see where your niece will be living?" Sophia asked.

"I would." Dean stood up and wheeled Peyton out of the office.

Dean took in every exit and entrance on their way to Peyton's room. Sophia insisted the residents didn't have rooms they had suites as if it was a fancy hotel, but the truth was it was probably where his niece would spend the rest of her short life.

Stop that train of thought.

They stopped at the door with one hundred and two written across the ivory wood, Sophia unlocked it and pushed the door open.

"I hope you find it comfortable." Sophia stepped back for them to go ahead of her.

"Wow," was Peyton's first response as they entered the massive room taking the word right out of his mouth.

The entire far wall was nothing but windows that allowed tons of natural light into the room. On the left side, a larger than the typical hospital bed was in the center of the wall. The bathroom door was on the same side and was wide enough to drive a truck through. The right side of the suite was set up as a small sitting room with a couch, recliner, television and a square table in the middle of a colorful rug.

"I want to make you aware, you can only see out through the windows. Nobody can look in." Sophia stood next to the door with a look of pride on her face. "We ensure total privacy."

"That's comforting." Dean wandered closer to the window and checked them.

"The windows don't open. The building is fully air-conditioned." Sophia seemed to read his mind.

Dean turned toward the bed. That part of the room resembled a hospital with a heart monitor, oxygen tanks and other medical equipment. He didn't show it, but he was impressed.

"Everything Ms. Flynn needs to make her comfortable and ensure the best medical care is in this room. We deliver meals to the room and menus are brought to each resident on Monday to make their choices for their meals that week. There is also a dining hall if you prefer to eat there." Sophia stepped to a part of the wall he hadn't noticed until she pushed the small door. "This cupboard contains all tubes, needles, ventilator supplies, suction machines, Tracheostomy supplies…" Dean held up his hands to stop Sophia.

"I'm afraid my uncle may be a little squeamish when we talk about all this stuff." Peyton giggled.

"Not squeamish but I feel that's for the professionals caring for my niece." Dean did know what a tracheotomy was and the thought that Peyton would possibly need it made him ill.

"I understand, and it will be. We have four nurses trained for Ms. Flynn's care. Three of them have been here for some time, and one is new to us but equally qualified and trained." Sophia closed the cupboard and turned.

"I'd appreciate if I could meet the staff that will directly be dealing with Pey." Dean eased into the recliner and steepled his fingers in front of his face.

"I'll arrange that for the morning." Sophia smiled.

"Who'll be caring for her tonight?" Dean asked, and Peyton's sigh told him she was annoyed with him.

"I'll bring Ms. Howell in right away." Sophia hurried out through the door which left him alone with Peyton.

"Do you have to act like some rich asshole, D?" Peyton rolled her eyes.

"Don't start, Pey," Dean warned.

"Isn't the reason I'm here because it's the best place in the province?" What could he say to that? She was right.

"Yeah," Dean nodded.

"Then the medical staff have to be competent and well trained." Peyton stared out through the window. "The view here is incredible."

"It is." Dean turned his head.

"Mr. Flynn, this is Zoey Howell." Sophia entered the room followed by a young woman. She appeared to be about his age.

"It's nice to meet you, Ms. Howell." Dean nodded.

"Please, we like to make everyone comfortable here, call me Zoey." The perky nurse practically skipped over to Peyton and held out her hand.

"So nice to meet you, Zoey." Peyton smiled.

While his niece got acquainted with the young nurse, Dean took the chance to speak privately with Sophia. He motioned for her to follow him outside.

"I assure you, Mr. Flynn, Zoey is one of the best staff we have." Sophia looked concerned.

"I don't doubt that, but she won't be with Peyton twenty-four hours a day, seven days a week." Dean shoved his hands into his pants pocket.

"No, we have a four-nurse rotation. They work twelve-hour day shifts from eight to eight for three days then they are off for three, then they work three-night shifts." Sophia explained. "Unless there's a staff change, Ms. Flynn will have the same nurses caring for her while she's here. Zoey and two of the other nurses have been here for a while the other nurse is only here for a few weeks until the permanent nurse returns from leave."

"I'm not sure about this new one." The fact that the nurse wasn't a current staff member made Dean uncomfortable.

"I assure you she came highly recommended from a dear friend who would not have sent her to me if she weren't confident she would be the perfect fit. I saw her during training last week, and I have no doubts about her abilities either." For some reason, Dean trusted Sophia's opinion, but he had no idea why.

"I still want to meet the other three as well as any doctors." Dean reminded her.

"I'll have the night nurse come see you as soon as she comes in and since the other two start their rotation tomorrow, you can meet them as well." Sophia pulled out her phone.

"That would be great. You did say I could spend a few days here with Pey while she settles in." Dean wasn't leaving until his niece was comfortable.

"Oh yes. We'll bring in a cot for you to sleep on." Sophia tapped into her phone and smiled when she received a text seconds later. "Done."

Dean didn't know how Peyton could sleep with the constant hiss and hum of her breathing machine. It was as annoying as hell and the fact that the night nurse Vivian Jones came in every couple of hours to check her didn't help his sleep situation.

At five in the morning, he finally decided three hours of sleep was all he could get. Peyton still slept soundly, and Vivian checked the supplies in the cupboard.

"Would you mind if I ran out to grab a coffee?" Dean felt the need to ask if it was okay.

"Mr. Flynn, don't worry she's in great hands here." Vivian smiled.

He nodded and grabbed his jacket from the back of the couch. Dean took one more glance at Peyton and left the room. Sophia scheduled a meeting for him with the other staff later in the morning. That gave him time to run to the closest Tim Horton's and check in with Keith.

The favorite Canadian coffee shop was about fifteen minutes from the care center. Dean proceeded through the drive-thru and called Keith once he'd gotten his order.

"Do you ever fucking sleep?" Keith grumbled when he answered.

"When I have to." Dean chuckled.

"Wait until you have to deal with a newborn screaming all night," Keith complained.

"Yeah, don't see that happening. Although, dealing with you over the years gives me lots of practice." Dean parked in the lot and sipped his coffee.

"Fuck you, Asshat," Keith growled. "Hang on a sec."

Dean heard Keith tell Emily to go back to sleep that it was work related. He laughed when she mumbled something about her hating work.

Emily gave birth to their first child two months earlier. A little boy with auburn hair and blue eyes. Dean thought the kid was cute as a button, but Keith would lose all intelligent thoughts when he was near the baby. They named him Noah Keith O'Connor he was the second boy born to the O'Connor family in less than a year. Stephanie and John had a second child, Brenden John O'Connor six months earlier.

"Noah giving mom and dad a hard time?" Dean chuckled.

"It's a new phase where he wants to sleep all day and keep us up all night." Keith sighed.

"I'm sure he'll grow out of it." Dean closed his eyes and rested his head against the headrest.

"I know you didn't call at the crack ass of dawn to discuss my son's sleeping patterns, What's up, Bull?" Keith knew him almost as well as he knew himself.

"Can you get Smash do a check on a couple of people for me?" Dean knew Keith wouldn't agree without some answers.

40

"I can, but the question is, will I? Why the fuck are you checking out people? I'm pretty sure that place don't hire just anyone." Dean heard Keith sip something.

"I'm being cautious." Dean knew Keith was right.

"Do you have any idea when you'll be able to come back?" It was shitty for him to leave Keith with all the business shit. He seemed to be doing that on all ends lately.

"Not sure but hopefully I can get back for a few days once she's settled." It was all he could say.

"You disappeared from Mike's wedding and tell Cannon the job is over. You should have given me a heads up." Keith continued. "You know you don't have to do this alone?"

"I know, and I'll fill you in when I get back. Can you get Smash to check out the names I emailed you before I called?" Dean had sent the email before he left the Center.

"Why not Sandy?" Keith chuckled.

"Because she's too fucking nosy and would dig into things I don't need to know about." Dean laughed.

"Fine, but you know she'll find out somehow." Keith was right. When that woman wanted information, she got it. Plus, she was probably breathing down Keith's back for information.

Dean emailed the names of the staff he'd met so far as well as Eric Humphrey. When Keith asked what other information he had about them, he cursed under his breath. The only thing Dean knew about Sophia, Gemma and Vivian were that they worked at Comfort Life Care. Eric, on the other hand, he had everything he needed.

"I only know the names and where they work for the three women," Dean explained.

"Not much to go on but I'm sure if there's anything to worry about Smash will find it. You want him to email the results?" Keith asked.

"Yeah," Dean finished the last of his coffee and tossed the cup into the nearby garbage bucket.

"No questions about a certain cousin of mine?" Keith chuckled.

"You know, you're spending way too much time with Emily and Sandy. I want Kristy to have a great life." That was the truth. "I'll stay in touch."

"You fucking better." Keith was interrupted by the wail of the baby and ended the call before he could lecture Dean about Kristy. He couldn't involve her in all his shit.

Kristy or the rest of the family didn't need any more drama. They'd had enough, and he wasn't about to put them or her in danger. Dean cared about them too much. Who was he kidding? He loved Kristy too much to ruin her life with him.

Chapter 4

Kristy plopped down on the couch and groaned. Her sisters helped her settle into her new apartment two weeks before, but it was lonely.

Kristy was accustomed to a family member close by, so it was hard when her sisters left to go back to Hopedale. It was too quiet, and she constantly heard every little creak and squeak in the apartment. She couldn't even sleep in her room because she convinced herself something was in there. She hated it.

She'd trained all week with three other nurses to care for a young woman with Cystic Fibrosis, an elderly man with dementia as well as another man a little younger. It was a lot to take in at once, but the place was incredible, and she liked the staff she'd met so far.

She started with the patients the next day and looked forward to the new change in her life. The position was for a month because she was there to replace someone on sick leave. Kristy didn't care because she was out of Hopedale and maybe it would help her get over Dean Nash.

Of course, she told her family she'd come back on her days off, but the truth was it was fall. If her position got extended which was possible, then it would go into the winter months. Knowing her father, he would insist she didn't drive in bad weather, and she would roll her eyes. It wouldn't be as if he could see her unless he used Facetime.

Unless he uses Facetime. Does dad know how to Facetime?

As if on cue, her phone vibrated on the table. Kristy jumped to her feet and scuffed to the kitchen where her phone sat on the counter. She didn't recognize the number.

"Hello," Kristy singsonged.

"Can I speak with Kristy O'Connor, please?" A soft female voice asked.

"Speaking,"

"Ms. O'Connor this is Sophia Frost from Comfort Life Care."

"Oh hello, Mrs. Frost." Kristy made her way to the kettle and flicked on the switch.

"I know you'll be starting in the morning, but Ms. Flynn's uncle wants to meet with all the staff who will be interacting with his niece." Sophia sounded almost apologetic.

"I understand, I'm sure he wants to make sure she's comfortable with the staff." Kristy couldn't blame the man.

"Yes, Mr. Flynn is a little, how should I put it? Overwhelming." Sofia chuckled.

"I grew up with seven male cousins, two uncles and a father who would probably put Mr. Flynn to shame." Kristy laughed.

"Then you're fully prepared to meet him."

"Trust me; I've dealt with worse." Dean came to mind.

"Good, your shift starts at eight and the meeting will be in suite one, zero, two," Sophia said. "Looking forward to seeing you again, Cora speaks highly of you. Oh, and nobody knows your aunt recommended you."

"Thanks, I wasn't aware you knew her well." Kristy felt slightly embarrassed because Cora probably pushed the issue.

"She and I went to college together, and if your work ethic is the same as hers, I'm sure you'll do fine." Kristy did work hard.

"I'll see you in the morning, Mrs. Frost." Kristy ended the call and groaned. "Great, I get rid of a bunch of overbearing men and have to meet another on my first day."

Just another day in my life.

Kristy pulled her car into the parking lot. The place looked more like a country club than a long-term care facility. The only thing to even hint it was for sick and seniors was the medical staff entering and exiting the building.

Kristy tucked her stethoscope into the pocket of her scrubs, grabbed her cell phone and got out of her car. A tall man with dark hair held open the door as she made her way to the entrance.

"Thank you." Kristy smiled.

"Anything for a pretty nurse." The man smiled, and all Kristy could think was Dean could snap you in half. She'd seen the man many times while she trained and knew the type. It would never happen, but she had to work with the guy.

"Kristy O'Connor, it's my first official day." She held out her hand and almost gagged when he put her hand to his lips.

"Doctor Kevin Dickson, at your service. Anything you need, and I do mean anything." Yep, he was a dick.

He held onto Kristy's hand a little longer than was comfortable and she pulled it away with a forced smile. He was attractive with hair to his shoulders that he continued to push back from his narrow face. She wanted to shout, 'cut it.' His hazel eyes sparkled with mischief, or he was horny, either way, she wasn't interested.

"Doctor Dickson, I'm sure you have a shift to start." A soft voice echoed in the vestibule.

It was comical the way he spun around and stammered something about a friendly welcome for the new staff member. Kristy rolled her eyes because there was no welcome in the way he greeted her.

"If you're finished. You have patients waiting." Sophia stood with her hands folded in front of her.

"Sure, glad to have you on the team, Ms. O'Connor." Dr. Dick scurried off down the hall.

"I'm sorry about your welcome committee." Sophia shook her head.

"It's fine. Mrs. Frost, it's a pleasure to see you again." Kristy held out her hand.

"Oh honey, you can call me Sophia but not in the presence of the other staff." She motioned for Kristy to follow her into the office.

"Do all the staff jump like Dr. Dick; I mean Dr. Dickson?" Kristy hoped her boss missed a slip of the tongue.

"No, you were right the first time. Kevin is a dick, but a great doctor and the female patients love him. Mostly because he has a pretty face and he flirts with them." Sophia pulled an envelope out of her desk.

"He's a little over the top." Kristy laughed.

"Yes, and he tries that with all the new female staff. It never works which is why he's probably still single. This is your identification card. It has a security chip inside for entering the building as well as secure areas." Sophia stared at her.

"Thank you." Kristy accepted the card attached to a clip that attached to her scrubs.

"I'm sorry, I don't mean to stare, but I still can't get over how much you resemble your mom." Sophia smiled.

"You know my mom?" After she asked the question, she remembered Cora and her mom had gone to the same college.

"Yes, Alice started dating your father during her last year of university. Your aunt's doing." Sophia chuckled.

"Oh yeah, Cora the Cupid." Kristy laughed. "Maybe we should have Aunt Cora come out here and talk to Dr. Dickson."

"Ha, I never thought of that." Sophia opened the door of her office. "Come on because you're about to meet another type of man. Quite handsome but not sure he knows how to smile."

"I've met men like that." Kristy knew one for sure.

When they arrived at suite one hundred and two, the two other women were in the middle of a chat outside the door.

"Ladies, right on time. You remember Kristy she'll be on rotation with you, Leah." Sophia spoke to the two women.

Kristy met the two women when they trained. Vivian Jones was shorter than Kristy with short blonde hair. Leah Sellers was taller with brown hair a little darker than Kristy's and cut close to her scalp. It reminded Kristy of the way men wore their hair in the military.

"So nice to see you again, oh and I'm a hugger." Leah grabbed Kristy and gave her a quick hug.

"Sorry about that." Vivian rolled her eyes. "She has no personal space boundaries."

"It's okay; I've got several little cousins who have the same issue." Kristy chuckled.

"Has anyone seen Zoey?" Sophia asked.

"She's inside with Peyton." Vivian smiled.

"Yeah, apparently her uncle is running late. He had some business to attend to." Vivian explained.

"Probably, out bench pressing a car." Leah fanned herself.

"You should have seen him in that T-shirt this morning." Vivian sighed.

"I'm not usually a fan of tattoos but holy baloney." Leah grinned.

"Ladies, professionalism please." The smile on Sophia's face said she understood.

"Sorry," Leah chuckled.

"Why don't we at least have everyone go inside and chat with Ms. Flynn." Sophia pushed open the door, and Kristy followed the three women inside.

Kristy was in awe of the beautiful room, and tried to take it all in but she was distracted by the pretty woman in the wheelchair with the nasal cannula. It wasn't something she was unfamiliar with but to see someone so young hooked up to oxygen was sobering. It didn't seem to affect the woman because she had a lovely smile on her face.

"Hello, Ms. Flynn." Sophia sat in the chair next to the young woman.

"Please call me Peyton. I feel like an old lady when you act so formal." Peyton glanced at Kristy and the others.

"I understand your uncle is running late, but I wanted to introduce you to your permanent nurses all together. Kristy will be on days for the next three days." Sophia motioned to Kristy.

"Kristy O'Connor," She held out her hand to Peyton.

"You're so pretty." Peyton smiled.

"Thank you; you're a real knock out." Kristy winked and stepped back.

Sophia introduced Leah who got the same compliment from sweet Peyton. Since Zoey and Vivian already met the elusive Mr. Flynn, Sophia told Vivian to take Kristy to the nurse's station and go over the reports, and she sent the other two home. Sophia seemed annoyed that Peyton's uncle demanded to meet all the nurses but didn't show up.

"He can meet Leah tonight and you when he comes in." Sophia told Kristy as they left Peyton's room.

Vivian explained there were sixty residents in the facility and the ratio was one nurse for three patients. Obviously, the place was for very wealthy people. Not that Kristy cared one way or the other.

"We care for the same patients on every shift unless there's a problem." Vivian held out the three charts. "You've met Peyton, and she's a sweetheart. So sad to be so young and so ill."

"Cystic Fibrosis is horrible," Kristy flipped through the chart.

"Yes, and there's no hope for a transplant as far as I can tell." Vivian sighed.

"So sad." Kristy shook her head.

"Anyway, Owen Bailey is eighty-three and can do most things himself. He enjoys checkers and spends a lot of time in the activity room. Chances are you'll have to track him down for his medication. He's an adorable gentleman. Walter Stone is sixty-nine, and according to him we're holding him, hostage, so his family can steal his money." Vivian gave her a smile that said I'm sorry.

"He's the one with dementia?" Kristy sighed.

"Yes, but most of the time he's lucid and grumpy, but when he gets out of sorts, we just agree with him. Honestly, I feel for the poor man, his kids put him here and visit once a month. I sometimes think maybe he's not wrong." Vivian shrugged her shoulders.

"Are most of the residents, seniors?" Kristy asked.

"Yes, most are, but we have a couple who are terminal. The people here pay big money to get the best of care and trust me they get it. It's the best job I've ever had." Vivian pulled on her jacket.

"How long have you been here?" Kristy asked.

"Four years and I wouldn't want to go anywhere else." Vivian pulled her purse onto her shoulder. "The room numbers are on the cards attached to the front, make sure you note everything, and I usually do vitals every two hours unless I see something out of the ordinary then I check every hour."

"Is there anyone I can call if I have issues?" Talk about getting tossed into the lion's cage.

"Don't worry; there's a list next to the phone with all the nurses on duty with your shift. If you've got any issues, you can call one of them. The computer system is the same one we used last week at training." Vivian didn't seem to be in a hurry to leave.

"It's pretty straightforward." Kristy also used the system when she did her nursing rotations at the hospitals in St. John's.

"Is there anything else, you need?" Vivian glanced up the hallway.

"I think I'm good." Kristy glanced in the same direction but couldn't see anything. "Is something wrong, Vivian?"

"I don't want to run into Dr. Dickson." Vivian rolled her eyes.

"Oh, I met Dr. Dick." Kristy chuckled.

"Oh my God, I love it." Vivian laughed.

"He's a little full of himself." Kristy stood up and wrapped her stethoscope around her neck.

"You have no idea." Vivian groaned. "He's harmless, but he annoys the hell out of me."

"I can understand why." Kristy stepped around the desk and glanced down at the first chart.

Vivian's notes were very detailed, and Kristy was quiet comfortable with her first rotation. Peyton's uncle had not returned but contacted Sophia to apologize. He would be back by the afternoon to meet Kristy. Leah would meet with him when she came in for her shift. He didn't want them to give up their day off because he'd gotten held up. At least he was not completely unreasonable.

Kristy found Owen very easy going and she didn't have any issues with Walter either. She was on her way to Peyton's room when her phone buzzed.

She pulled it out of her pocket. A text from Keith popped up with a picture of his new baby. Kristy smiled when she opened it and saw Noah with a huge smile.

Keith: He wanted to say hi to his favorite big cousin.

It was odd for Keith to text her out of the blue, but it seemed her cousin's new baby had softened the big burly man.

Kristy: He's so adorable.

Keith: Like his dad.

Kristy: Whatever gets you through the day, cuz.

Keith: How's the new job? Meet any interesting people yet?

Kristy: On shift now. I'll call when I get home.

Kristy shoved the phone back into her pocket and made her way to Peyton's suite. She knocked on the door as she slowly pushed open the door. Peyton was in her bed and a little paler than earlier.

"Hi, Peyton," Kristy smiled as she moved next to the bed.

"Hey," Peyton smiled.

"How are you feeling?" Kristy pulled off her stethoscope and proceeded to check Peyton's vitals.

"Good. I got a text from D to say he's here with a muffin for me." Peyton smiled.

"Lucky you." Kristy laughed.

"Yeah, I guess you'll get to meet him." Peyton sat on the bed while Kristy checked her breathing.

"Looking forward to it." Kristy smiled as she made her way to the supply cupboard to retrieve Peyton's medication. She'd just poured a glass of water when the door to the room opened. Kristy couldn't see who entered from where she stood.

"Oh my God, chocolate chip." Peyton was very excited about it. "This is huge. Kristy, do you want some?"

Kristy turned and sucked in a breath. On the other side of Peyton's bed was the last man she expected and the very one she didn't want to see. Kristy gasped, and the tray of medication clattered to the floor.

Dean.

She knew at that moment the reason she received the random message from her cousin and why her aunt pushed her to take the short-term position. They both had to know, and she was ready to give both of them a piece of her mind.

Chapter 5

Dean's morning went way off schedule. He'd gotten a call from his sister's lawyer about a deal offered to her by the Crown Attorney. It meant if she admitted to the murder there would be no trial and reduce the charge to manslaughter. The lawyer added pressure for her to accept it, but Dean had no idea why.

It was only a thirty-minute drive to the women's prison. It made him appear unprofessional to miss the meeting he'd demanded with the staff at Comfort Life Care, but something was off with his sister and her lawyer.

He waited for the guard to open the door to the entrance. Since he visited so often, he knew most of them by name. As usual, he removed his belt and left his phone in a locker before he could go into the visiting room.

Dean waited for Hannah to be escorted into the visiting room. He glanced around at the other visitors and prisoners currently in the room. He noticed a small woman on the other side of the room with her head down as a man leaned over the table. The woman looked scared, and the man looked pissed. Before he could get the guards attention to warn him, he heard his sister.

"Hey," Hannah moved slowly toward him.

"Hi," He wanted to jump up and hug her, but it wasn't permitted. He couldn't even hold her hand.

"Is everything okay with Peyton?" Hannah folded her hands together on the table in front of her.

"She's great. Sassy as ever." Dean smiled, but Hannah dropped her head and sighed.

Hannah was different over the last few weeks. Who could blame her? She was in jail for something she didn't do and no way out. She never even had a chance to mourn the man she loved.

"Han, why are you thinking about taking this deal? I know you didn't do this." Dean folded his hands in front of him.

"Trevor said there was gonna be another delay on my trial." Hannah lifted her head, and her eyes filled with tears. "I want to get this over with, and if I take this, I won't get as much time."

"Why the delay?" Dean didn't trust Trevor Poole. Hannah hired the lawyer, and Dean told her several times to get another, but the guy convinced her he was the best. The only thing Dean could see was the huge invoices from the man.

"Something about missing statements and it could be months before it gets figured out. He said the deal is the best option." Hannah's hands shook.

"I'm finding another lawyer. That guy's an idiot, and I told you from the beginning." Dean clenched his jaw when she closed her eyes. "I'm sorry, Han but something doesn't add up with that guy. I seem to remember he promised you this would be over in a couple of weeks when you hired him."

"I had the gun in my hand, but I don't remember anything from that night. I don't even know how I got to bed and it's the Crown Attorney that's holding things up. Every time he asks for something they put him off." Hannah swiped her hands across her cheeks to wipe the tears away.

"Did you have to sign for the chocolate's that you thought Ivan sent?" Dean asked.

"We've been over this, Dean. It was left on the step. Please, stop worrying about me and take care of my daughter." Hannah whispered.

"I'm doing that, Han but I'm going to take care of you too." Dean met his sister's Hazel eyes.

"It's no use, Dean. Either way, I'm not going home." Hannah sobbed.

"If I've got anything to do with it you'll be home sooner rather than later," Dean growled.

Hannah waved her hand in front of her to show she no longer wanted to talk about her situation. Dean hated to see his sister so upset.

Dean changed the subject and chatted for the rest of the visit about Peyton, his business, and life in Hopedale.

"Sounds like you found a wonderful place to call home." Hannah smiled.

"Yes, and there's one there for you and Pey, too." Dean smiled.

The smile she gave him didn't reach her eyes, and it was apparent she couldn't see a future out of prison. What the hell was he supposed to do?

He'd stopped to grab a coffee and a muffin for Peyton and made his way back to CLC. He arrived after lunch with the hopes he'd at least get to meet the day shift nurse at some point during the day. He needed to get back to Hopedale at least for a few days, but he hated to leave Peyton.

"Hello, Mr. Flynn." Dean had to force himself to stop the roll of his eyes as Gemma glided by him on his way to Peyton's room.

"Ms. Grimes." Dean nodded his head.

"You can call me Gemma, and I'll call you Dean." She smiled. It seemed a supposed married man didn't keep her at a distance. She looked even more interested.

"I think we need to keep this on a professional level." Dean nodded again and continued down the corridor.

He pushed open the door to Peyton's suite and smiled at her excitement. Not over his return but over her muffin. She held out her hand like a child to receive her treat.

"Oh my, God, chocolate chip." Peyton tried to squeal. "This is huge. Kristy, do you want some?"

The name caused his head to snap up, but it was the woman on the other side of the bed that made his heart pound in his chest.

"Kristy, are you okay?" Peyton sat straight up on the bed when whatever Kristy held clattered to the floor. If anyone asked him what it was, he wouldn't be able to tell them because he couldn't pull his gaze from her.

"Umm… no… I mean yes. I've got to get….." Kristy spun around, yanked open the door and stomped through it.

"I'll be right back, Pey." Dean hurried out of the room in time to see Kristy disappear through a door leading to one of the viewing decks.

In nothing flat, Dean made his way down the hallway and pushed open the door. Kristy paced the small deck while she mumbled under her breath. Her hands flailed around in the air, and it made him smile because that was the Kristy he knew and loved. Feisty and beautiful.

"I'll kill aunt Cora for this. She knew. She definitely knew. I bet Keith did too. Asshole, that's why he wanted to know about interesting people." Kristy babbled while she shook her hands in front of her.

"She didn't know, but I don't know about Keith." Dean braced his shoulder against the door and crossed his arms over his chest.

"Don't you think you should be in there with your... ummm.... niece." Kristy rolled her eyes.

"Peyton is my niece," Dean emphasized the word niece because Kristy seemed to have other ideas.

"Sure, she is. You have a niece my age." Kristy rested her back against the rail and braced hands on the top behind her back.

"My sister Hannah is fourteen years older than I am and she had Peyton when she was twenty." Did he just tell her that?

"Where's your sister?" Kristy narrowed her eyes.

"It's a long story and ...." Dean began but got cut off before he could finish.

"Oh right, nobody can know about the secret life of Mr. Dean Nash." Kristy stomped toward him and motioned for him to move.

"It's not a secret life, Kitten." The scent of apples surrounded him, and he stifled a groan. Every fucking time his dick reacted to her scent. He wasn't sure if it was her shampoo, body wash or perfume but it drove him crazy.

"Can you move?" Kristy reached around him and grabbed the door handle.

"You can't talk to anyone about Peyton or me." That wasn't going to go over well with Kristy. He knew that before he even uttered the words.

"Why not? Wait, your name isn't Flynn." Kristy dropped her hand from the door handle and crossed her arms over her chest. He was thankful she wasn't wearing anything to accentuate her incredible breasts.

"No, it isn't." Dean met her beautiful blue gaze.

"Why does everyone here think you have the same last name as Peyton?" She wasn't going to let it go.

"Kristy, I'll explain, but you've got to keep this quiet." She glared at him.

"Dean, this is my job and why should I jeopardize it for you?" Kristy grabbed the handle again and pulled. Dean pulled her hand from the door and backed her against the enclosed wall. Her breath hitched, and it took all his strength not to cover her mouth with his and do what he'd wanted for more than five years.

"Kristy," Dean dipped his head until his mouth was only inches away from her lips. "This is why I've kept you at a distance."

"I don't understand." Kristy's voice trembled, and she rested her hands on his chest. She had to feel his heart and how it pounded in his chest.

"I don't want you tangled up in all this shit." Dean brushed his cheek against hers, and she held her breath.

"Dean, please. Tell me." Kristy's warm breath against his ear sent a shiver of desire through him.

"Fuck," Dean pulled back and cupped her face in his hands. "I shouldn't do this, but I can't fight this anymore."

"Dean," Kristy turned her head, and her lips grazed his cheek.

He turned his head and lightly touched his mouth to her plump, trembling lips. He knew the second he kissed her there was no turning back. It both terrified him and thrilled him.

"Kitten," Dean sighed when her eyes fluttered closed, and her mouth opened enough that the urge to drive his tongue between her lips overpowered every reasonable thought.

Dean moved his hand to the back of her head and tilted it, so he could finally kiss her the way he'd always wanted. His lips moved to hers, and she flicked her tongue against his lower lip. With a groan, he plunged his tongue into her warm mouth and ran it across her teeth. She gently bit down on it, and his cock hardened instantly.

Kristy fisted the front of his shirt and pulled him against her as he devoured her mouth. It was as if he'd been starved for years

63

and finally gotten his first taste of nourishment. It was better than he ever could have dreamed. Kissing her was addictive and so fucking wrong, but he didn't want to stop.

Kristy seemed to be able to think rationally because she pulled her lips from his. Dean opened his eyes, but it took a minute to focus. Kristy licked her lips as she tried to catch her breath. He was equally low on oxygen, and his dick strained behind his zipper. It begged to be released, but that was his life since he met her.

"Dean, eight years you push me away, and now you decide to give in." Kristy flopped back against the wall. "What the hell is going on?"

It wasn't that he didn't trust Kristy, because he trusted her completely. He didn't know if his family drama would put her in danger, but he couldn't take any chances because if anything happened to her, it would kill him.

"It was the hardest thing I've done in my life to keep away from you, Kitten." Dean ran his knuckle down her cheek. "It's complicated. A fucked up can of worms, and I don't want to get you involved."

"Seriously? Complicated? You've met my family, right? Complicated is something I can deal with." Kristy rolled her eyes.

"But you've never been in the middle of it, and I always made sure you were safe. Even if you didn't know it and no matter how pissed you got with me." Dean made sure anytime danger hit the O'Connor family, Kristy was out of it.

"This is so stupid." Kristy pushed him away and headed for the door.

"Can you trust me?" Dean threw his hands in the air.

"Trust you? Are you serious?" Kristy spun around and rested her fists on her hips. "I trust you with my life Dean, but obviously you don't trust my family or me. I can't believe you haven't even told Keith about this. He's gonna be so hurt, but I won't tell anyone. Not because I don't want to but because I can't. I'm not permitted to talk about patients." With that, she yanked open the door and stomped inside.

Dean turned and punched the wall several times until his frustration subsided a little. She was right. Keith would kick his ass not because he didn't know but because the truth was Dean needed help. He knew Kristy would never jeopardize her job, but he hated to put her in this situation.

You're a stupid fucking asshole, Bull.

Dean entered Peyton's suite about fifteen minutes later careful not to let them see his cut knuckles. Kristy and his niece were deep in conversation. Dean made his way to the recliner and pulled out his phone as he pretended not to listen to them.

"You've got such a big family." Peyton chuckled.

"Yes, too big sometimes but I love them. I hate being away from them but it's nice to be able to hear myself think." Kristy held up her phone in front of Peyton.

"Who's the sweet baby?" Peyton cooed.

"That's my cousin Keith's baby. We actually have two new babies added to our family this year, and I've got a feeling there will be more in the near future." Dean didn't miss the emphasis she put on Keith's name.

"Isn't Keith your business partner, D?" Peyton asked.

"Mm-hmm." Dean didn't look up, but Kristy must have told Peyton she knew him from Hopedale.

"This was at Keith's wedding," Kristy said.

"Wow, D you look so handsome, and you both look great together." Peyton sounded way too excited. "You two dated?"

"No, I'm too young for Dean. We were in Keith's wedding party but this guy," Kristy swiped her phone. "He's the guy I brought to my cousin Mike's wedding a couple of weeks ago."

"He's hot." Peyton gasped, and Dean stifled a growl.

"I know, right?" Kristy sighed as she looked down at the phone.

"He was okay for a pretty boy," Dean mumbled loud enough he knew Kristy would hear him.

"Trust me he's way more than a pretty boy." Kristy fanned herself.

Dean clenched his teeth because the thought of another man with his hands on her made him want to punch something or someone. Mainly the pretty boy from the wedding.

"Well, I need to check on my other patients. I'll be back in a bit." Kristy waved to Peyton as she left the room.

"You're such an idiot." Peyton sat straight up on the bed.

"Thanks, and why am I an idiot?" Dean didn't bother to look up from his phone.

"I saw her reaction when she saw you and the way you ran after her was pretty obvious how you feel about her." Peyton was way too perceptive.

"It's complicated," Dean grumbled.

"That's only because you make it that way. Let me see if I can figure this out." Peyton tapped her finger against her chin.

"Let's not and say we did." Dean groaned.

"You're keeping your distance because of what's going on with mom and me." It was partly true but the truth was he kept his distance from her because of who he was.

Between the reporters printing stories before his father died about him making questionable business connections and then his death the reports got out of control. Then there was the fact that he'd hidden his true identity from most of the people that he considered family.

"Not talking about this, Pey," Dean shrugged out of his jacket.

"Of course not, mom always said you weren't the best at communicating." Peyton sighed.

"I communicate fine. One has nothing to do with the other." Dean sat back in the recliner and closed his eyes.

"Why are you staying here again?" Peyton groaned.

"You don't want me here?" Dean lifted his head and stared at his niece.

"I think you would be more comfortable in a hotel bed or maybe Kristy could…" She stopped when Dean held up his hand.

"I'm not asking Kristy." Dean held his breath as he tried to calm the thoughts he could spend the night alone with Kristy. It would be heaven for him, but he had to stay in hell.

"Again, doth protest too much." Peyton closed her eyes and let out a long sigh.

A few minutes later Peyton had fallen asleep. She always seemed to get tired in the late afternoon. More so lately. It killed him that there was nothing he could do to save her, and she'd moved up on the transplant list, but her pulmonologist wasn't sure she'd survive the surgery even with the respiratory therapy she received.

Dean quietly left the suite to grab a cup of coffee in the small kitchen next to the nurse's station. It had nothing to do with the possibility he'd run into Kristy.

He walked by the nurse's desk, but it was empty. He turned into the door across the hall and was happy to see a full pot of coffee on the coffee brewer. As he grabbed the pot and poured the hot coffee into the cup, someone moved behind him. Before he turned to see who, it was, he felt a hand squeeze his ass.

"Fuck," Dean growled when the coffee slopped onto his hand when he spun around.

"Mr. Flynn, we keep running into each other." Gemma ran her well-manicured finger across the top of her pushed up breasts. Her blouse opened a little more than he'd seen earlier.

"Yes, but I guess since you work here that'll happen." Dean stepped to the left to leave, but she moved in front of him.

"Mr. Flynn, you don't have to leave on my account." She took a step closer.

"I came to get a cup of coffee and head back to my niece." Dean glared at the woman.

"I'm sure she wouldn't mind if you sat and had a cup of coffee with me." Gemma pressed her finger against his chest.

"No, but my wife may." Dean smiled as her flirty expression changed to annoyance.

"I guess your wife might mind you sticking your tongue down the throat of one of our nurses as well." Gemma stepped back and smoothed the front of her hair back. The bitch saw him with Kristy.

"If you'll excuse me, I need to get back to my niece." Dean stepped around her but stopped with her next statement.

"I will have to inform Mrs. Frost of Ms. O'Connor's indiscretion." Gemma gave an exaggerated sigh.

Dean could always control his anger and speak calmly to people to ensure a situation didn't get out of control. This woman was testing that control, but Dean didn't want Kristy to get hurt. Dean turned around slowly to face Gemma.

"Ms. Grimes, I don't know what kind of game you're trying to play here but let me give you a warning. If you do anything to interfere with Kristy, my niece or myself, I will file sexual harassment charges against you." Dean would never do it, but she didn't have to know that. He pointed to the camera in the corner of the room. "I'm sure that recorded your little flirtation with me and the less than subtle grab of my ass."

Gemma's mouth dropped open and closed again. She pressed her hand against her chest and let out a fake chuckle.

"Mr. Flynn, are you threatening me?" She spoke loud enough that he was sure someone had either walked by or entered the kitchen behind him.

"It didn't sound like a threat to me." Dean turned around to see an older man casually propped against the door of the kitchen. "Looking for a rich fuck again?"

Gemma narrowed her eyes, but a second later she stomped out of the room. The man stepped aside with a chuckle.

"Sorry about her. Submit a complaint with Sophia. Not many men turn that woman down, so there's only one other complaint about that bitch."

"She does this a lot?" Dean shook his head.

"Gemma's what I would call a pussy looking for a golden dick." The man's language put Dean in total shock. He looked in his mid to late fifties and dressed in a very expensive suit. If he remembered correctly, it was probably Ralph Lauren or Gucci.

He chuckled to himself because if the guys in Hopedale knew he could pick out name brand clothing, they'd give him such shit.

"She's a piece of work, that's for sure." Dean refilled his cup.

"I'm Graham Frost by the way." He held out his hand to Dean.

"I'm Dean N... Flynn." Dean quickly caught his slip up. "Wait, Frost? As in Sophia Frost?"

"That beautiful lady is my wife." The way Graham's face lit up it made it more than obvious he loved his wife.

"I get the feeling the complaint on Gemma is from you." Dean raised an eyebrow, and the man laughed.

"No, she's not that stupid. First, I'm her boss, and second, Sophia would scratch her eyes out and come back for the sockets." Graham chuckled.

"She seems pretty mild-mannered." Dean laughed.

"Most of the time she is but don't piss her off. That woman is beautiful, sexy and sweet but she can rip you a new asshole if you cross her." Graham poured the coffee into a cup he'd pulled out of the cupboard.

"Darling, are you spreading lies about me?" Dean laughed when he heard Sophia's voice, and Graham almost dropped the cup of coffee he poured.

"I was raving to Mr. Flynn here on what an incredibly wonderful wife I have and how lucky I am to have her." Graham grinned.

"Graham, after almost thirty years don't you know I can see when you spew bullshit from that sexy mouth of yours." Sophia twirled her finger as she walked toward her husband.

"On that note, I'm going to go back to check on Peyton." Dean laughed.

"Traitor," Graham called out as Dean left the kitchen.

Over the next three days, Dean spent most of his time with Peyton. Kristy did her rounds and would be there when his niece had her therapy. Mostly, she ignored Dean, and as much as he wanted to pull her aside and tell her everything, he let it be.

He'd made a point to join Graham in the kitchen a couple of times a day for coffee and a chat. Dean liked the man. He and his wife reminded him of Kathleen and Sean O'Connor. They teased each other, but the love was undeniable. When he thought about it, all the couples he knew had this deep love that people dreamed about.

He wasn't sure if he'd ever have that. He loved Kristy more than he ever thought he could love anyone. It was as if Kristy gave him the piece of his heart that he missed but until Hannah was out of jail, and he was sure Peyton wasn't in danger that happiness had to wait. The worst part was by the time he'd be free of his obligations, Kristy would have moved on.

"Peyton was looking for you a little while ago. She buzzed the desk." Dean stopped when he heard Kristy behind him.

"Is she alright?" Kristy stood with her back braced against the wall looking beautiful.

"Dean, she wants to talk to her mom." Kristy tucked her hands into the pockets of her scrubs.

"She told you that?" Peyton asked him several times to call her mother, but inmates were only permitted inbound calls from their lawyers or in the case of an emergency.

"Look, I know she's your niece, and I don't know how much you know about her illness but …" He stopped her before she said it.

"Peyton doesn't have much time left." Dean finished what he knew before anyone ever mentioned it.

"I'm sorry." Kristy's eyes filled with tears.

"You know the only friends Peyton ever had was the nurses who cared for her and me." Dean stepped toward her.

"She's delightful." Kristy didn't move when he took another step.

"Yes, she is. So are you." Dean ran his knuckle down her cheek.

"Don't, Dean. That screws with my head." Kristy pulled back and turned away.

"I'm sorry." Dean took several steps away from her. "I don't want to do that to you."

"You've been telling me for eight years that you weren't interested. Eight years, Dean. Then three days here and you kiss me and give me that look." Kristy pulled her hands down over her face. "I've wanted you to look at me like that since the first day I saw you at James and Marina's house."

"Kitten," Dean closed his eyes and tipped back his head.

"I want the truth," Kristy demanded in a soft but firm voice.

"About how I feel?" Dean dropped his chin to his chest and sighed.

"Yes, but I want to know why you're not telling my cousin what's going on." Kristy put her finger under his chin and forced him to look at her. "You know Keith would do anything for you."

"Kitten, I know that, but with all the shit your family has dealt with over the last few years. They don't need anymore, and Keith knows most of what's going on here." Her touch calmed him.

"Peyton's in danger?" Kristy whispered.

"Possibly," Dean couldn't lie to her.

"From who?" She cupped his cheek.

"I don't want to talk about this. Not here." Dean glanced around to ensure nobody was close enough to hear the conversation.

"I'm off at seven. Come to my place and tell me what's going on. Maybe I can help." Kristy dropped her hand to her side.

"I'm not letting you put yourself in the middle of this. Not for me." Dean shook his head.

"You're not letting me?" Kristy raised her eyebrow and grinned. "You're not the boss of me, Dean. If you don't tell me, I'll ask Peyton."

Kristy stepped around him and headed in the direction of his niece's room. He caught her hand and squeezed it gently. When she turned back to him, she linked her fingers with his.

"It gets harder and harder to say no to you." Dean smiled.

"Good to know." Kristy winked and released his hand.

"When Peyton's settled for the night, I'll come over. Text me your address." Dean backed away from her toward Peyton's room.

"I will." Kristy turned and walked back to the nurse's station. As if he had no control his eyes dropped to her sweet ass. He was sure she swayed her hips a little more to tease him.

"She's trying to kill me." Dean groaned under his breath as his cock twitched.

He walked to the suite with a lighter feeling. Almost as if the weight of the world lifted off his shoulders. He'd pushed how he felt about Kristy deep down for so long that he wasn't sure if he could keep it there any longer. Cora had to be right because something in the universe kept them on the same path.

Peyton was on her side with her hand hung over the edge of the bed. He glanced at his watch to check the time. It was odd for her to sleep so long, but then again, she slept longer over the last few days. He knew what that meant, but he hated the thought.

Dean walked closer to the bed to push her hand back on the bed. Then he saw it. Her lips were blue, and her machines were turned off. Dean pressed his fingers against her neck. No pulse.

"Pey?" Dean shook her, but her head flopped forward.

Dean's heart pounded as he ran from the room his shouts for help echoed in the corridor. Medical staff seemed to come from all direction as they ran toward him. He couldn't speak as he pointed to the room.

"Mr. Flynn, come sit here." Dean looked up to see Gemma above him. He couldn't remember how he got to his knees, but she and another woman tried to help him up.

"Code blue, suite one zero two. Code blue, suite one zero two." A voice echoed over the intercom.

Dean's chest felt as if an elephant sat on it and he gasped for air. He felt someone push his head down and heard something about keep his head between his legs.

"Take slow deep breaths, Mr. Flynn." He recognized the voice and turned his head to see Leah crouched next to him.

"She... she's... not.... She... blue." Dean couldn't remember the last time he'd felt so out of control of his emotions. He thought he'd prepared himself for this, but the truth was he didn't want to believe it would happen.

"Here's some water." Gemma handed him a glass and knelt on the floor next to him.

Dean glanced up as another doctor scurried into Peyton's room. He could see the crowd of people inside as the door slowly closed again.

Twenty-eight minutes later a doctor walked out of the room followed by Kristy. Dean knew what he was about to say, and it took every ounce of strength he had to get to his feet.

"I'm sorry, Mr. Flynn. We did everything we could." Dean glanced at his name tag. It was the same doctor he'd heard the nurses complain about. Someone even called him Dr. Dick.

"All her machines were off. I don't understand. Who turned them off?" Dean asked.

"Dean, it appears that she disconnected everything. Her oxygen was turned off, and she had her phone next to her. She was sending you a text, but she didn't hit send." Kristy held out the phone.

Dean met her gaze as he took the phone from her. He glanced down at the screen and shook his head when he read the unsent text.

Peyton: Dean, I can't do this anymore. It hurts every time they have to help me clear the mucus and I know its only a matter of time before I'm gasping for air. My last breath needs to be on my terms not on this horrible disease. You're the best uncle anyone could ever have, and I love you for caring for me. Please don't be sad because I'm going to a place where I won't be sick anymore. Be happy. Live your life. Love Peyton.

Dean read the text three times and still didn't believe it. Peyton committed suicide? She was gone, and he felt numb. What was he going to tell his sister? Hannah asked him to protect her daughter, and he tried, but he didn't realize Peyton was in danger from herself. He'd only been gone from her room a little over an hour.

"Do you want to see her?" The doctor asked.

"Yeah," Dean pressed send and shoved the phone into his pocket. He didn't want to take the chance of any of what she wrote getting deleted.

"I'll go in with you." Gemma offered.

"No, I'd rather Ms. O'Connor come in with me." Dean pushed away Gemma's hand on his shoulder.

"As you wish." Gemma stepped back.

Dean pushed the door open slowly. It was too quiet. He'd gotten used to the sound of the machines, but now it seemed eerily quiet in the room with all the machines off. He stopped inside the door and glanced toward the bed.

"Are you sure you want to see her right now?" Kristy closed the door behind them and slid her hand into his.

"Yes, I have to." Dean squeezed her hand and hoped he wasn't hurting her with how tightly he held it.

They moved slowly to the side of the bed. Peyton was on her back with her hands next to her sides. Except for the slight bluish color of her lips, she looked as if she was asleep. Her mouth looked as if it was turned up with a slight smile and she appeared happy. Peaceful.

"She's not suffering anymore," Kristy whispered and rested her head against his shoulder.

"She suffered her whole life." Dean swallowed the lump in his throat as he forced out the words. Memories of a little girl with tears in her eyes because it hurt to cough filled his thoughts. A beautiful teenage girl on the floor of her bedroom with cut-outs of prom dresses she'd never wear. He couldn't stop the flashes of memories.

"Do you want me to go with you to tell her mom?" Kristy lifted her head, and he turned to look down into her eyes.

"This is going to kill her, but I'll have to call the jail to get special permission to talk to her alone." Dean couldn't stop the tears that slipped from his eyes. He didn't even cry when his dad died, but Peyton was different. She didn't deserve to die the way she did.

"Jail?" Kristy whispered.

"It's what I was going to tell you about tonight." Dean reached down and smoothed his hand over the top of Peyton's head.

"Well, come home with me when I leave, and we'll talk about everything. I'll go with you tomorrow to tell your sister." He felt her hand tighten in his.

He didn't know how long they stood next to the bed, but Kristy didn't speak as he sobbed over the loss of a beautiful soul.

Another member of his family was gone. At that moment he decided Hannah was not about to spend the rest of her life in prison for something she didn't do.

"You're in the arms of the angels, Pey. Fly with the angels, sweet girl. Fly with the angels." Dean bent over and kissed her forehead.

Chapter 6

Kristy hurried to Sophia's office as soon as she left Dean to speak with the doctor. Something didn't make sense. She'd left Peyton not two hours before, and she had a huge smile on her face, but when she buzzed Kristy, she sounded weird.

The fact that all the machines were turned off made the hair on the back of Kristy's neck stand up. Peyton's breathing was worse but for her to choose such a painful way to die didn't make sense. She would have gasped for air once she removed the oxygen.

Sophia sat behind her desk with her head in her hands and Gemma stood in front of the desk. An older gentleman was next to her, and he looked pissed.

"I'm sorry, I don't mean to interrupt." Kristy didn't care, she needed to get Dean out of the place where he could get his head around everything.

"I was about to page you, Kristy." Sophia sighed and lifted her head.

"Okay?" Kristy stepped further into the office.

"You can go, Gemma." Sophia glared at the woman. "Close the door behind you."

Gemma turned to leave but not before she gave Kristy a look that made her shudder. It was pure hate.

"Did I do something?" Kristy stepped toward the desk still anxious to tell Sophia something was off with Peyton's death.

"No, it's what you didn't do." Sophia leaned back in the chair.

"What are you talking about?" Kristy glanced at the man.

"Before we go any further, this is my husband, Graham." Sophia motioned to the man.

"It's nice to meet you," Kristy said, and the man nodded.

"Kristy, it's come to my attention that you may have been inappropriate with one of the patient's family members" Sophia raised her head and met Kristy's shocked expression.

"I'm sorry, say that again?" Kristy practically fell into the chair behind her.

"Sophia, I told you that you need to take into consideration who the information came from." The man sighed.

"Graham, please let me take care of this." Sophia glanced up at her husband and then back to Kristy.

"Sophia, I don't know where you got this information, but I swear to you I haven't been inappropriate with anyone. My God, I haven't even been here for a full week." Kristy felt as if she would burst into tears, but she swallowed hard and sat up straight in the chair.

"Did you know Mr. Flynn and his niece before you started to work here?" Sophia folded her hands in front of her.

"I've known Dean for eight years, but I didn't know his niece or that he even had one." Kristy felt a sense of panic because she wasn't sure how much Sophia knew about Dean.

"So, you've dated?" Sophia tipped her head to the side.

"No, he and my cousin are business partners, and he's become a close family friend." Kristy's heart pounded in her chest.

"Have you been intimate with him while on duty today?" Sophia appeared embarrassed to ask the question.

"What? Absolutely not." Kristy stood up and fisted her hands at her sides. "Look, I don't know where you got this information, but I've got a feeling I can guess. Yes, I've known Dean a long time, and I have deep feelings for him, but even if we were a couple, I'd never, ever, do such a thing while I was at work."

"Kristy, what's going on here?" Dean's voice boomed from behind her.

"Mr. Flynn, I was about to come see you. I've…" Sophia's ramble stopped with the slam of her office door.

"I've been outside your slightly open door since your assistant left. I've heard everything you've been discussing." Dean stomped over to stand next to Kristy.

"Mr. Flynn, I…" Sophia stopped again when Dean held up his hand.

"Graham, have you discussed with Sophia what you witnessed in the kitchen not long before Sophia joined us the other day?" Dean's face was red, and he looked about ready to explode.

"I tried, but my wife seemed to think Ms. Grimes is as innocent as a newborn baby." Graham's sarcasm was obvious.

"I didn't say that." Sophia sighed.

"Well, you should know your assistant has been less than innocent. Not only did she proposition me that day, but she did get a little hands on, shall we say." Dean's voice rumbled.

"I walked in during the conversation and can vouch for everything Dean said." Graham propped his fists on the desk next to Sophia.

"I've had other staff complain she does this, but nobody has complained other than the staff. They never have proof, and Gemma always denies it." Sophia pulled a file from the drawer of the desk.

"Honey, the truth is that girl is only here to hook some rich guy." Graham crouched next to her.

Kristy was about to run out of patience. She didn't care about all the crap with Gemma. She needed Sophia to concentrate on Peyton because something in her gut told her Peyton didn't take her own life.

"Look, can we deal with this crap over Gemma later. Ms. Flynn just passed away and what happens to me is not important." Kristy blurted out.

"I'm sorry, what did you say?" Sophia stood up slowly.

"Didn't Gemma tell you?" Kristy motioned toward the door that Gemma had exited.

"No. My God. Mr. Flynn. I'm so sorry." Sophia walked around the desk and touched Dean's shoulder.

"What happened?" Graham asked.

"It seems Pey was tired of suffering and removed her oxygen and turned off all the machines. She sent me…." Kristy cut Dean off because they needed to know what she suspected.

"Stop. I don't believe Peyton took her own life." Kristy cringed when she realized she'd yelled over Dean.

"What are you talking about?" Sophia's eyes opened wide, and her mouth dropped open.

"First of all, the last time I checked on her, she was smiling and laughing. She even teased me about beating me at cards." Kristy held out her hand. "Dean read the text she sent. She called you Dean and ended it with Peyton. The last few days I've only heard her refer to you as D and I've only heard you call her Pey. Then there was when she buzzed me at the nurse's desk. She asked if I knew where Dean was and that she needed to talk to him. She called him Dean."

"Kristy, the names could be…." Kristy held up her hand to stop him.

"Look at all the messages she's sent you. I bet not one of them says Dean. She doesn't use your name. Maybe I'm jumping to conclusions, but my gut tells me I'm not. Dad's a cop, and he's always told us to trust our instincts." Kristy blew out a heavy breath. "Get someone to check it out. I don't believe she turned off all her machines and hung up her nasal cannula on the wall. I imagine suffocating is very painful and for her to get back into the bed and cover herself up would be impossible."

Kristy glanced between the Frosts and Dean. They all seemed at a loss for words, but Kristy wasn't about to let this go until there was an investigation.

"Who was the last one in the room?" Sophia asked.

"I think I was. When I left the room, Pey was sleeping and connected to her oxygen, and all the machines were on." Dean pulled his phone from his pocket.

"I can vouch for the time he left the room," Graham said. "I was walking down the hall when he came out."

"How long were you gone from the room?" Sophia asked.

"We were in the kitchen at least an hour or more," Graham answered.

"Kristy, you do your rounds every two hours, right?" Sophia hurried behind the desk.

"Yes, I was on my way back to the room when Dean came out yelling." The memory of his panicked voice made her stomach clench.

"We need to have everyone questioned." Graham pulled off his suit jacket and tossed it on the chair.

"We need to call the police and have an autopsy done on Peyton." Kristy couldn't believe that wasn't the first thought of her new bosses.

"Kristy, we can't jump the gun here." Sophia snapped.

"Are you kidding me? We need the police to check the room for any evidence." Kristy didn't appreciate Sophia's tone.

"Evidence is probably compromised." Dean's voice cracked.

"Why?" Kristy turned, and the tears in his eyes almost broke her.

"They called a code blue. There were at least ten people in and out of that room." Dean tipped back his head, and she saw his Adam's apple move up and down.

"There still could be something there," Kristy didn't care who watched, she grabbed his hands and squeezed them. "I know I'm right, Dean."

"Fine but I'm not letting anyone do this. I want your cousins and your dad out here." Dean looked down, and she met his gaze.

"We have local police, Mr. Flynn." Sophia sounded as if she'd been insulted.

"I trust the police from Hopedale. I'm sure Kurt can get authority from the local department to have them do this investigation." Dean looked over her shoulder at Sophia.

"Honestly, I know the family too, and maybe you're right." Sophia sighed. "Do you want to call, or will I?"

"Before I call them, I've got to be honest with you." Dean glanced at Kristy, and she nodded.

She didn't know the whole story herself, but she did know that Dean's last name wasn't Flynn. She also wondered why he picked that moment to reveal his secret.

"Why do I get the feeling we are about to be thrown a curve ball." Graham plopped down in the armchair next to the desk.

"First of all, my niece's name is not Peyton Flynn." Dean pulled his wallet from his pocket and removed something from the inside.

"What's her name?" Sophia sighed.

"Peyton Decker-Humphrey." Dean dropped an identification card on the desk in front of Sophia.

"Why does that name sound familiar?" Graham squinted his eyes as if it would help him remember.

"Her father was Ivan Humphrey, and her mother is Hannah Decker-Humphrey." Dean glanced at Kristy and back to Sophia.

The names sounded familiar to her, but she couldn't figure out why. Another thing bothered her was the fact that Dean's sister had a different last name then Dean.

"Maybe this will help, my given name is Augustus Dean Decker. My father was Aiden Decker." Dean glanced at her.

Kristy knew the name Aiden Decker very well. The man was a billionaire and very well-known businessman and philanthropist. She remembered the tragic news of his death all over the news and the bad press since his death. It was a shock to her to know Dean was the man's son.

"Oh dear. Now I remember. Your sister's been accused of killing her husband." Sophia closed her eyes and then took a deep breath before opening them again. "Can I ask the reason for the dishonesty?"

Kristy noticed him wince. If there was one thing she'd learned about him, it was he didn't like to be called a liar.

"I needed keep her out of the media and hide her location from her father's brother." Dean's jaw clenched.

"I'm sure there's a reason to keep him away from your niece, but you've put us in a complicated situation." Graham stood up.

"I understand, but I assure you that it was for Pey's best interest." Dean met the man's gaze.

"How much of this does Kurt know about?" Sophia glanced at Kristy and Dean.

"Nobody outside of myself, my sister and Pey knew about any of this. Well, Keith knows most of it as well." Dean stood with his hands clasped in front of him.

Kristy pulled out her phone and hit Facetime for her father. He was about to be pissed. Dean didn't ask for help, and she knew her father thought a lot of Dean.

"Hi, sweetheart." Her father's smiling face filled her screen.

"Hey, dad." Kristy tried to force a smile.

"Kristy, what's wrong?" His smile disappeared, and concern filled his expression. "Are you okay?"

"Dad, I'm fine, but there's a problem here that we need your help with." Kristy didn't get a chance to explain when Dean took the phone from her hand.

"Bull, what the hell are you doing with my daughter?" Her father sounded like a bear about to attack, and Kristy rolled her eyes.

"Kurt, I need your help."

Chapter 7

By the rage in Kurt's eyes, Dean would be lucky if the man didn't shoot him as soon as they were face to face. Kristy's father had warned Dean not to play with Kristy's heart and if he did Kurt would make him sorry he was ever born.

"Why the fuck didn't you tell us about this? Does Keith know?" Kurt shouted, and Dean glanced up at Kristy.

She rolled her eyes again because it was typical of her father to shout and roar when he was worried. He could be a bear but with a heart the size of Newfoundland.

"He knows some but not all. I didn't want to involve any of you in this." Dean certainly didn't want Kristy anywhere near any of this.

"Well, now that worked out great, didn't it?" Kurt snapped and then took a huge breath "I don't know anything about this guy but is he capable of hurting his own niece? What about his parents?" Dean could only see Kurt's profile, and he heard the rapid clicks of a keyboard.

"Lucy and Henry are both deceased. Ivan didn't trust Eric and said he could be a mean son of a bitch. Ivan never trusted him." Dean remembered one conversation in particular with his late brother-in-law.

Eight years ago….

Dean entered his father's den for the first time since the funeral. His father was dead and in such an unnecessary way. Dean was furious with his dad for his stupidity, but he had nowhere to direct his anger.

"The last of the caters just left." Dean looked up from behind his father's old oak desk. Ivan stood inside the door with his hand shoved into his front pockets. His brother-in-law had been a rock for Hannah through the whole thing.

"Have they been paid?" Dean motioned to the chair across from him.

"Yes, I've got the invoice right here." Ivan reached into his jacket pocket and pulled out an envelope.

"Ivan, I want you to deal with all this. Dad knew I had no interest in his company." Dean motioned around the room where his father did all his business "He groomed you for all this because he knew I wanted nothing to do with it."

"Dean, you know the will divides everything between you and Hannah. I was only your father's lawyer and assistant." Ivan leaned back in the chair and rested his ankle on top of his other leg.

"Ivan, you might have been dad's lawyer, but you know about all this crap. It's not something I want, and I know Hannah doesn't." Dean rested his elbows on the desk.

"You know what everyone's gonna say." Ivan sighed and linked his hands behind his head.

"I don't give a fuck what anyone says. I know you married my sister because you love her. I also know you treat her like a queen and you worship Peyton." Dean never for a moment thought Ivan was after his sister for her money.

"My brother told me I stuck my dick in a gold mine and he wished Hannah had a sister." Ivan's jaw clenched, and it was obvious the man disliked his brother.

There'd been trouble with Ivan's brother ever since they moved to St. John's. The police were called more than once to have him removed from the Decker property.

"I am happy to believe that your dick has gone nowhere near my sister and immaculate conception conceived Peyton." Dean chuckled, but Ivan's expression remained serious.

"I love Hannah with all my heart, and I'd do anything to keep her happy. I don't give a fuck about money or position, Dean, but my brother, he worries me. Things he says makes me wonder what the man is capable of." Ivan stood up and pulled his hands down over his face. *"Look, I'll manage everything, but no decisions will be made without you or Hannah. Okay?"*

"That's fine with me." As long as he didn't have to be the one dealing with CEO's and business meetings, Dean didn't give a shit.

"I need you to do one thing for me?" Ivan rested his fists on the desk and met Dean's gaze.

"What?"

"Help me keep my crazy brother away from my family. My mom and dad are probably not going to be around much longer. I mean they're in their eighties. Dad's on borrowed time, and mom doesn't know she's in the world or out. I'm worried when they're gone; Eric will get desperate." Ivan swallowed hard. *"I don't trust him. I know it's a terrible thing to say about my own brother, but he's hated me for years, and I don't know why. He says I get what I want whether it was mine or not. I'm sure if he could find a way to do away with me he'd do it with a smile on his face."*

The memory of the conversation caused more pain then he wanted to admit. Now, Ivan was dead, and Hannah in jail for his death. Eric had to be involved, but Dean didn't know how.

"You don't believe your sister killed her husband." Kurt must have seen something in Dean's expression.

"No, but there's no way to explain away the evidence." Dean hated how vulnerable he felt with everyone's eyes focused on him.

"I really should kick your fucking arse for not trusting us to help, but right now we'll deal with what happened with your niece and then work on your sister's case after that. Then you've got a real shit knocking coming to you." Kurt's forehead wrinkled as he leaned into the screen. "Do you want me to call Keith or do you want to do that. I'm gonna send the coroner and forensics unit from St. John's."

"I'd feel more comfortable with you guys …" Kurt stopped him.

"They're the best." Kurt's expression softened. "I wouldn't send them otherwise, Bull."

"Thanks, Kurt." Dean did appreciate it more than he could ever say.

"You're family, no thanks necessary but don't think that gets you out of my bad books." Kurt's lips quirked. "We'll get this figured out, son."

The screen went black, but the last word Kurt said hit Dean straight in the heart. It was stupid but to have a man he idolized call him, son, gave him hope that everything would be okay.

"I'll call Keith and make sure he has Noah in his arms. That way he won't yell." Kristy smiled as she took her phone from his hand.

"Rusty's yelling doesn't bother me." Dean referred to Keith by the nickname they used for him at work.

"Me either but it will bother him when he can't." Kristy tapped the screen, and he heard the ring go through.

"Hey, cuz." Keith's voice echoed.

"Where's baby Noah?" Kristy glanced over the top of the phone at Dean.

"He's right here." Emily's laugh made him smile.

"You should let Keith hold him while we talk." Kristy pressed her lips together.

"Why?" Keith knew something was up by his tone.

"Just do it." Kristy sighed.

There was a rustle, and Kristy turned the phone so that he could see Keith and Emily. If it weren't such a fucked up situation, the couple's expressions would have been laughable.

"What the f... What are you doing there?" So, Keith did censor his language around the baby. This call was about to get interesting.

"Remember you can't yell with Noah in your arms and don't pretend you didn't know Dean was here with his niece. I'm not stupid." Kristy leaned her head against Dean's shoulder and then pulled away.

"Bull, what the fudge cake is going on?" Dean couldn't help but chuckle at the child appropriate language Keith used.

"See, babe. It's so easy to use other words." Emily grinned and then turned back to the camera. "What are you doing there with Kristy?"

Dean was sure there was smoke about to come out of Keith's ears as he told his friend everything. Emily looked annoyed as well, and she was another one Dean didn't want to piss off.

"Bull, I can't use the type of words I want to use right now or tell you what I'm going to do when I get my hands on you but trust me in about an hour you better be wearing earplugs and body armor." Keith sounded so idiotic with the soft tone of voice he used.

"Get in line because your uncle already gave me a list of hurt he's going to rain down on me." Dean snapped.

"How could you keep this from us? You're family for heaven's sake." Emily looked about ready to burst into tears.

"I'm sorry and please don't cry." Dean hated to hurt any of these people.

"You aren't making me cry it's the darn hormones, but I can't believe you wouldn't ask for help. Especially after all the help you've given this family." Emily shook her head and pulled Noah from Keith's arms.

"That's why. You guys have been through hell and…" Dean got stopped again when Keith's face filled the screen.

"Bull, are you kidding me right now? If one of us needed you tomorrow wouldn't you drop everything and be here?" Keith growled.

"Yeah, but…"

"So why the hell would you think we would do anything else? I knew you weren't telling me everything. If you had, I could have told you where Kristy was going to work, and my cousin wouldn't be involved." Keith's face wasn't as red, but he was hurt.

"Keith, will you stop being a bum. He's a big dummy we know, but now he needs us, and it's none of your business how I'm involved. I can take care of myself." Kristy snatched the phone from Dean.

"I know you can but … never mind. How much of this did you know about?" Keith snapped at her, and that didn't sit well with Dean.

"Not as much as you, apparently." Kristy's snarky response made her cousin wince.

"She didn't know anything." Dean stepped behind her and Keith was quiet for a moment.

"Uncle Kurt has help on the way?" Keith glanced behind him at Emily.

"Yes," Kristy answered.

"Bull, I'll be there as soon as I can, and I'm sure I won't be alone." Keith stopped and sighed. "Hang in there, brother."

Dean raised his arms and linked his fingers behind his head as he turned toward the window. The last thing he wanted was to involve this family in any more drama.

"Dean, it'll be okay." Kristy touched his arm, and he spun around.

Her blue eyes always mesmerized him because they were like a mirror to her beautiful soul. She was kind and thoughtful, but when he gazed into her eyes, he felt at peace. Nobody had ever been able to make him feel that way.

"Dean, I don't know what kind of connections Kurt has, but the police and coroner are here." He'd almost forgotten Sophia and Graham were in the room.

"I guess when the Chief of police of Newfoundland calls, everyone jumps." Graham glanced out through the window.

"I'll have them come in here to talk to you." Sophia opened the door. "I'll also show them to the suite."

"Thanks, Sophia." Dean nodded.

"If I haven't already said it, I'm very sorry for your loss." Sophia and Graham walked out of the office, and he was left alone with Kristy.

"Do you really believe Pey, didn't do this herself?" Dean took Kristy's hand and linked his fingers with hers.

"It's a gut feeling, but no I don't think she would do it. I know I've only known her a few days, but she kept talking about the future." Kristy took his other hand and held it the same way.

"I don't know how. Without a transplant, Pey didn't have a chance." Dean pressed his forehead against hers. "Not the best first week of a new job for you, is it?"

"Dean, I don't give a shit about this job right now. I do care about you. More than you know." Kristy pulled back and stared into his eyes.

"I know, Kitten. I'm so sorry for hurting you." Dean released her hands and cupped her face.

"You did hurt me, but it didn't change how I feel." Kristy turned her head and pressed her lips to his wrist.

"I need to tell you before your family comes and probably kills me. Kristy, I…" The door of the office opened, and he dropped his hands.

Dean recognized the man that entered as one of the officers who helped when Mike's wife was on a human trafficking list.

"Steve?" Kristy pushed back from Dean.

"Hey, Kristy." Steve Parker smiled at her and it irritated Dean.

"I didn't realize you were coming," Dean tried not to snap at the police officer, but it was hard.

"I was out this way to interview a witness for a case." He reached out to shake Dean's hand.

"Thanks." Kristy smiled.

"Hey, the Chief calls we jump." Steve motioned for them to sit.

"I appreciate it." Dean practically fell into the armchair and waited for the interrogation.

It was standard procedure for Steve to ask another officer to take Kristy out of the room, but Dean wanted to punch him. Of course, the constant questions about why he hid their identity not only from Comfort Life Care and his friends made him feel about three inches tall.

"I'll need her phone." Steve held out an evidence bag.

"I've touched it and so did Kristy." Dean pulled it from his pocket and dropped it in the bag.

"It's okay, we've got both of your prints on file." Steve zipped up the bag and handed it to the officer he called into the room.

Since Dean owned and worked with a security firm his fingerprints were on record, and he assumed because Kristy worked with the hospitals they would have done the same to her as well.

Two hours later Dean watched through the window as a man pushed a covered gurney out to the awaiting ambulance. It was déjà vu. He'd observed that day someone wheeled Ivan out of his sister's home in the same way.

Four months ago ....

Dean couldn't believe his eyes. Hannah handcuffed and shoved into the back of a police cruiser and his brother-in-law, dead, in a body bag.

What the hell happened? Hannah wouldn't hurt a fly how the hell could she kill the man she loved more than life itself. She seemed to stagger when the police led her out of the house. Then again, she was probably in shock.

"Your niece is looking for you, Mr. Decker." Dean glanced at the young officer in the doorway. He was relieved not to see anyone he recognized or who would know him.

"Thank you." Dean walked to where they'd brought Peyton when he arrived.

"Keep all the family separated." he'd heard one of them say.

"D, oh God." She sobbed as she practically fell into his arms. "Mom... she.... she wouldn't... hurt dad." Peyton sobbed through heavy gasps.

"Shhh... Pey, the police will figure out the truth." Dean held her while she sobbed and helped her when she struggled to breathe.

Peyton's condition declined more then he thought. His sister had hired a full-time nurse to be with his niece when Hannah couldn't.

He wished he knew what happened because now he was in the middle of a shit storm and no fucking idea what to do. He couldn't involve his friends in any of this. They just got through their own version of hell with Mike's wife and her niece.

Dean had to deal with his family trouble on his own. His father's death had been plastered all over the papers for years and still showed up around the anniversary of his accident. He managed to keep out of that without it coming out who he was.

Now it was about to hit the fan, again. He'd protected his sister and niece from most of the media blowback back then, but he couldn't protect them from it now.

Present….

Dean paced the office while he waited for Steve to give him the okay to leave. It would take a couple of days for the autopsy report but the more he thought about it, the more he knew the truth.

"Bull," Dean stopped in the middle of the office but didn't turn toward the door. He knew the voice, and for the first time in years, he was ashamed to look his friend in the eyes.

"Not now, Rusty." Dean's eyes zoned in on a nail in the wall as he referred to his friend by the nickname given to him years before.

"Brother, I'm not here to give you shit. I'm here to help. We're here to help." Keith stepped further into the room, and Dean heard the shuffle of several feet.

When he turned to face the door, James, Aaron, Nick, Caden 'Rex' Dixon, Hunter 'Crunch' Crawford, Ben 'Trunk' Murphy and Sandy formed a semi-circle at the entrance of the office.

"Don't all of you have jobs to do?" Dean found it difficult to speak.

"Family first." James smiled.

"Brothers always help each other." Nick winked.

"We got your back." Aaron slapped Dean on the shoulder.

"I might want to kick you in the jewels for holding out, Chrome Dome, but I'll wait until your sister is out of jail and we find out what happened to your niece." Sandy stood in front of him as she poked him in the chest.

Dean couldn't help himself he pulled the feisty woman into a hug and was relieved she hugged him back without the damage to his balls.

"Right now, we need to get out of here. Kristy's taking you back to her place. She said you haven't eaten or slept and it's after eleven." Kurt squeezed through the men and stepped in front of Dean.

"I'm not tired, and I've got to go see my sister." Dean sighed.

"Bull, I'm not in the mood for another fucking argument. My daughter practically bit my head off because I told her you were not going back to her apartment. I'm about this far from pounding the piss out of you." Kurt held up his thumb and index finger about a centimeter apart. "I know how my daughter feels about you and I swear on my life if you hurt her again I'll rip your arm off and beat you to death with it."

"Wow, that's the most words I've ever heard Kurt say at once." Sandy chuckled but stopped when Kurt glared at her. "Oh, don't be such a grump or I'll call Nan and tell her you're picking on Chrome Dome." Sandy pushed Kurt's shoulder playfully.

"Why the hell did we let you come?" Kurt covered his eyes with his hand and groaned.

"You didn't let me. I told you I was coming with or without your permission." Sandy nudged Kurt with her shoulder and left the room.

"How the fuck does Ian handle that woman?" Kurt turned around and shook his head.

"Please don't ask her that. She'll start telling you about their sex games." Aaron laughed.

"Guys, if you don't mind, can I talk to Kurt alone for a minute." Dean glanced over Kurt's shoulder at the men behind him.

The group filed out of the room, and Keith closed the door but didn't leave the room. Dean knew it was useless to ask him for a chance to speak with his uncle in private.

"Kurt, I want to apologize for all this." Dean met Kurt's blue eyes. "I do want you to know that I never wanted to hurt Kristy."

"Not now, Bull. Go and get in the car before she gets her mother on the phone again or worse, she could call my mother." Kurt put his phone to his ear.

Dean didn't say another word as he walked toward the office door. Keith opened it and met Dean's gaze. It was obvious his friend wanted to say something, but he held back. Either Keith was worried about his grandmother giving him grief or too pissed off to be civil.

The last thing Dean heard as he left the office was Kurt's booming voice giving orders to whoever he called.

"I don't give a fuck what it takes. I want every piece of information you have on Ivan Humphrey's murder and I want it yesterday."

Chapter 8

Kristy made her way to the staff room to grab her things before she headed home. The shouting match with her father had given her a headache. It wasn't her fault Dean didn't tell her or her family about his business. It didn't reveal all his secrets to her because the truth was he'd gone out of his way to avoid her.

Still, no matter how much she hurt over him there was no way she'd let him push her away anymore. The kiss they'd shared earlier in the day proved that Dean Nash wanted her more than he'd admit.

Kristy plopped down on the bench in front of her locker. Dean had so much more to deal with at the moment than a relationship.

Poor Peyton.

Why would someone want to hurt her? It didn't matter that the sweet girl probably didn't have much time left, but there was still a slim chance. How could someone be heartless enough to hurt a terminally ill woman?

"You okay?" Kristy looked up.

"It's been a hard day, Sandy." Her cousin's wife sat next to her and draped her arm around Kristy's shoulder.

"Chrome Dome has kept a lot from us." Sandy squeezed her shoulder.

"Will you please stop calling him that?" Kristy sighed.

"Sorry. Do you want to talk about it?" Sandy was a bit of a hardass, but she did have a heart as big as Newfoundland.

"Peyton was such a sweet woman. It was bad enough that she's been sick her whole life, but someone kills her. For what?" It took a lot to make Kristy cry, but the tears spilled out and ran down her cheeks. "She didn't deserve this."

"Honey, we'll figure this out." Sandy grabbed the box of tissues next to the cabinet by the entrance of the staff room.

"Dean is lost. I'm sure he's worried about his sister's reaction to this." Kristy wiped her face with a tissue. "His sister. I didn't even know he had one. Hell, we didn't even know who he really was."

"Oh, I sort of knew," Sandy grumbled. "I didn't know all of it."

"How come you never told me? How could you not know everything? Don't you search the entire internet for things you want to know?" Kristy nudged Sandy with her shoulder.

"I would never do such a thing." Sandy's fake shock made Kristy laugh.

"No, not you." Kristy stood up and closed her locker. She threw her knapsack upon her shoulder and linked her arm into Sandy. "Let's get out of here. Dean's coming back to my place so he can get some sleep."

"Ohhh… are you sure he'll get sleep with you there?" Sandy winked.

"You're a pervert." Kristy rolled her eyes.

"It's what your cousin loves most about me." Sandy sighed.

Sometimes Kristy wished she was more like Sandy. The woman had tenacity and said whatever was on her mind. It's not that Kristy didn't have confidence or afraid, to be honest with people but when it came to Dean the only time she had the guts to make a move she felt stupid.

She didn't want to read more into their kiss, but he wanted her as much as she wanted him. The problem was Kristy more than wanted him; she was in love with him.

"Bull's in there talking to uncle Kurt," Nick told her when they met everyone outside of Sophia's office.

"Probably getting the '*keep your hands to yourself*' speech." Aaron laughed.

"Shut up, A.J." James slapped Aaron on the back of the head.

"I swear, between my brothers and uncle Kurt it's a wonder I don't have brain damage." Aaron rubbed the back of his head.

"Oh, you do, Honey." Sandy slapped Aaron on the shoulder.

"You took the words right out of my mouth, Sandy." James laughed.

"Why do I stay around you people?" Aaron feigned a sigh as he leaned on the small reception desk.

That was her family. Always teasing but they loved each other. It's the way Kristy felt about them and Dean. If only he felt the same way about her. Sure, he was attracted to her, that was obvious, but that's not all she wanted from him. He was about to tell her something when Steve showed up, but he didn't finish.

Kristy glanced over her shoulder toward the exit. Leah and Gemma looked as if they were in a heated discussion. She found it odd because Leah told her during training that she disliked Sofia's assistant.

"That looks intense." Nick nodded his head toward the two girls.

"Yeah, I'll be right back." Kristy liked Leah and was more than a little pissed at Gemma for her attempt to get her in shit. The woman had her priorities entirely out of whack. Her priority should have been to tell Sophia about Peyton's death not trying to get Kristy fired.

"You had no right to be in that room." Leah snapped.

"I had every right to be there. I've got to check and make sure you're doing your job." Gemma flicked her hair over her shoulder, and Leah looked ready to strangle her.

"That isn't your job. You're Sophia's assistant and not the head of the medical staff. That's Dr. Dickson's job." Leah took a step toward Gemma.

"Leah, what's going on?" Kristy touched Leah's arm because the girl looked about ready to give Gemma a black eye.

"This doesn't concern you, Ms. O'Connor. I'm sure you need to make sure you've got all your things so that you can leave." Gemma raised an eyebrow. Maybe she should have let Leah punch the woman.

"I have my things, Ms. Grimes." Kristy glared at the arrogant bitch.

"I'm sorry we couldn't work together longer, but your inappropriate actions can't get swept under the rug." Gemma tucked her hair behind her ear.

"What are you talking about, Gemma?" Kristy remembered Sophia asking about what happened with Dean, but the woman didn't say anything about being fired.

"Your contract states that you can't fraternize with patients or families of the patients. It's immediate dismissal." Gemma's expression changed to anger.

"Considering what happened today, I doubt Sophia was concerned with your gossip." Leah snapped at Gemma.

"It wasn't gossip. I was doing my job." Gemma raised her voice.

"So, is it your job to try and seduce Peyton's uncle?" Kristy spun around at the sound of the male voice.

Graham stood behind Kristy and looked mad enough to kill. Gemma's cocky attitude vanished. Leah crossed her arms over her chest, and it was all Kristy could do not to laugh at the grin the young nurse now had on her pretty face.

"I… I didn't…. I didn't try to seduce anyone." Gemma stammered over her words.

"I'm going to say this once and once only. You may be Sophia's assistant, but I own this place as well, and I can tell you without a doubt Ms. O'Connor still has a job here as does Leah. You're walking a thin line." Graham's voice was deep and threatening. "Do you understand Ms. Grimes?"

"I…Yes, Mr. Frost." Gemma spun around and practically ran away.

"Thank you, Mr. Frost." Kristy was relieved her job was safe because getting fired on her first week would be humiliating.

"I think considering the circumstances of what happened today, we've much more to worry about then that vindictive bitch."

Graham squeezed Kristy's shoulder. "It's possible someone took a life here tonight, and I won't rest until we find out for sure."

"Mr. Frost, I understand how you feel, but you need to let the police handle this." James stepped next to Kristy. "It's why we're here."

"Officer, I understand it's your job, but my wife and I have worked our asses off to create a safe and comfortable place for the patients. To know that someone may have got in here to murder that girl makes me sick to my stomach." Graham looked as if he was about to burst into tears.

"Yes, Mr. Frost, this is my job, but it's also personal to all these people and me. Bull's practically a brother and Kristy's my cousin." James was right they would move heaven and earth to help anyone in trouble.

"Bull?" Graham glanced between her and James.

"It's Dean's nickname." Kristy smiled.

"Well, he's about the size of one." Graham chuckled.

"Not sure if that's where he got the name or not." James glanced over his shoulder toward the office. "I hope we can figure this out. He's gone out of his way to help us over the last few years."

James wasn't wrong. Dean had been one of the first to volunteer whenever there was any family drama. It was the O'Connors turn to help him. Maybe one of the other staff saw something.

She turned to speak to Leah, but the nurse stepped back when Graham chastised Gemma. Kristy scanned the foyer, and at first, she didn't see her friend, but out of the corner of her eye, she caught sight of her outside with her back against the window.

"Tell Dean I'll be outside." Kristy kissed James cheek and then made her way through the door.

Leah didn't seem to notice when Kristy walked toward her. The young nurse was deep in concentration with something on her phone. There was a lot of tension in Leah's stance.

"Hey," Kristy stood next to her.

"Sorry about that in there." Leah shoved her phone into her pocket.

"Don't worry about it. I don't know what the hell Gemma has against me, but she seems to want me out of here." Kristy shook her head and gazed out at the grounds. It was dark, except for the street lights around the perimeter of the parking lot.

"She hates anyone that gets more attention than she does. Especially, from men." Leah leaned her head back against the wall.

"Why were you here so early? You weren't supposed to start until eight?" Kristy asked.

"One of the other nurses was out sick today, and Sophia asked if I wanted to split a shift with the other night nurse. I need the money, so I said yes. What a night to do over time?" Leah sighed.

The door to the building opened, and Nick ran down the front steps to one of the cars parked in front of the door. He dug around in the trunk for a bit and then made his way inside the building again. Gave her a quick wave before he disappeared inside.

"At least the view is amazing." Leah nodded toward Nick.

"Yeah, he does nothing for me." Kristy smiled.

"Are you freaking blind?" Leah stared at her.

"Nick's my cousin. Most of the bunch in there are related to me or might as well be related." Kristy chuckled.

"Damn, I'm moving to Hopedale." Leah sighed.

"You want to tell me what the argument with Gemma was about?" Kristy asked.

"I was in the staff room earlier, and she was in there," Leah glanced at her then to the ground.

"What's the big deal about her being in the staff room?" Kristy didn't understand.

"It's the staff room. Management has offices with bathrooms. That bitch had no right to be in there." Leah grumbled. "She was in there to show me who has the most power in this place."

"What do you mean?"

"Put it this way. If she doesn't like you, it wouldn't surprise me if she tried to put something in your locker or spread a rumor about you." Leah stood up and stretched. "Be careful around her."

"You sound as if you know from experience." Kristy stood as well.

"Not me but she manipulates people." Leah sighed.

"Do you know if she was near Peyton's room earlier?" It was a long shot and getting someone fired was a far cry from murder.

"I don't know. When the code was called everyone came running." Leah stood next to the entrance.

"You aren't going home?" Kristy started to head down the steps.

"I'm here until eight in the morning." Leah smiled.

"You need sleep, Leah." Leah looked exhausted.

"I'll sleep on my day off tomorrow. Plus, I'll get a couple of hours when everyone is down for the night." Leah stopped. "I just realized, I only have two patients now."

"Yeah, poor Peyton." Kristy swallowed the lump in her throat. "I'll see you tomorrow."

Kristy hurried through the parking lot to her car. It was creepy to walk through it at night, and after what happened she probably should have gotten someone to walk her to her car. A feeling tickled the back of her neck, and she increased her pace toward the vehicle.

Kristy glanced behind her as she got to her car. Trunk jogged down the front steps and made his way to his jeep in front of the building. He looked agitated and had his phone to his ear. Kristy laughed as she got into her car. Trunk had gotten close to a friend of Mike's wife. From what Kristy had gotten from Jess, Abbie Martin had Trunk in a spin.

Kristy pulled her car directly in front of the entrance and waited for Dean. She'd warned her father not to give him shit about staying at her place. Her dad was aware how Kristy felt about the man thanks to Cora. Not that she'd said anything to her aunt but with her cupid thing she made it very clear Kristy was meant to be with Dean.

It caused a bit of a shouting match between her dad and Cora. When it came to his sister's weird gift, he didn't deal well with her playing cupid with his daughters. Although up until Dean had kissed her earlier, Kristy figured it would be the first time Cora the Cupid would be wrong, but there was a sliver of hope in her heart now. She hoped it didn't get broken again.

Chapter 9

Outside the office, the rest of the group stood around quietly in conversation. Well, except Aaron. He seemed to have found his next conquest in one of the pretty nurses behind the reception desk.

As he left the building, Dean shook his head. Aaron would pick up a woman anywhere. The guy was a walking hormone, and at thirty years old he showed no signs of settling down.

Kristy parked in front of the main entrance leaned against the passenger side door. It was dark out, but the light from the doorway fell on her beautiful face as she gazed up at him. It was as if all the stress in his body disappeared and when she smiled his heart fluttered in his chest.

God, he loved her, but he was terrified to admit it out loud. Everyone he loved was slowly getting ripped from his life. It started almost ten years ago with his mother's death, then his father and now Peyton. If he lost Kristy, it would kill him.

"I thought I was going to have to come in and drag you out." Kristy pushed off the car and walked around to the driver's side.

"I needed to talk to Kurt." Dean didn't get into her car.

"Did he give you a hard time?" Kristy groaned.

"Not as much as he should have." Dean shoved his hands into his front pockets.

"Should you have talked to Keith or dad about all this? Yes. Was it your choice to do so? Yes. Were you a big idiot? That would be a big yes." Kristy crossed her arms over her chest.

"Gee, thanks." Dean kept a safe distance from her.

"You're welcome but Dean it was your family and your business. None of us know what it's like to be involved in this type of situation, but the fact of the matter is, it's in the past, and the only thing that's important is finding out who killed Peyton and get your sister out of jail." Kristy opened the car door. "Come on. We'll get a bite to eat on the way to my apartment."

"I'm not going with you." Dean stepped back from the car.

"Dean, you need to sleep and eat. Dad and the rest of the guys can deal with things while you get some rest. They need to start their investigation, and you can't get involved. You know that." Kristy motioned toward the building.

"I'm not hungry, and I doubt I can sleep." Especially if he was alone in a small apartment with Kristy. Even with all the shit on his mind, he knew that it was too tempting to be close to her.

"Dean, I'm not arguing over this. Get in the damn car and come on." Kristy snapped.

"Kitten, I can't." Dean shook his head.

"For fuck sake, do I have to get Nan out here because I will if I have to." Kristy pointed her finger at him.

"What's your grandmother going to do? Pick me up and put me in the car." Dean chuckled.

Before he finished, Kristy pulled out her phone, and her fingers tapped furiously on the screen. Dean had no idea what she was doing. At least not until his phone buzzed in his rear pocket.

He pulled it out and glanced at the screen. He knew the number because Nanny Betty added him to the family text group, but she wasn't texting him. She was calling.

"You gonna answer?" Kristy grinned as she tucked her phone into her pocket.

"Hello," Dean glared at Kristy as he put the phone to his ear.

"Now young man, get in dat car wit Kristy. Yar not gonna be any good fer anyone if ya falls flat on yer face because ya aren't lookin' after yerself." Nanny Betty's demanding voice echoed through his phone.

"I'm fine, Nan." Dean pointed his finger at Kristy, but it only made her grin more.

121

"No yar not. Don't have me get Tom ta drive me out der ta duff ya in da arse." Nanny Betty's voice was firm, and there was no use arguing with the woman who was like a grandmother because she would make poor Tom drive out over the highway to give him that kick in the ass.

"Alright, Nan. Don't go making Tom drive at this hour. I'll go and get a bite to eat." Dean sighed.

"Good, we're all here for ya." Nanny Betty's voice cracked.

"Thank you, Nan." Dean ended the call.

"Well?" Kristy wasn't even trying to hide her laugh.

"That was mean." Dean held his phone up. "But I'm not getting in your car."

"I'll call her again." Kristy pulled her phone out.

"Your car is a sardine can. I'll follow you in my truck." Dean didn't give her a chance to respond as he turned and made his way to his vehicle.

"I'll text you the address," Kristy shouted as he yanked open the door of his truck.

Dean slammed the door and tipped his head back. He rubbed his hand over the stubble on his bald head. He'd given up on shaving his beard, but at the point he kind of liked it. He wondered what Kristy thought of it.

Dean pulled into the parking space next to Kristy's car. She'd sent a text and told him he had fifteen minutes to get to her place or she was going to call her grandmother again. At that moment Dean didn't know if he was afraid she'd do that or if he only wanted to spend time alone with Kristy. After the kiss, he knew he didn't have the willpower to deny himself of the very thing he'd wanted since the day he met her.

He grabbed his bag from the back seat and hopped out of his truck. The building was two stories with ten apartments in total. They had separate entrances, and Kristy was in number seven. He walked down the brick path toward her door, but he didn't miss the little dangers around the place. There wasn't a lot of light in the parking lot or the walkway for that matter. It didn't sit well with him.

He stood in number seven and tried to calm his racing heart. He was a six-foot-four man that could bench press three hundred pounds and took down men that were as big or bigger than him but Dean 'Bull' Nash was terrified of what would happen when he entered the apartment.

"Fucking coward." He grumbled as he knocked on the door.

"It's open." Kristy's muffled voice shouted from inside the apartment.

"Are you out of your fucking mind?" Dean snapped when he stomped into the apartment. "That could have been anyone knocking on your door."

"Wow, for a man who has his own security firm you aren't very observant." Kristy placed two plates on the small table in her little kitchen.

"What are you talking about?" Dean dropped his bag inside the door.

She pointed to the small television screen on her counter. How the hell did he miss the camera outside? He knew how. He'd been preoccupied with his racing heart and looking for non-existent danger.

Dean slipped out of his jacket and hung it on the hook next to the entrance. When he walked further into the apartment, she placed two bottles of beer next to the plates.

"Sit and eat. Nan sent lots of food out with Dad." Kristy sat in one of the chairs and picked up her fork. "I heated it up, so dig in before it cools off."

The aroma of the roast beef with dark rich gravy made his mouth water. Nanny Betty's food was the best, and he was a lot hungrier than he thought. He pulled out the chair and glanced at Kristy. She giggled as he eased into the small chair.

"If you'd be more comfortable on the sofa you can take your food over there." Kristy hitched her thumb over her shoulder. "Those chairs aren't exactly built for someone of your size."

"Great, now you're calling me fat." Dean grabbed the fork and picked up a piece of the thick, rich beef. He shoved it into his mouth and moaned. "Damn that woman can cook."

"Yep," Kristy smiled as she slowly ate her meal.

"Thank you." Dean smiled at her.

"For what?" Kristy tilted her head to the side.

"For being so wonderful to Peyton and ..." Dean swallowed hard.

"And what?" Her bright blue eyes met his.

"For being there for me today." Dean pushed the plate back because the memory of Peyton's lifeless body flashed in his head.

"You need to finish eating." Kristy stood and picked up her plate. "And you're welcome, but you don't need to thank me."

Dean watched her place her plate in the dishwasher and wiped down the counter for the third time. She'd changed into a pair of pajama pants and tank top that fit snuggly against her firm breasts.

He hadn't moved from the chair because his cock was painfully hard. He wanted to strip Kristy naked and worship every inch of her body and forget every reason he'd listed in his head why he had to keep his distance from her.

"Do you want it?" She stood next to the table and gazed down at him.

"Huh?" Did he say what he wanted to do out loud?

"Your food. Are you finished?" Kristy pointed to the plate.

"Oh, yeah. I'm done." Dean pushed back from the table and made his way to her small living room.

"You didn't eat very much," Kristy called after him.

"I'm not hungry." Dean plopped down on the couch to lay down. It was a good thing he probably wasn't going to sleep because he'd never get comfortable. A man his size would never get comfortable on the lumpy couch.

He tucked the throw pillow under his head and draped his arm over his eyes. One leg hung over the end of the couch, and the other stretched out on the floor.

"Dean, the bed is more comfortable." She startled him when she touched his arm.

"Yeah, that's not a good idea." Dean kept his eyes closed.

"Don't trust me?" She laughed, and he opened one eye to look up at her.

"It's not you I don't trust." He growled because she had her arms crossed under her breasts. It pushed them up and enhanced the fact she wasn't wearing a bra.

Fuck my life.

126

"Dean, I'll sleep on the couch. I've been sleeping there anyway. You need to sleep." She crouched next to him.

"Kitten, why do you sleep on the couch?" Dean turned on his side and rested his cheek on his fist.

"I don't know. I've only been here a little while, and I feel more comfortable in the living room." Kristy looked down at her leg and picked off what appeared to be an invisible piece of lint.

"You're not used to being so far away from your family." Her whole family was never more than a few minutes apart from each other.

"Dean, I've been living on my own since I was twenty." The cute way she plopped down in the small armchair and sighed made his dick twitch.

"Yes, but someone in your family was always at least two minutes away." Dean turned his head so that he couldn't see her.

"Stop changing the subject and go sleep in the bed." He hadn't noticed how close she was until she tugged on his arm and his hand curled around her forearm.

He looked up, and her gaze met his. It would be so easy to pull her on top of him and get lost in her, but that wouldn't be fair. Kristy had feelings for him, and it would give her hope that they could have a future. It wouldn't be a good idea until his sister was out of jail and he found out who killed Peyton.

"Go to bed, Kitten." Dean released her arm and turned into the back of the couch.

"No, if you don't go in there and get off my couch then I'll sleep in the chair. So, either you go in the bedroom, or we'll be sleeping in the living room together." Kristy grabbed his shoulder and pulled him, so he had to turn over onto his back.

"Kristy, go to bed." Dean snapped.

"I can't because your overgrown ass is on it." Kristy yanked on his arm again.

"Are you calling me fat?" Dean chuckled.

"Dean, will you please go to bed and let me go to sleep. I'm exhausted….." Dean jumped up, and Kristy stepped back.

"You are going to tell me why you don't want to sleep in the bedroom." Dean stood up slowly and took a step toward her.

"I won't be telling you anything because there's nothing to tell. I like sleeping here." Kristy stepped around him and quickly made herself comfortable on the lumpy couch.

Dean stared at her for a moment as she made herself comfortable. He crossed his arms over his chest and waited until she looked back up at him. She didn't. Kristy turned into the back of the couch and tucked her arm under the pillow.

"Turn off the light on your way to the bedroom." Kristy yawned, and he shook his head.

Dean switched off the light and made his way to the bedroom at the back of the apartment. He found the light switch and flicked it on. The bedroom was average size with a double bed in the center of two windows. A white dresser with a large mirror was on the left side of the room with only a lamp on top of it.

Dean found it odd that there was very little of Kristy's things in her bedroom and she'd been so determined not to sleep in the room. He didn't see anything off as he sat on the bed. It was definitely more comfortable than the couch.

"So why don't you want to sleep in here, Kitten," Dean whispered.

Dean lay back on the bed and tucked his hands under his head. He stared at the ceiling, and for the first time since he'd left Comfort Life Care, he allowed what happened to Peyton back into his thoughts. He should have stayed at the place to help, but he had to figure out how to tell Hannah.

His sister seemed ready to give up on ever getting cleared of the murder charges. Now with Peyton gone, Hannah probably wouldn't fight at all. He had to do something about getting a new lawyer for her because Trevor Poole wasn't doing a damn thing to help her.

Dean closed his eyes and tried to relax. It was quiet in the apartment it was why the soft scratching had him slowly sitting up. He flicked on the lamp next to the bed and glanced toward the corner of the room. At first, he wasn't sure what he saw, but then it moved again. The small brown figure scratched at a box on the floor and Dean glanced around the room.

The little mouse didn't seem the least bit concerned when Dean eased his way off the bed to grab the empty glass on the nightstand. He was pretty sure catching the thing would be impossible, but he wasn't getting any sleep he might as well do something.

To his surprise, he managed to scoop the mouse into the glass with minimal effort.

"So, are you the reason she avoids sleeping in here?" Dean whispered as the mouse stretched it's body up trying to escape his small confines.

He glanced out through the bedroom window but decided it would be cruel to put the thing out on the window sill eight feet off the ground. He opened the bedroom door and tried to ease his way to the front door quietly.

"Okay little fella, you need to find another home," Dean whispered as he eased open the front door.

"Who are you talking too?" Kristy startled him, and he spun around.

When she noticed what was in his hand, Kristy jumped up off the couch and ran out of the living room. It would have been comical if it had been any other day.

"Get that damn thing out of here. Where the hell did you get that?" Kristy shouted from behind the bathroom door.

"I'm bringing it outside." Dean shook his head as he opened the door.

Dean walked to the end of the parking lot to a grassy area away from the building. He crouched and tipped the glass slowly allowing the mouse to scurry into the grass and disappear behind a tree.

When he came back into the apartment, Kristy was back on the couch with her feet curled under her and the blanket wrapped around her shoulders.

"Toss that glass in the garbage." Kristy squeaked.

"You can wash it and disinfect it." Dean chuckled.

"Eww, toss it out and scrub your hands." Kristy shivered.

"Is Mickey the reason you haven't been sleeping in your room, Kitten?" Dean dropped the glass into the garbage bucket.

"I told the landlord, and he didn't believe me." Kristy pulled the blanket tighter around her.

"He's gone now so why don't you go sleep in the bed. I'm not going to sleep tonight." Dean plopped down on the couch next to her.

"Are you freaking kidding me? I'm not going to sleep either. I need to find another apartment." Kristy pulled out her phone and tapped the screen.

"What are you doing?" Dean turned his head and studied her profile. She was so damn beautiful.

"I can't stay here." Kristy shivered as she scrolled through something on her phone.

"The mouse is gone." Dean folded his hands together over his stomach.

"There is never only one mouse." Kristy cringed.

"I didn't realize you were afraid of mice." Dean chuckled.

"I'm not afraid. I hate rodents." Kristy turned to glare at him.

"I guess Kitten was the wrong nickname for you." Dean laughed.

"Asshole," Kristy flicked her hand against his chest, and he grabbed her wrist.

"Glad you realize what I am." Dean gave her hand a gentle squeeze before he released her.

Kristy sighed as she tossed her phone on the table next to the couch. She turned to face him, and he smiled as she was careful not to allow the blanket or her legs to touch the floor.

"Why do you do that?" Kristy tilted her head, and her blue eyes met his. It took all his strength not to pull her into his arms and kiss her until they were both breathless, but he wouldn't be able to stop at just that.

"Do what?" He didn't even recognize his own voice.

"Try to make me dislike you." He'd pushed her away for so long he didn't even know he did it anymore.

"The question is, why do you like me?" Dean couldn't understand how someone as smart and beautiful as Kristy would want him. Sure, he knew women were attracted to him and not because of his glowing personality.

"That's a stupid question." Kristy huffed.

"Why is that stupid?"

"Have you looked in a mirror in your life?" Kristy waved her hand up and down in front of him.

"Yes, but is that it?" Physical attraction wasn't something to build any kind of relationship.

"Sure, your looks were the first thing that got my attention but watching you over the years helping my family and protecting them made you a hell of a lot more attractive than your looks ever could." Kristy's hand cupped his cheek, and he covered it with his own hand.

"It was my job, Kitten." Dean closed his eyes when her thumb stroked his lower lip.

"It might be your job, but that's not the only reason." She moved closer, and he was powerless.

"Kitten, I'm not the right guy for you," Dean whispered.

"That's not what Aunt Cora says."

Dean rolled his eyes. He was well aware of Cora's opinion on the subject of them as a couple, and no matter how often she'd been right it was hard for him to believe Kristy was meant to be with him.

"I thought you didn't believe your aunt's special gift." Dean sighed.

"She's never been wrong." Kristy moved her face closer, and he kept his gaze locked on hers. "Never." She whispered as her lips brushed against his.

"Kitten, this isn't a good idea." Dean rasped.

"Are you telling me you don't want this?" Kristy moved closer to him and allowed her lips to linger longer against his.

"It doesn't matter what I want, Kitten." He really should stop her but fuck she felt so good. The memory of the kiss the first day had his cock aching for the last three days.

"Does it matter what I want? Don't you want to get lost for a while and put this terrible day in the back of your mind? If only for a short time." Kristy lightly nipped his jaw it sent a shiver through his body.

"You don't need to be involved in the middle of all this shit." Dean lifted her until she straddled his legs. "I told you earlier today that I'd tell you everything and I did mostly."

"Mostly?" Kristy pulled back and gazed into his eyes.

"I didn't tell you about how I feel about you." Dean cupped his hands on her cheeks.

"Are you going to tell me now?" Kristy turned her face and kissed his palm.

"You deserve so much more than I can give you right now." Dean studied her face as if she would disappear at any second. Her long brown hair was braided and hung over her shoulder above her breast. Her tiny button nose wrinkled when she stared at him with confusion. Her plump lips were slightly open as she waited for him to continue.

"Everything in my life is so fucked up right now. My sister is facing a long time in jail for a murder I know she didn't commit, my niece, her daughter, is dead, and I have no idea who would want to kill her."

"My dad's here to help, and I'm going to call a lawyer friend tomorrow." Kristy ran her hands over the top of his head, and he couldn't keep the groan inside. Her touch was heaven.

"Kitten, I don't want you involved in my sister's shit, and she has a lawyer. He's not doing much, but she does have one." He had trouble getting the words out because she'd allowed her hands to move from his head down the sides of his face to his neck.

"I'm not letting you push me away anymore, Dean Nash." Kristy leaned forward until her nose was touching his and stared into his eyes. "Or should I call you Augustus."

"Nobody ever called me that." Dean chuckled.

"Dean is better. By the way, the way that beard is coming in is sexy as hell." It was the last thing she said before she covered his mouth with hers. He dropped his hands to her waist and pulled her tighter against him. He couldn't fight it anymore, and he didn't want to.

Dean plunged his tongue into her mouth as Kristy tugged at his shirt. He didn't want to let her go to remove it but she was stronger than he ever thought and she pushed back to lift it over his head.

"Your body's a work of art," Kristy whispered as her hand glided over his chest and arms.

"Kitten, you're a work of art." Dean slid her tank top up and over her head. Her nipples were hard and a shade darker than her pale skin.

"I have two tattoos, but they aren't as beautiful as yours."

"I've only seen the one here." Dean ran his fingers over her shoulder where she had the O'Connor family crest inked. He knew everyone one in Kristy's family had the same tattoo somewhere on their body. It was a family tradition.

"The other is a little lower." Kristy smiled and eased the waistband of her pajamas on the left side. Next to her left hip was a small tattoo with the word love written in such a way that it resembled a heart.

"That's pretty cute." Dean ran his finger over the ink.

"You're pretty cute." Kristy ran her finger across one of his nipples and smiled. "I always wanted to see these piercings up close and wondered if it's the only piercing you have."

"It's the only one." Dean chuckled because he knew what type of piercing she meant.

"Aww. I was kind of hoping…" Kristy slid her hand between them and cupped his rock-hard cock.

"Mmm… Sorry to disappoint." Dean closed his eyes as she rubbed him through his jeans.

"This isn't a disappointment." Kristy popped the button on his jeans.

"I think this would go much better if we could go to your bedroom." Dean grinned.

"You think I'm afraid to go in there?" Kristy narrowed her eyes as she leaned in to nip his bottom lip.

"You've been spending all your nights out here, right?" Dean twirled his finger in the air referring to the living room.

"That's different. I won't be in there alone tonight, now will I?" Kristy eased off his lap and slid her pajama pants off, so she stood in front of him with only a green pair of boy short underwear.

"Fuck," Dean's breath came out in a long whoosh.

"Maybe we can if you'd stop sitting there and follow me." Kristy backed away from him crooking her finger in that come here motion.

"Are you sure about this?" Dean stood slowly.

"Dean, I've wanted this for more than eight years." Kristy moved toward him and pressed against him.

Her warm skin against his made him shudder with need. He grabbed her around her waist and lifted her off the floor. Her legs wrapped around his waist as he made his way to the bedroom. He held her with one hand as he squirmed to open the door to the bedroom. It wasn't easy with her sucking on his ear and whispering all the dirty things she wanted them to do together.

"Kitten, you're gonna make me come before we get to the bed."

"Don't you have more stamina than that, Big guy." Kristy grinned when he lowered her to the bed.

"Sweetheart, you've been giving me a bad case of blue balls for so long I'm surprised I didn't come when you took off your top." Dean eased down next to her.

"Oh no, you don't. Jeans off." Kristy purred as she slid her hand down the length of her leg.

Dean rolled over and quickly discarded the rest of his clothes. Once he was naked, he positioned himself above her. Her blue eyes darkened as she let her gaze travel down his body.

"You really are a big boy." Kristy grinned and wrapped her small hand around his engorged cock.

"Kitten, you're killing me." Dean groaned when she stroked him painfully slow.

"I want you, Dean," Kristy whispered and pulled him down on top of her, and he covered her mouth with his. He plunged his tongue into her mouth and swirled it around.

Her moans had him on the brink of losing all control and when she grabbed his ass and squeezed. It took everything he had to pull back before he slammed into her.

"Con.. fuck…. Condom." Dean panted.

"Drawer," Kristy breathed as she nipped at his neck.

Dean fumbled with the small drawer in the nightstand, and she wiggled under him to rid herself of the only piece of clothing between them.

What was he doing? He was about to bury himself inside the one woman he knew was not going to be a one night stand. Kristy worked her way into his heart and taken up residence. He loved her there was no doubt in his mind but he sure as hell wasn't ready to tell her that.

"Dean, what's wrong?" He hadn't realized that he'd sat up and was staring into space.

Kristy knelt next to him with her hand on his shoulder like a wet dream come to life and so beautiful that it took his breath away.

"You're having second thoughts, aren't you?" Kristy sighed.

"Not second thoughts because I want you more than I could ever tell you. All you have to do is look between my legs and see that but Kitten, is this what you want?" Dean lay down and pulled her down next to him. "Do you want to start something with me in the middle of this shit storm?"

Kristy tilted her head back and turned his face toward her. For a moment she stared into his eyes and stroked his face. As aroused as he was he would have been perfectly happy to lay there staring into her blue gaze.

"It seemed to work for my cousins." Kristy smiled.

She wasn't wrong because all five of her cousins that were married didn't exactly have a calm and smooth start to their relationships.

"You may be right there, but I despise the thought of you being in any kind of danger. Your father will kick my ass if you get hurt." Dean picked up a piece of her hair and twisted it around his finger.

"How can a guy your size be afraid of my dad?" She smiled.

"I respect your father." Dean tapped his finger against her button nose.

"My dad respects you too, and all of my family he cares about you." Kristy pushed herself up on her elbow and pressed her body against his.

"If he knew I was in your bed right now with both of us naked he'd have my nuts in a vice." Dean chuckled.

"Dean, are we just going to lay here and talk about my dad because I've got to tell you, it's kind of a turn-off." Kristy lowered her head and flicked her tongue against his piercing moving the barbell.

"You aren't playing fair." Dean moaned.

"Why are you fighting it?" Kristy swirled her tongue around his nipple and lightly suck it into her mouth.

"Jesus, …. I don't … Fuck…. I don't want you to regret being with me down the road." Dean's voice cracked not only because she wasn't easing her teasing but because the thought of losing her made it hard to breathe.

"The only thing I will regret is it taking so damn long to be with you." Kristy slid her hand down the center of his chest and over his stomach.

"I don't want you to get hurt." Dean groaned when her hand closed around his erection.

"I can protect myself." Kristy kissed her way down the middle of his chest. "Can we forget the outside world for tonight and give in to what we've wanted for so long."

Kristy's hand slowly stroked his throbbing dick, and her hot mouth moved down over his stomach. It was making it so hard to catch his breath. Never in his life had a woman had such an effect on him. Kristy was barely touching him with her mouth, and it was driving him crazy.

"You're so damn sexy, Dean." She whispered as she released his cock from her grip and ran her two index fingers down over his hips. "Every time I've seen this V it makes me drool."

"Kitten, you're torturing me." Dean flipped her over onto her back, and she squeaked.

"Then stop torturing me." She whispered, and he couldn't hold back anymore as he covered her mouth with his.

Dean slid his hand up over her smooth hip while his tongue plunged into her mouth. Her moans had him ready to explode. He pulled his mouth away from hers to pull in much-needed air. She took his hand and guided it to her breast. Dean lowered his head to suck her hard nipple into his mouth.

"Yes, Dean." Kristy gasped, and her back arched off the bed.

"So responsive, Kitten," Dean growled. "Makes me wonder if other parts of you are the same way."

He lifted his head and moved his hand down her flat stomach to between her legs. Dean didn't like when women shaved themselves bare but appreciated when they trimmed the area. Kristy definitely kept herself groomed, and the auburn curls was lighter than the hair on her head.

"You aren't a real brunette, Kitten." Dean places soft kisses across her stomach.

"No, but not many people know that. Consider yourself a member of the private club." She gasped when he flicked his tongue quickly against her swollen clit.

"Why do you cover up that you're a natural redhead." Dean flicked his tongue against her clit again.

"Ahh…. Years of being teased… ahh… in school." Kristy groaned when he slowly slid a finger inside her wet heat.

"You shouldn't hide who you truly are." Dean ran his tongue between her folds.

"God, yes. Do we have to discuss my hair color right now because we could also discuss why you shave your head?" Kristy groaned.

Dean didn't say another word. He pressed his tongue against her clit and slid a second finger inside her. She arched off the bed when he rolled her clit between his teeth. It was fucking beautiful.

"Ahh… Dean…. Yes." She moaned a few seconds later, and he pulled his fingers from inside her and drove his tongue into her wetness.

"So damn tasty," Dean growled as he moved over her.

"You're pretty great with that mouth. Are you gonna show me how you do with the big boy?" Kristy purred and ran her nails lightly down his back making him shiver.

"Big boy does just fine." Dean grabbed the condom he'd dropped earlier and ripped it open with his teeth.

As he slid between her legs and rolled the condom on to his erection, Kristy reached for him. She pulled him down until he was laying on top of her. She placed a soft kiss against his lips and ran her hand over the top of his head. There was something about her caressing his bald head that was erotic, and he could feel it in his cock.

"How do you do that?" Dean moaned and dropped his head to the crook of her neck.

"I want you inside me," Kristy whispered into his ear right before she nibbled his earlobe.

Dean moved his hips until the head of his cock slid between her slippery folds. He could feel the heat from her entrance even through the condom. He eased his hips forward until the head slipped inside her.

"Ahhh… deeper." Kristy lifted her hips, and he slipped deeper inside.

"You're so tight." Dean panted.

"It's been a while." Kristy wrapped her legs around his hips and pulled him deeper.

"I know this makes me a fucking ass, but that's so good to hear." Dean gave one more thrust, and he buried himself completely inside her. "Fuck."

"Yes… you feel so damn good inside. I feel so full." Kristy whispered.

Dean slowly moved his hips thrusting his throbbing cock deep inside her over and over. Keith had told him the first time he made love to his wife that he knew he'd never want anyone else. At that moment Dean knew exactly what his friend meant.

"You're so damn beautiful." Dean cupped her cheek and slowly made love to her.

"I've wanted to be with you for so long. It's so much better than I imagined." Kristy pulled his head down and covered his mouth with hers.

Their tongues twisted together as he plunged inside her over and over. His orgasm hit him fast, and his body convulsed. Seconds later Kristy shuddered under him.

He did his best to keep the bulk of his weight from crushing her. Her warm breath blew across his ear making him shiver. Dean raised his head to gaze down at her, and she grinned as she ran her hands over the top of his head. His dick jumped as if she'd touched it. He never thought light touches over his bald head could arouse him, but every time Kristy did it was as she touched every intimate part of his body.

"You like when I do that don't you?" Kristy chuckled.

"When you do it, yes." Dean brushed his lips across her cheek.

"I wish I'd figured that out years ago." Kristy smiled.

Dean flipped them over, so he was on his back it elicited the cutest squeak from her. She lay on top of him his cock still buried inside her. With everything that happened over the last twenty-four hours, the last thing he expected was to be holding the woman who burrowed into his heart and taken up residence. She didn't know that.

Kristy crossed her hands over his chest and rested her chin on her folded hands. Her blue eyes sparkled in the moonlight shining through her window. Her hair hung over her shoulder and pooled on top of his chest. He wasn't sure when she removed the braid. She seemed to be studying his face, and his body tensed when her face turned serious.

"Are you okay?" Her voice was slightly above a whisper.

"I'm grrrreat." Dean smiled as he did his version of Tony the Tiger.

"Dean, I mean… Peyton." Kristy stared into his eyes.

His smile disappeared, and he took a deep breath. He hadn't forgotten what had happened, but he couldn't let himself go there until he knew who took Peyton's life before her time. Sure, she probably didn't have a lot of time, but that didn't give anyone the right to take what she did have left away from her.

"Kitten, I'm okay. I don't have time not to be. In less than six hours I've got to tell my sister that her only child is not only dead but murdered. The daughter she asked me to protect." Dean swallowed the lump in his throat. He didn't want to talk about Peyton at that moment.

"It wasn't your fault." Kristy cupped his cheek.

"I picked that place because it's the best in the province." Dean closed his eyes.

"Please, don't blame yourself. Keith, my dad, and cousins, will find out what happened." A tear escaped her eye and ran down her cheek.

"Kitten, don't cry." Dean wiped the tear away.

"Sorry, it's … Peyton didn't deserve…" Kristy took a deep breath and closed her eyes.

"Shh…" Dean turned on his side and pulled her into his arms. He'd slipped from inside her, but he didn't care. Having her in his arms was soothing.

"God, I'm such a bitch. You're the one who lost someone you loved, and here you are trying to comfort me." Kristy pushed herself up on her elbow.

"You're not a bitch, and I'm comforting you because you've got such a sensitive heart that you feel when someone is hurting. Comforting you helps me." It was true. It was also how he always dealt with grief. He'd put all his emotions into everyone else.

"Can I ask you something?" Kristy ran her finger down the center of his chest.

"Sure."

"Are you going to keep me at arm's length after tonight?" She looked everywhere except into his eyes.

He put his finger under her chin, so she had no choice but to meet his gaze. What he saw in her eyes made him want to kick himself in the balls. It was fear, but he didn't know why.

"I don't like that look in your eyes." Dean cupped her cheek.

"What look?"

"The one that makes me think you expect me to walk away from you as if nothing happened." Dean gazed into her eyes.

"Are you?" Kristy covered his hand with hers.

"I couldn't even if I tried. Kitten, I wouldn't do that to you. Especially you." Dean pressed his lips together. Should he tell her that he loved her? Was it fair to her when things were so fucked up?

"You did before." Kristy's reminder was the same as a punch to the chest.

"I know, and I'll never forgive myself for putting that look in your eyes back then. It gutted me every time I saw you after that." Dean couldn't forgive himself for the hurt he caused her, and it was why he did his best to avoid her.

"I know that feeling. It hurt me to watch you from a distance, but I'm ashamed to admit that I enjoyed the way you glared at Todd at Mike's wedding." Kristy wrinkled her nose and smiled. It was so fucking adorable.

"Enjoyed making me jealous, did you?" Dean pressed his forehead against hers.

"A little bit." Kristy cupped his cheek.

"I wanted to rip his head off," Dean admitted.

"Is that why you left Mike's wedding?" Kristy brushed her lips against his.

"No, I got the call to say a place opened up for Pey...." Dean stopped and rolled onto his back. "I should've left her where she was."

Kristy jumped to her knees and took his face in her hands. Her eyes filled with tears but her eyebrows furrowed, and her lips were in a straight line. She was pissed.

"Dean, don't you blame yourself for this. None of this was your fault. Whoever did this is a bastard and deserves to burn in hell for hurting someone as sweet as Peyton." A tear ran down her cheek. "Do you understand me? This. Isn't. Your. Fault."

Dean wrapped his arms around her and pulled her down on top of him. He hugged her naked body tightly against his and tucked his face into the nape of her neck. She was right, but it was hard not to blame himself. It was difficult for him to feel out of control of his emotions, but at that moment all he wanted to do was grieve for his niece. The soft sob from Kristy broke him, and for the first time in a long time, Dean cried.

Chapter 10

Whoever was pounding on the door to her apartment must not want to live very long. Kristy grumbled as she crawled out of her bed and glanced back to where Dean was still softly snoring. How he didn't hear the loud knocking was beyond her. She grabbed her clothes from where she dropped them in the living room the night before and quickly tossed Dean's shirt into her bedroom.

"For the love of God, I'm coming," Kristy yelled as she hurried to the door.

She yanked it open, and her annoyance increased. Nick and Aaron stood on the other side of the door with Tim Horton's coffee and a bag of what was probably breakfast sandwiches.

"Jesus Christ. Were you two dead or did we interrupt something." Aaron winked as he squeezed by her and headed into her kitchen.

"I was sleeping, asshole. We were up late." Kristy closed the door when Nick followed his brother.

"I bet you were." Nick chuckled.

"Don't be a jerk. Dean was upset." Her cousins didn't need to know what happened before Dean finally let the floodgate of sorrow escape.

"I'm sorry. How's he doing?" Nick asked.

"He blames himself for moving her to the place, and thinks his sister's going to give up and take the plea bargain they offered her."

"Not me. I'd want to get out and find the bastard that murdered my kid." Aaron growled as he opened one of the sandwiches he pulled out of the bag.

"That reminds me. Nick, Jason Brenton is a criminal lawyer now, right?" Kristy had found out her sister's ex-boyfriend switched from family law to criminal.

"I'm pretty sure, but you should check with Mike." Nick lifted himself onto her counter and took a huge bite out of his own sandwich. "There's food in there for you and Bull." He nodded toward the bag on the table.

"Thanks, but I'm not hungry. Dean said something last night about not having any faith in Hannah's lawyer. I don't think he has any faith in him. I know Jason is good." Kristy opened the coffee cup that Aaron handed her.

"He's working with Sandy's dad now." Nick glanced up from his phone. "Mike said, Stewart is one of the best defense lawyers in the city even if he is retired. He recruited Jason to take his place in the firm. Sandy's dad wouldn't do that if he didn't think Jason was worth the time."

"True but how pissed do you think Jess will be if we ask Jason to help?" Aaron asked.

The whole Jason and Jess situation was a complete mystery to everyone in their family. Kristy asked many times why Jess broke it off, but her sister explained it as they weren't meant to be together. Jess hadn't had a serious relationship since and still wouldn't talk about it.

"I don't see how this has anything to do with her. She's not pissed because he's still playing in the band with you guys."

Aaron, Nick, John, and Mike played in a band called Rockin the Law with Jason and another police officer, Cory. They weren't looking for fame and fortune. They enjoyed music and played at her mother's pub from time to time. They were also often hired to perform at charity events.

"Jason was playing with us long before they dated or broke up." Nick reminded her.

"I don't care. Dean needs our help, and Jess will have to deal with it. I love my sister, but this is important." Kristy snatched her phone off the coffee table where she'd left it the night before.

"Would you rather I call him?" Nick asked.

"No." Kristy found Jason's number and tapped her screen. "I've got nothing against him."

The phone rang several times before someone answered. Kristy was a little confused by the female voice.

"Hello," The soft-spoken woman said.

"I think I may have the wrong number." Kristy knew the number she'd dialed was supposed to be Jason's cell phone.

"Are you looking for Jason?" The woman asked.

"Yes,"

"He's taking a shower. I'll get him for you." The woman sounded pleasant enough, but Kristy felt a little odd.

"Thanks, doll. Hello." Jason answered the phone.

"Hey, it's Kristy O'Connor." She sat on the kitchen chair.

"Hi, Kristy. Nice to hear from you." Jason seemed a little surprised to hear from her.

"Am I interrupting?" Kristy didn't want to talk business if she didn't have Jason's full attention.

"No," He laughed. "What's up?"

"I need a favor." Kristy blurted it out and cringed.

"Is Jess okay?" Jason sounded panicked.

"Yes, she's fine. It's nothing to do with my sister." Kristy sighed. "How fast can you get to the women's prison in Conception Bay?"

"Jesus, what did you do?" Jason gasped.

"Not me, but a friend needs my help and yours." Kristy caught Nick out of the corner of her eye. He glanced over her shoulder, and she turned. Dean stood with his arms folded across his chest and his face was expressionless.

"I can be there in an hour." Jason didn't ask what it was about, but he had to know she wouldn't call him if she had another choice. Mike didn't deal with criminal law and Nick was no longer a lawyer.

"Thanks, I'll explain when I see you." Kristy ended the call and turned to Dean.

"What are you doing?" He asked as soon as she dropped her phone on the table.

"I'm getting your sister a new lawyer." Kristy smiled.

"You think I can't do that myself?" He raised an eyebrow, and she rolled her eyes.

"I know you can, but you need the best and Jason is working with the best." Kristy met his stance by crossing her arms over her chest. She didn't miss his gaze drop to her chest and back up again.

"Who?" He demanded.

"Sandy's dad, Stewart Michaels." Kristy saw his shoulders relax because everyone in Newfoundland knew Stewart was the best in the province.

"Jason is Jess's ex, right?" Dean glanced at Nick.

"Yes," Nick answered.

"No way." Dean shook his head.

"I'm sorry?" Kristy narrowed.

"I'm not upsetting your sister." Dean looked away from her and nodded toward the coffee on the counter.

"Jess won't care." Kristy didn't know that for sure.

"You asked her?" Dean was back to the standoffish way he acted when he had no choice but to be close to her when he wanted to run away.

"She won't give a damn." Kristy snapped.

"You know that for sure?" He turned to face her and flipped open the cover of the coffee cup.

Kristy narrowed her eyes and snatched her phone off the table. She wasn't letting him do this again. She tapped her sister's phone number and prayed she wasn't at work. Jess answered on the second ring.

"I was waiting for you to call. How's Dean doing?" Jess had apparently been waiting for her call.

"Being an ass." Kristy snapped as she met Dean's gaze.

"So, nothing's different." Jess chuckled.

"Listen, I need you to be honest with me. I just got off the phone with Jason and asked him to help with Dean's sister's case.

He's working with Stewart which means he has the means to give Hannah the best defense she can get here. Dean, however, thinks that it will upset you." Kristy babbled so fast that she wasn't even sure Jess was still on the phone.

"Why would I care what Jason does? If he can help, tell Dean to use him. It's his sister for heaven's sake and Jason knows what he's doing." Kristy breathed a sigh of relief because although she said Jess wouldn't care, she wasn't sure her sister would be okay with it.

"I'm going to put you on speaker. Can you tell Dean what you said?" Kristy glared at the man she'd made love to a few hours earlier.

"Of course," Jess laughed.

Kristy tapped the speaker and held up the phone. Jess repeated every word. It was subtle, but Kristy saw the slight change in Dean's stone expression.

"You're sure, Jess?" He asked.

"I'm sure, ya big dummy. She's your sister." Kristy swallowed hard when she heard the slight crack in Jess's voice.

"Thanks, Shorty," Dean started the nickname a while back because Jess was the shortest out of all the O'Connor girls.

"Oh, and, Bull?" Jess only used Dean's nickname when he called her Shorty.

"Yeah," He smiled.

"I can still kick your ass," Jess growled. "Talk to all of you later."

"That I don't doubt." Dean chuckled.

"Can I talk to Dean alone guys?" Kristy shoved her phone into her back pocket and met his gaze.

"Yeah, we dropped by to see if Bull was okay and to let you know Uncle Kurt put a rush on the autopsy for Peyton." Aaron stood up and headed out of the kitchen.

"Forensics finished in her room around four this morning. They collected some things in the room, but we'll know more when they give us their reports." Nick followed Aaron out of the room. "Uncle Kurt said to call him after you see your sister, Bull."

Kristy didn't drop her gaze from Dean until she heard the door to her apartment close. He sipped his coffee but kept his eyes glued to her.

"Do you want to tell me why you are acting this way?" Kristy snapped.

"What way?" Dean sauntered toward the living room, but she grabbed his arm.

"As if nothing happened between us last night and you didn't completely open up to me or promise you wouldn't treat me like this again." Kristy raised her voice.

"I don't…" Dean started, and Kristy lost it.

"If you say you don't know what I'm talking about I swear I will hit you over the head with a frying pan." Kristy fisted her hands at her sides.

"Kitten, I …. I didn't know how to act with Nick and A.J. here." Dean braced his back against the door jamb.

She stared at him for a moment as she allowed her body to relax. Kristy should have known it would be awkward for him considering how close he was to her cousins and how long he had kept his distance from her.

Kristy stepped toward him and rested her hands on his chest. He covered them with his own and pressed his forehead to hers.

"I don't know how to do this. I've never cared about someone so much." His voice was barely above a whisper.

"You're not alone here, Dean. I've never been in…" Kristy stopped because she hadn't told him she loved him yet.

"I haven't either." Dean must have read her thoughts.

"I guess it's why we both find it so hard to say it." Kristy closed her eyes and raised her head.

"I'm terrified to say it." Dean's voice sounded strangled.

Kristy opened her eyes and met his gaze. His hazel eyes glistened and she swallowed hard.

"Dean, I... I love you. I have for a long time." Kristy watched his eyes widen, and then a smile crossed his sexy mouth.

"I'm captivated by you, and I've told my heart to shut up more often than I can count but it calls out to you. There are a million men who are so much better for you than I am, but the truth is, nobody could ever love you more than I do. I'm sorry it took me so long to get my head out of my ass but Kristy O'Connor, I love you with every bit of my heart and soul." Dean cupped her face in his large hands and brushed the tears from her cheeks.

His words were so beautiful, and she'd wanted to hear them from him for so long it moved her that it caused all those locked up emotions to spill out.

"No more pushing me away?" Kristy whispered.

"No, I promise." Dean touched her lips with his.

"Let's go talk to Hannah." Kristy hugged him and pressed her lips to his.

Nothing would ever put a wedge between her and Dean ever again. She'd fight to her death to make sure that didn't happen. All was left to do was to figure out who killed Peyton and who set up Hannah. That should be a breeze.

Yeah, right.

Chapter 11

A vast weigh lifted off Dean's shoulders, or it felt that way. He didn't understand how finally admitting how he felt about Kristy could make him feel so relieved. There was still a shit storm hanging over his head, but for some reason with Kristy next to him, it felt less of an impossible situation.

"They're bringing her in now, Dean." The guard informed him. Dean didn't like the way the man stared at Kristy and was about to tell him such when Kristy spoke up.

"Is something wrong?" She asked.

"No, I'm sorry. I'm used to Dean coming alone." He smiled at Kristy.

"It's not a place that you want to bring your girl to for a date," Dean grumbled.

"True." The guard nodded and walked away.

"Jason should be here by now." Kristy glanced toward the entrance, and he could feel her shake her leg next to him.

"He'll be here." Dean squeezed her hand.

161

A few minutes later the gate opened, and Hannah moved slowly through it. He'd seen her less than a week ago, but she seemed to age. How was that possible?

He stood up and released Kristy's hand. Hannah didn't look at him as she moved toward him. When she was next to the table, it was when he noticed it. A bruise on her left cheek below her eye.

"What the fuck happened to you, Han?" Dean lifted her chin to get a better look.

"I slipped off my bunk and smashed my cheek against the desk," Hannah whispered and glanced behind him.

"That looks like someone hit you," Dean growled.

"Dean, please. I fell. Let it go." She was still looking over his shoulder.

Dean turned and met Kristy's gaze. She stood behind him with Jason. He must have arrived while Dean was concentrating on his sister.

"Please, sit," Dean whispered as he made his way to the other side of the table and sat next to Kristy.

"What's going on?" Hannah's body was stiff, and he didn't miss the cringe as she sat down. It was as if she was in pain.

"Han, this is Kristy O'Connor and Jason Breton." Dean didn't move his eyes from his sister.

"So, you're Kristy." Hannah smiled, and it was the first real smile he'd seen from her in a long time.

"It's nice to meet you," Kristy said softly.

"You look like a lawyer." Hannah glanced toward Jason.

"I am." He said.

"Dean, what's going on?"

Dean stared at his sister for a moment as he tried to find the best way to tell her about Peyton. He hoped it didn't cause her to give up entirely.

"Han, I've got terrible news." Dean took his sister's hands in his.

"No. No… please… don't say it." Hannah's eyes filled with tears and she squeezed his hands.

"I'm sorry, Han but last night …." Dean swallowed hard.

"I thought she had more time." Hannah sobbed.

"Han, we think …" How was he supposed to say this?

"We don't think it was natural." Kristy covered his arm with her hand.

"What? You think someone… murdered…" Hannah's eyes widened, and she started to tremble.

"Yes." Dean didn't know whether to pull her into his arms or wait and see what she did first.

"I thought that place was secure." Hannah yanked her hands from his. "You said, it was the best place for her."

"I'm sorry, Han." Guilt bubbled in his stomach.

"Hannah, this isn't Dean's fault. I'm a nurse there, and it is one of the best places in the province." Kristy reached across the table toward her. "Your brother was right to put her there."

"She's dead. Tell me exactly how she was safe there?" Hannah snapped at Kristy.

"Don't do this, Han. Kristy didn't do anything to you or Pey, but her family is bending over backwards to find out what happened and to find out who the hell set you up." Dean wasn't about to let his sister turn on Kristy no matter what emotions she felt at the moment.

"How the hell are they going to help me? Trevor said I don't have any other choice but to take the plea and since my daughter is gone, I'm going to do it." Hannah tried to stand up, but Dean grabbed her hand.

"No, you're not. I've fired that ass. Jason is your new lawyer, and he's good. Damn good." Dean wasn't sure how good the man was, but he didn't want his sister to know that.

"You had no right to fire my lawyer." Hannah snapped.

"I'm your power of attorney, Han. You gave me that right." Dean hated to throw that at his sister, but she wasn't acting like herself.

"Only because I needed to do that because of Peyton." Hannah slapped her hands on the table.

"Look, I don't know you, and you don't know me, but I will tell you, I work for the best defense lawyer in the province and I'll do everything in my power to get you out of here. There will be no deal because from the email I got from your brother, you didn't do this." Jason interrupted. Dean had emailed him all the information he'd received from Trevor. He was sure Jason didn't have enough time to go over it, but Dean assumed that Jason was stalling for time.

"What if I did do it?" Hannah growled.

"I don't think you did." Dean was impressed with Jason's confidence with Hannah.

"You don't know me." Hannah stood.

"I don't, but by the end of this week I'll know more about you than you know about yourself." Jason stood as well.

"Will I be able to leave to bury my daughter?" She snapped at Jason.

"I'll guarantee it." Jason buttoned his jacket and picked up his briefcase.

"You're pretty cocky." Hannah narrowed her eyes.

"You've got no idea." Kristy chuckled.

"I'll be in touch." Jason turned and walked out of the visiting room.

"How did she die?" Hannah's eyes focused on where Jason exited.

"We'll know after the autopsy." Dean didn't want to tell her that her daughter suffocated.

"I can't believe she's gone." Hannah's expression softened, and a tear ran down her cheek.

"She's in a better place now." Dean didn't know if he believed in heaven, but if it existed, he was sure Peyton had a direct flight there.

"Yes," Hannah sighed and sat down.

"Hannah, you don't know me, but my family will move heaven and earth to find out what happened to your daughter." Kristy reached across the table and touched Hannah's hand.

His sister looked at him and then back to Kristy. She seemed to be debating on what to say, but the only thing Dean had on his mind was to find out how Hannah ended up with a bruised face. There was no way she fell and ended up with a fist-sized bruise on her face.

"Dean speaks very highly of your family," Hannah glanced back to Kristy. "And of you."

"When you get out of here, you can come to Hopedale and meet them. You're family now." Kristy smiled, and Dean fell in love all over again.

"I'd like that," Hannah whispered, but something in her expression told Dean his sister didn't expect to leave the prison.

Dean wasn't sure how he would get his sister out for Peyton's funeral, but he was sure Kurt could tell him. He would have to talk to him and get all the information. It was possible that Jason already put that wheel in motion.

"Dean, she didn't get that bruise from a fall," Kristy said on the drive back to her apartment.

"I know." He wanted to find out, but if Hannah didn't tell him, he was damn well sure she didn't mention it to any of the guards. He'd never been inside, but he knew that inmates didn't complain for fear of retaliation.

"Do you think it was one of the other inmates?" Kristy asked.

"Probably, but we have no way of finding out unless she's willing to tell us." Dean sighed as he pulled into the parking space in front of her apartment.

"What the hell?" Kristy growled and hopped out of his truck.

Dean looked up and shook his head when he figured out why she was pissed. Her father stood outside her door with a truck parked in front of the door. Nick and Aaron were carrying her bed out through the door.

Dean stepped out of the truck as Kristy threw her hands up in the air. Her father didn't seem the least bit bothered by her rant. As he got in the front of the door, he understood why Kristy was pissed.

"So who gave you permission to move my things?" Kristy shouted.

"Kristy Elizabeth, stop shouting. I don't care if you're twenty-nine years old. You got away with it last night because of what happened, but you better watch yourself, little girl." Kurt sounded pissed himself.

"Fine, but why are you taking my things out of my apartment?" Kristy lowered her voice, but it was apparent she was still fuming.

"We got here not long after you two left to go see Bull's sister. I walked in, and the first thing I see is a mouse running out of your kitchen." Kurt snapped.

"Really?" Kristy's dislike for the small rodents seemed to calm her anger.

"There is no reason for you to live in a rodent infested place. I check around, and there is more than one of them in there. Your work is not that far from Hopedale, and if the weather is bad I'll drive you there myself if I have to, but you aren't living here anymore." Kurt turned toward Dean. "I need to talk to you too."

"Dad, don't start on Dean, please." Kristy sighed.

"This is about the case of his sister, but unless you want your cousins packing your clothes, you better get in there and pack it yourself." Kurt turned away from her and Dean almost laughed when she stuck out her tongue. It was childish but cute as hell.

"I saw that little girl." Kurt nodded toward Dean's truck.

"Why do I feel this is going to be more bad news?" Dean said when they were inside his truck.

"How much do you know about your brother-in-law's death?" Kurt held a folder in his hand, and Dean reached across to take it. "Sorry, Bull, I can't give you this."

"I know he was shot twice in the head." Dean cringed because he remembered parts of Ivan's head splattered all over the room.

"Do you know why they suspected your sister?" Kurt asked.

"Because she had the gun in her hand and she was next to him on the bed." Dean had no idea why Kurt was bringing this up considering they were supposed to be investigating Peyton's death.

"Yes, but my problem is the investigation has major holes in it. I don't understand how your sister's lawyer didn't bring this up." Kurt turned to face him.

"What do you mean?" Dean remembered police running up and down the stairs to his sister's bedroom with evidence bags.

"First, your sister had the gun in her left hand." Kurt opened the folder.

"I guess." Dean shrugged his shoulders.

"She's left-handed?" Kurt glanced up at him.

"Yes," Dean was also left-handed. He remembered she taught him how to use a pencil because both their parents were right handed.

"I'm not an expert, but I've seen more crime scenes than I care to remember and with their position on the bed, I can't see how it would be possible for her to shoot him the way she did." Kurt shook his head. "This is shitty police work, and I'm going to have to check with the officers that were first on the scene because something doesn't sit right."

"What are you saying?" Dean stared at the man as if he was about to give him the best news of his life.

"I think someone's going to get their ass fired. Your sister didn't do this unless she shot him with her right hand and had an umbrella over her head to keep from getting splattered with blood." Kurt slapped the folder closed.

"Shouldn't her lawyer have had a copy of that report?" Dean knew the answer, but he had to hear it.

"Yes, and I'll make sure Jason gets this." Kurt clenched his teeth together. "I'll try to be civil when I contact him."

"You don't like him?" Dean chuckled.

"He hurt my daughter. Remember that. You're still on my list. You better watch yourself." Kurt opened the door and jumped out of the truck. "You should probably make sure you throw away the condom wrappers in the future."

When Kurt slammed the door to the truck, Dean blew out a breath. A wave of hope came over him as he stared out through the windshield. All this could clear his sister. Now they had to find out who killed his niece.

"Can you believe that man?" Kristy yanked open the door to the truck pulling Dean from his thoughts.

"He is his mother's son." Dean chuckled.

"I'm moving back to Hopedale." Kristy waved her hand toward her apartment. "It would have been nice if I'd made that decision, but apparently Dad thinks I'm two years old and can't make a logical decision to save my life."

Her feistiness was one of the things he adored about her. Her cheeks were red with anger, and she was throwing her hands all over the place as she ranted.

"Why did he make this decision?" Dean grabbed one of her hands and kissed the palm.

"When he walked in he saw a …." Kristy shuddered, "mouse run out of the kitchen."

"Another one," Dean had a feeling there would be more.

"Yeah," Kristy sighed when he kissed her hand again.

"He's looking out for you." Dean squeezed her hand.

"You're making it difficult to be mad at him. Stop kissing my hand." Kristy sighed when he pressed his lips against her wrist.

"Good," Dean smiled. "Where are you going to stay when you go back to Hopedale?"

"Dad talked to Isabelle about staying with her until I can find something else. I should move into the shack next to her to piss him off." Kristy laughed.

"Shack?" Dean linked his fingers with hers.

"There's a house next to Isabelle's. It's for sale but needs a lot of work. I love that area, and when I look at it, I can see how beautiful the house could be. I even thought about talking to Billie's brother Matt to see what he thought. He designed Mike's house." She flopped back on the seat and turned her face toward him.

"I thought he was a carpenter?" He knew Matt worked for Keith's construction company.

"He is, but apparently he always wanted to be an architect and Keith's helping him do it. He's taking night classes and online classes while he works. He has a daughter to raise now so he wants to make sure he can take care of her." Kristy smiled.

"Have you checked on what they want for the house?" Dean asked.

"No, I couldn't afford to buy it right now anyway." Kristy glanced at her apartment.

"Your dad had some interesting information for me." Dean watched Aaron drop another box into the back of a truck.

"About Peyton?" Kristy didn't turn toward him.

"No, my sister and how he thinks the investigation of Ivan's death was not handled right." Dean felt the wave of hope overwhelm him again.

"Really?" Kristy spun in the seat toward him.

"Yeah, someone is about to get fired was his words." Dean rested his head against the back of the seat.

"If Dad said that, you can be sure the shit is about to hit the fan." Kristy sighed.

"Why don't you drive back to Hopedale with me?" Dean wanted to talk to her some more about that little house.

"And how am I supposed to get my car home?" She raised an eyebrow.

Dean started his truck and lowered the window on the passenger side. He waited for one of the guys to walk out of the apartment. When he saw James toss a bag in the back, he called out to him. James jogged over to the truck with a grin.

"Can you drive Kristy's car back to Hopedale?" Dean asked.

"Hey, what if I want to drive it myself?" Kristy grumbled.

"Kitten, do you want to drive back to Hopedale in your car or my truck?" Dean asked.

"I'll drive back with you." She sighed. "Here's my keys." She pulled a set of keys out of her purse and pulled the car key off the link.

"I'll get Sandy to drive it. I won't fit in that damn thing." James chuckled.

"I'm sure she'll appreciate that." Kristy laughed.

"At least I won't have to listen to her complain that I drive too slow." James rolled his eyes.

"I need to drop by the landlord's house and hand in the key. He'll probably give me shit about not giving notice." Kristy pulled on her seatbelt.

"I can give him the key." Dean grinned. "Better yet, tell him to call your father the Chief of police."

"I might do both." Kristy waved to her father as they pulled out of the parking lot.

Once they left the grumpy landlord, who pulled in his attitude when Dean got out of the truck. They hit the highway toward Hopedale. He had so much on his mind as he drove that he barely heard Kristy say his name.

"Are you okay?" Kristy asked when he turned toward her.

"A lot on my mind." Dean reached over and brushed his knuckle against her cheek.

"I understand but you know if you need to talk, I have a great ear." Kristy unhooked her seatbelt and moved to the center of the seat. She pulled on the other belt and rested her head on his shoulder.

"Thanks, Kitten." Dean kissed the top of her head.

He was afraid to get his hopes up but no matter what happened over the last twenty-four hours, it was possible his sister could be out of jail sooner rather than later. The problem is, who the hell killed Ivan and set up his sister. Eric's name was the first one to pop in his head. Could the man kill his brother and try to make it look as if Hannah did it? The other question was, if he did do it, what made him hate his brother so much?

Chapter 12

"I can't believe dad moved your things out of that apartment without even asking." Jess shook her head as she dropped a box at the foot of the bed.

"How can you be surprised? You have met Nan, right? She did raise dad." Isabelle chuckled from the closet where she hung up the last of the clothes they brought in from Aaron's truck.

"I can't believe you guys didn't say anything." Jess slapped Nick on the shoulder.

"What were we supposed to say?" Aaron helped Nick put the bed together.

"For the record, I did say it wasn't a good idea." James was crouched behind the headboard attaching it to the frame.

"Honestly, I wasn't staying there much longer anyway," Kristy admitted. "Dean, caught a mouse last night in my bedroom." She shuddered as she proceeded to put clothes in the dresser.

"What was Dean doing in your bedroom, missy?" Isabelle peaked around the door of the closet.

176

"Has it been that long for you, cuz? You can't remember what you do with a man in a bedroom." Aaron laughed but ducked when Isabelle threw a shoe at him.

"Dean was sleeping in there because your sister took the couch. She wouldn't sleep in there because she heard the mice but didn't tell anyone." Kristy spun around at the sound of his voice and immediately her heart fluttered when he smiled at her.

"I can't believe the guy can rent a place crawling with rodents." Jess wrinkled her nose.

Kristy barely heard her because her gaze locked with Dean and the rest of the world faded. He braced his shoulder against the door jamb and crossed his arms over his chest. It was the sexiest damn thing she'd ever seen.

"Dean, I'm sorry about your niece." Isabelle walked over to him and rested her hand on his arm. "I'm sure that doesn't help with the loss but we're all here for you."

"It means a lot, Iz, and thanks." Dean seemed to enjoy giving nicknames to everyone. At least Isabelle's was from her name.

Her family quickly completed what they were doing and filed out of the bedroom Kristy had taken over in Isabelle's house. For a moment Dean didn't move. He gazed out through the large window across the room.

"You're right about the view here." He spoke after a few minutes.

"Yeah, my sister is a lucky duck." Kristy sat on the bed and followed his gaze. "She got this house for a song."

"Didn't know Isabelle sang." Dean walked into the room and closed the door behind him.

"Did Dean Nash make a joke?" Kristy feigned shock.

"Never, I'm too serious for that." He smiled and plopped down on the bed next to her.

"Are you okay?" Kristy didn't get a chance to talk to him about his conversation with Jason after they'd returned to Hopedale.

Dean had dropped her off and met Jason at the police station. She waited at Isabelle's house for Aaron and Nick to show up with their trucks filled with her things.

"I can't believe how the investigation was botched." Dean shook his head. "I still can't believe that I didn't know at least one of the cops at the house that day."

"I guess they were all from town. Most of the police you've met or know work in Hopedale or the surrounding communities. Hell, I don't know if anyone I know is with the city department anymore." Kristy went through the list of police she knew in her head outside her family, but none came to mind.

"According to Jason, Kurt is doing an inquiry into the investigation. He said he'd have Hannah out by the end of the week." The spark of hope in his eyes made her breathe a sigh of relief.

"Are you going back to her home with her?" Kristy hoped not because the thought of Dean being back in town when she was in Hopedale made her sick to her stomach.

"I don't think Hannah will ever go into that house again." Dean took her hand and linked his fingers with hers. "Keith has the guys cleaning up one of the bunkhouses for her."

"Do you really think she'll be comfortable there? Isabelle has another room here. I'm sure she wouldn't mind having Hannah stay here." Kristy traced the tattoo that ended at his wrist with her finger.

"Kitten, I know Isabelle would put Hannah up if I asked, but my sister won't be comfortable with someone she doesn't know, and besides I'll be there with her." Dean put his finger under her chin and pulled her face up, so she had to look at him. "You want to tell me why you're worried?"

"I'm not." Kristy lied. Although, terrified described how she felt a little more accurately.

"Yeah, you are, and I know what's going through the beautiful brain of yours." He tucked her hair behind her ear.

"Oh so not only are you a joker, you're a mind reader now. You should really take that show on the road." Kristy rolled her eyes.

"Maybe after this is all over. I'll need a lovely assistant. You want to moonlight as my assistant?" He smiled and cupped her cheek.

"Sure," Kristy laughed.

"Stop worrying." Dean brushed his thumb across her lower lip.

"I'm not." She couldn't lie and look him in the eye which was why she glanced toward the window.

"You are, and if you would stop avoiding eye contact with me, I'll tell you why you need to stop worrying." Dean released her hand and held her face between both his hands.

"What?"

"My feelings for you haven't changed in the last twenty-four hours. I. Love. You." Dean pressed his lips against hers and pulled back.

"I know that, and I love you too." Kristy cupped her hands on his forearms.

"I'm also not about to lose you now that I've got my head out of my ass and had a taste of those sweet lips." He smiled.

"Dean, you've got so much more to worry about than me." Kristy met his eyes. "I don't want you to forget I'm here if you need anything."

"I won't because I can't forget about you. You're in my every thought, and there isn't a second of the day I don't think about you. Even with all the shit going on in my family, you were always my first thought in the morning and the last one before I go to sleep.

I wish I hadn't waited so long to tell you how I feel." Dean pulled her into his arms and pressed his lips against the top of her head.

"I love you so much, Dean." Kristy wrapped her arms tightly around him.

"Kitten, even with the hell of all my family shit the last couple of days, I feel lighter because I have you." Dean kissed the top of her head.

Kristy swallowed the lump in her throat. He'd finally said the words she'd wanted to hear. She was so happy she could cry, but the truth was, their relationship couldn't move forward. Not until Hannah was out from behind bars and Peyton's murderer was in jail.

"I'm sorry, the last thing you need on your plate is to be concerned about my insecurities." Kristy pulled back and saw the tears in his eyes. "Dean, what is it?"

"Pey told me if I didn't tell you how I felt soon I would lose the chance and I'd be kicking myself in the ass for the rest of my life." Dean smiled and blew out a breath. "She wasn't wrong."

For a long time, they sat together on the bed and held each other. It felt intimate, and for the first time in her life, Kristy understood what her mom meant about intimacy being more than sex.

A loud knock on the bedroom door broke the spell, and Kristy pulled back from Dean's embrace. She still kept her hand linked with his, and she smiled when he didn't pull away.

"Come in," Kristy called out.

The door opened, and her father walked into the room followed by Keith. Neither of them looked pleased, but she couldn't help from rolling her eyes when her father raised an eyebrow at their intertwined fingers.

"Bull, we need to talk." Keith walked into the room and closed the door.

"Okay," Dean glanced between her uncle and cousin.

"Kristy, I think we need to talk to Bull about this alone." Her father's voice seemed strained.

"It's okay, Kurt. What is it?" She was relieved when Dean held her hand a little tighter and didn't ask her to leave.

"Bull, did you know your sister had another child?" Her dad asked.

"What? No. Hannah only had Pey." Dean's mouth hung open as he gaped at her dad.

"Sandy found a hospital record from when your sister was fourteen. It showed that she'd given birth." Keith stopped and dropped his head. "Sandy found a sealed adoption record that said she put the baby up for adoption."

"I didn't know. My parents never mentioned anything to me about her putting a baby up for adoption. For that matter neither did Hannah." Dean had started to squeeze her hand, and it began to hurt.

"Bull, the baby was a boy." Keith obviously wanted to say something else.

"Wow, I didn't know." Dean rubbed his hand over his head.

"There's something you're not saying." Kristy knew her father and cousin well enough to know when they were hiding something.

"The boy was born in November." Her dad stared at her.

"Wait, you think… no fucking way." Dean jumped to his feet and dropped her hand.

"Sandy hasn't been able to get the record open yet but Bull, it all lines up." Keith kept his focus on Dean.

Kristy watched Dean because she knew where they were going with this. Dean's birthday was the sixteenth of November. Was it possible he was Hannah's son and not her brother?

"There's no fucking way my family would keep something that big from me. Jesus Christ, they kept things close to the vest but no… no… fuck no. Hannah's not my mother." Dean stomped out of the room and almost knocked Keith over on his way out.

Kristy jumped up to run after him, but Keith caught her by the arm. She tried to pull out of his grasp, but he shook his head.

"Kristy, give him some time to digest this." He released her arm.

"Do you really think…" Kristy glanced at her father and then through the open door where Dean disappeared.

"I don't know what to think, but there were lots of rumors going around about that family over the years. It wouldn't surprise me, but I can't believe they would hide something so important from Bull." Her dad wrapped his arm around her shoulder and kissed the top of her head. "I know how you feel about him but listen to Keith. Give him some time."

Kristy rested her head against her father's shoulder and sighed. It was hard to let him run off without following, but she knew Dean needed time to get his head around what they told him. She hoped that this shock didn't cause him to push her away.

Chapter 13

Dean didn't know how long he'd been walking, but he was back at the bunkhouse where he stayed when he was in Hopedale. His head pounded, and his thoughts were swirling in all different directions.

There was no way Hannah was his mother. His mother had shown him pictures of herself when she was pregnant with him. He remembered her raving about how good she felt when she was pregnant and happy because she never thought she could have any more kids.

The records had to be fucked up. Even if Hannah did have another baby, he wasn't it. *No.* He couldn't believe his family would betray him in that way.

"Well, it's about fucking time." Dean spun around.

Matt Carter stood in his opened door with a clipboard in his hand. For a moment Dean forgot why the man was there. Then he remembered he'd called him when they got back to Hopedale about the house next to Isabelle. He'd also called Mike's wife Billie to see about buying the home. She and her friend were partners in a real

185

estate business, and he knew that if anyone could get him a good deal on the house, Billie and her friend Abbie could.

"Sorry, I got distracted with some family shit." Dean yanked open the cupboard and pulled out a bottle of whiskey. He needed something to calm his frayed nerves.

"I heard. I know what it's like to lose someone. My condolences." Matt's statement was filled with emotion. The love of his life had been murdered the year before and he was left to raise their daughter alone. The little girl was deaf, and Matt only found out before Peggy died that he was Chloe's father.

"Thanks," Dean held up the bottle.

"No, that shit'll kill ya." Matt laughed.

"Probably but I'll take that chance." Dean poured the dark amber liquid into a tumbler and pointed to the kitchen bench seat.

"Billie said you wanted me to take a look at the house on Beach Street next to Mike's cousin?" Matt sat down.

"Yeah, I'm thinking about buying it for… I wanted to know if it was worth buying and fixing it up." Dean didn't want too many people to know the real reason he wanted the house.

"I can drop by there and have a look, but Abbie or Billie will have to get me the key to the place so that I can look around. I drove by there on the way here, and from the outside, it has good bones." Matt leaned back on the bench and draped his arm over the back.

"If I buy this I need you to keep it quiet that I bought the house." Dean pressed his lips together.

"Even from Keith? Don't get me wrong, Bull but he's still my boss, and I can't do something on the side without letting him know." Matt worked for Keith's construction company while he studied architecture.

"I trust Keith to keep it to himself, and I know Billie and Abbie will as well." Billie had threatened to spill it to the whole town if he didn't tell her the reason he wanted information on the house.

"Give me a few days, and I'll get back to you." Matt stood up and made his way to the door. "I'm assuming this has something to do with the youngest of the O'Connor girls. If I run into her, I'll tell her I'm working on a project for school." Matt laughed.

"Thanks," Dean forced a smile as Matt disappeared down the path to the small parking lot Keith had for the staff.

He closed the door and slammed back the rest of the whiskey in his glass. He grabbed the bottle from the counter and made his way to the couch. He plopped down and poured another glass for himself. He didn't drink very often, but he needed something to take the edge off his confusion. Not that getting piss eyed drunk would help, but he just didn't want to believe what Kurt and Keith told him.

No fucking way.

"Dean, wake up." He heard her sweet voice, but he had to be dreaming. She wouldn't be at his place in the middle of the night.

Dean opened one eye and closed it immediately when he saw the empty whiskey bottle on the coffee table. He'd drank the whole thing and must have passed out.

"Dean, don't do this to yourself." Kristy knelt next to him and pressed her cool hand against his cheek.

"I didn't mean to." He mumbled and felt like he was about throw up all over himself.

"Wow, you smell really bad." Another reason he loved this woman. She didn't hold anything back.

"I need to get up and grab a shower and swallow a bottle of Tylenol." Dean cringed when Kristy grabbed his hands and pulled him to a seating position. "Or you could shoot me in the head now and put me out of my misery."

"Come on." Kristy pulled on his hands. "You go get a shower, and I'll make you something to eat."

"I don't think I could eat." The acid in his stomach burned.

"That's why you need to drink that bottle of water and take these." She put something into his hand, and when he opened his eyes, there were two pills in his hand and a one-liter bottle of water.

"I'm sorry." Dean sighed.

"Something upset you, but I know you aren't one to run and get drunk every time something upsets you." Kristy touched his cheek.

"No, I hate getting drunk. That bottle of whiskey has been there for over a year." Dean stood up and fell back down on the couch when the room started to spin. "I also don't like the room to spin when I stand up."

"Come on I'll help you to the bathroom." Kristy chuckled.

Dean stood under the shower spray until he felt somewhat human again. He couldn't remember the last time he drank so much. He stood outside the shower stall with a towel wrapped around his waist and stared at his disheveled self in the vanity mirror.

The memory of the conversation with Kurt and Keith echoed in his brain. He was thirty-seven years old and never even suspected Hannah could be his mother. It was hard to wrap his head around, but there were clues over the years. People wondered where he got his height because his mom was only a little over five feet tall and his dad barely hit five feet eight.

Lots of people had made comments over the years about how he didn't resemble either of his parents. Sure, he had his dad's hazel eyes and his mom's dark hair, but if Hannah was his mother, he could have inherited that from her.

"Although I enjoy the look of you only covered with a towel, I think you need to come eat." Kristy had walked into the bathroom without notice.

"I wonder who fathered Hannah's first kid," Dean whispered mostly to himself but loud enough that he knew Kristy couldn't miss what he said.

"Dean, don't do this to yourself. You don't know for sure and until you do, don't torture yourself." Kristy stood behind him and wrapped her arms around his waist. The warmth of her cheek against the middle of his back soothed him in a way he couldn't understand.

"I know you're right, in here." He pointed to his head, "But in here it's hard to deal with the fact my family hid something from me that could affect my life." He held his hand over his chest.

Kristy walked around to stand in front of him and placed one hand over his. She cupped his cheek with the other and gazed into his eyes.

"I'm sure it's a shock to find out all this but it doesn't change who you are. A strong, smart and protective man who cares about people and will walk through hell to keep someone safe. You are still Dean Nash, the man I love, and I don't care if your parents are Martians, nothing changes that. It's not going to change how I feel or how my family feels about you." Kristy stood on her toes and brushed her lips against his.

"Martians? Really?" Dean rested his hands on her hips.

"It was a rumor I'd heard from one of the girls who worked at the store. I think her exact words that nobody from this planet could look so good." Her arms wrapped around his neck and she pressed her body against his.

"If you keep rubbing against me that way, I'm afraid the food will get cold," Dean whispered into her ear then bit it gently.

"You have a microwave." She gasped.

"I do." Dean slowly nipped his way down the nape of her neck and nudged the loose collar of her t-shirt out of his way so that he could run his tongue over her shoulder.

"As much as I would love to continue this, I regret that I promised my mom I would help her train a new girl at the pub." Kristy grazed her nails down the center of his back and covered his ass with her tiny hands. She squeezed while she pressed him against her.

"Yet you have no problem teasing me." His hard cock rubbed against the material of the towel, and the pressure of being pressed against her firm stomach made him want to spin her around, rip off her clothes and bury himself inside her.

"I'm torturing myself as well here." Kristy flicked her tongue across his nipple and pulled gently on his piercing with her lips.

"I think you better go back out to the kitchen before I lose all rational thinking." Dean kissed her cheek as he stepped back. Her eyes dropped to the tented towel in front, and she grinned.

"Maybe I can stay here tonight." Kristy glided her fingernail across his abdomen above the towel.

"Great idea. Now go so I can try and force this thing to go down so I can get dressed." He slapped her ass as she walked away. "Oh, and Kitten,"

"Yeah," She turned her head around to look at him.

"Thanks, for distracting me from my thoughts." He smiled.

"I like distracting you." She winked and disappeared from the doorway.

He loved her so much. He wasn't going to fuck this up and no matter who turned out to be his parents, he wasn't about to let it ruin his budding relationship with Kristy.

Two hours later Dean had eaten the western omelet Kristy had made and drank a full pot of coffee. He actually felt himself again, but now he was pacing outside the courtroom where Jason had managed to get a judge to look into Hannah's release from custody.

Apparently, Sandy's father Stewart had called in a favor and if he was to believe Sandy, threats of secrets revealing themselves about a certain judge and his court reporter.

"You need to relax, Bull." Keith and John had come along for moral support because Kristy helped her mother to train a new girl which Kristy said needed very little instruction.

"I don't want to get Hannah's hopes up only to have her thrown back behind bars." Dean braced his back against the brick wall and rubbed his hands over his bald head.

"What are you more nervous about? That or finding out she could be your mother?" Keith stood next to him in a mirrored stance.

"She's not." Dean still couldn't believe it was possible.

"Sandy is still working on getting the record open." John didn't look at him. He gazed over his shoulder out through the window.

"I don't need her to open it to know Hannah is my sister and not my mother." Dean sighed.

Another hour passed, and Dean could have pulled hair out of his head if he actually had some there. He'd started to pace again because Jason wasn't answering his texts or phone calls.

"He probably has it turned off," Keith spoke when Dean pulled his phone out of his pocket for the tenth time.

"Why the fuck is it taking so damn long?" Dean plunged his phone back into his pocket.

"That judge could have a dozen cases today." John held out the tray of coffee he'd arrived with a few minutes earlier.

"Thanks." Dean took the cup.

"I see you guys are still here." Dean glanced behind him. Stewart Michaels walked toward them with Hannah linked into his arm.

"Hannah?" Dean placed his coffee on the window sill and hurried toward her. He pulled her into his arms and held her tight as if she'd disappear.

"Where's Jason?" John spoke from behind him.

"He's tying up some loose ends with the judge." Stewart smiled at Dean when he finally released his sister.

"I figured you'd be anxious to see this lovely young lady and take her home. She's spent way too much time in a place she never should have been in the first place." Stewart dropped his hand on Dean's shoulder.

"I don't know how to thank you, Mr. Michaels." Hannah held out her hand, and Stewart shook it.

"No thanks necessary. Jason got you out, and from what I've seen you won't be going back." Stewart smiled.

The man had mellowed since he'd developed a relationship with his children. Sandy was his daughter, but he also had another daughter and two sons. There was one more daughter, but she died when she was shot by her brother when she tried to have Sandy killed.

"Hannah is right. We owe you a debt of thanks as well." Dean shook Stewart's hand.

"We're family." He smiled. "Which reminds me, is it this weekend for the family supper?" He glanced at Keith.

"You know it. I think mom and dad are going to have to move, or we are going to have to start renting out a place." Keith laughed.

"Well, I have no issue with offering my place as a venue. At least before I sell it." Stewart buttoned his suit jacket.

"You're moving?" John asked.

"Yes." Stewart nodded. "Hopedale is about to become my home. I've purchased a smaller place for myself and the little woman. Plus, I'll be closer to my kids and grandkids. I've spent way too much of my life away from them."

"I'm sure they'll love that." John smiled.

Dean hadn't taken his arm from around his sister as he listened to the conversation going on around him. Hannah clung to him and remained quiet as well. He couldn't believe all the time wasted with her inside when all he had to do was get her a competent lawyer.

"I want to go." Hannah peered up at him. The bruise on her cheek faded, but the sadness in her eyes remained. Why wouldn't it be? She had to bury her daughter in a couple of days.

"Come on; we've got a comfortable place all set up for you." Keith winked at her. "I'm Keith O'Connor by the way, and this is one of my older brothers, John."

"It's nice to meet you." Hannah smiled, but she obviously forced it.

"There are a lot of people in Hopedale that want to meet you." John smiled, but Hannah tensed.

"I think that can wait." Keith must have noticed. "I'm sure Hannah wants to go home and relax."

Jason appeared as they were about to leave and from the huge grin on his face, Dean could tell he was pretty proud of himself.

"Stew, Judge Smallwood said to tell you he'll meet you at the club for that drink." Jason chuckled.

"A drink. That lush owes me more than a drink." Stewart laughed. "Care to join us, boy. You might learn a thing or two about schmoozing the likes of someone like Smallwood."

"I'd be glad to." Jason laughed. "Hannah, I'll drop by on Monday to see you and your brother and talk about getting this case thrown out."

"Thanks so much." Hannah shook his hand.

"My pleasure." Jason nodded and followed Stewart down the hallway toward the exit.

"Let's go home, Han." Dean guided his sister down the hall followed by Keith and John. They walked in silence, but Dean's thoughts were loud, and thousands of questions swirled around his head. He couldn't drop them on Hannah right away, but he would. He needed answers and soon.

Chapter 14

Kristy couldn't sit still as she waited for news from Dean about Hannah. He'd been surprised Jason got her case brought up before a judge so quickly. The truth was, so was Kristy.

"When does your mom open the pub part?" Kristy turned to see Lora the new waitress at Jack's Place.

Kristy liked her. Mostly because she knew what she was doing, and she wasn't a teenager or a woman her mother's age. Not that over fifty was a bad thing, but it was nice to have someone her own age to work with at the pub.

"Usually after supper. Mom swore she wasn't going to have the bar opened all day, so people could spend all day drinking instead of home with their family. Nan told her Grandda would roll over in his grave if he thought about people not being home with their families at supper time." Kristy chuckled.

"Your family is close." Lora sat next to her while they waited for the supper rush.

"Yeah," Kristy sipped on a cup of tea she'd poured for herself.

"That's wonderful." Lora smiled shyly.

"You aren't close with your family?" Lora hadn't said much about her life except she had a little girl.

"My dad died a few years ago and Molly, my mom and me rent a place on Knob Lane." Lora stood up and glanced around as if she was uncomfortable with talking about herself.

"No siblings?" Kristy should have taken the hint, but she was nosey.

"I have a brother, but he's a pilot and is only home a week or so every few months." Lora sighed. "Would you mind if I call home to check on Molly?"

"No, go ahead. Hell, you need a break. You haven't stopped since you got here."

The conversation distracted Kristy for a short time, but as she watched Lora walk to the back of the pub, her thoughts went back to Dean and his sister. He said he would text her when he knew something, but it had been hours, and her phone remained silent.

She snatched a cloth off the bar and started toward some of the empty tables to wipe them down. Not because they needed to be but because she had to distract herself. She was off from the Comfort Life Center for the next three days, and if she was honest, she wasn't sure she wanted to return there.

It wasn't that she didn't love the job but considering what happened she wasn't sure how she could go back there. Kristy didn't have much of a choice because she'd made a commitment to Sophia and she didn't want to let her down.

"If you keep wiping down that table you're going to wipe the coating off it." Kristy turned around.

Her cousins Mike and Ian were at the end of the counter holding menus. Ian always dropped in on Thursday because he worked late at the clinic and Billie spent Thursday evenings at the real estate agency until nine. So, Mike would drop by and have supper.

"Why exactly are you looking at the those when you probably know it by heart?" Kristy walked around the counter and stood in front of her cousins.

"We had to do something until you figured out that table was clean." Mike laughed.

"So that will be a spit seasoning for whatever you order." Kristy held up the notepad and smiled at her cousin.

"Don't mind her she's kidding." Lora seemed shocked by the way Kristy spoke to Mike and Ian.

"I doubt that." Ian laughed.

"It's okay, Lora. These are two of my cousins. Mike and Ian." Kristy pointed her pen at each cousin.

"Oh, sorry. Nice to meet you." Lora backed away from where Kristy stood.

"Lora is the new waitress mom hired. She doesn't live far from Keith's compound." Kristy remembered Knob Lane ran across the back end of Keith's property.

"Nice to meet you. I'm sure you'll do great." Ian nodded.

"She can't do worse than this one." Mike laughed.

"That will be spit seasoning on…" Kristy stared at Mike. "What was it you wanted?"

"Lora to serve me." Mike pointed toward the new waitress.

The supper rush came and went. Still no word from Dean and when she messaged Keith and Jason the only response she got was give him a bit of time. That didn't help her at all. Either Hannah didn't get released, or he found out she was his mother. Maybe both.

"Lora, you did amazing today." Kristy's mom walked out from the kitchen and unlocked the entrance to the bar part of the pub.

"Thanks so much, Mrs. O'Connor." Lora removed her apron.

"Please call me Alice. I'll see you in the morning at nine." Her mother handed Lora an envelope.

"What's this?" Lora glanced down at the sealed envelope.

"It's today's tips." Her mom smiled at the expression on Lora's face.

"But Kristy worked too. This is way too much." Lora gasped when she opened the envelope.

"Kristy has the same amount." Her mom handed her an envelope as well, but Kristy knew there was less in hers because she'd told her mother to give most of it to Lora. The woman had a daughter, and this wasn't a full-time job for Kristy.

"People in Hopedale are very generous when they get top notch service." Kristy smiled and wrapped her arm around her mother's shoulder.

"Thanks, I'll see you in the morning, Mrs…. Alice. Will you be here tomorrow too, Kristy?" Lora had a huge smile on her face.

"Actually, tomorrow my other daughter Jess is going to be helping out. After that, I think you'll be fine." Kristy didn't doubt it for a minute. Her mom asked Kristy several times how Lora was doing.

"That's great. Bye." Lora smiled as she opened the door and left the pub.

"I think she's going to be a good choice." Her mother smiled.

"Yeah," Kristy glanced out through the front of the pub.

"Still haven't heard from him?" Her mother cupped Kristy's cheek in her hand.

"No, I don't know what happened. I wanted to head over to his place and see if he's there, but then I feel like I'd be intruding." Kristy plopped down on one of the seats next to the counter.

"You could call him." Her mother suggested.

"I tried, it goes to voicemail." Kristy called before the supper rush started.

"What does Jason say?" The way her mother said his name told her she disliked Jason almost as much as her father did.

"Give him some time." Kristy sighed. "But I don't want him to go pushing me away."

"Well, maybe ya should march right over dere and find out wat happened." Kristy turned around to the sound of her grandmother's voice.

"Hi, Nan." Kristy hugged the tiny woman and kissed Tom's cheek.

Tom Roberts was Nanny Betty's boyfriend, but it wasn't exactly what her grandmother called him. He was her companion. He was also her first love, and after years of being estranged, they finally reconnected a few years earlier. They'd been inseparable ever since.

"Don't hi me, lassie. Get over dere and let dat man know yar worried." Nanny Betty pushed her toward the exit.

"Nan, maybe he wants to be alone." Kristy knew it was pointless to argue with her grandmother, but she had to try.

"I doubt dat. Now get. Text us and let us know how he is." Nanny Betty pushed her through the door and closed it once she was outside.

It was a beautiful late September day, and if she weren't in such a hurry to see Dean, she would have walked home. She jumped in her car and drove up Harbour Street toward Main Road. Keith's property was the only residence on the road that lead out of Hopedale.

Keith's property was a huge compound and required a code on the main gate to enter. If you didn't know the system or didn't have a code of your own, you had to buzz the security office. It seemed a little over the top to Kristy, but since Keith and Dean ran a security firm, it made sense to them. Especially if they had to bring clients to the property for protection.

Keith had given each of the family their own code to enter, so she punched it in, and the gate slowly opened. She drove through and waited for it to close again.

Dean's bunkhouse was on the back of the property next to five others. Keith and Dean had them built for staff that lived in Hopedale. It made sense, and the guys seemed to enjoy the town.

Dean's truck sat in front of his bunkhouse and the porch light was on. She pulled her car up next to it and turned off the engine.

She was still debating whether to intrude or not, but she had to see what happened at court.

"Are you going to stay in the car, or are you coming in?" Kristy jumped at the sound of his voice next to her open window.

"Damn it, warn a girl next time." Kristy rolled up her windows and stepped out of the car.

Before she had a chance to ask anything Dean pulled her into his arms and covered her mouth with his. She melted into his kiss and wrapped her arms around his neck as he pulled her against him.

"I fucking missed you." Dean smiled down at her when he ended the kiss.

"Really? Is that why you're ignoring my texts and calls." Kristy tapped her finger against his nose.

"I wasn't. When we got back here this afternoon, I got out of the truck and dropped my phone." He reached into his pocket and pulled out his phone with the screen shattered.

"That sucks." Kristy cringed.

"Keith picked up the new one while he was in town. It's where I was coming from when you pulled up." Dean kissed the top of her head. "You don't look in your rearview mirror at all do you?" He chuckled.

"Yes, I do."

"Oh, then you were ignoring my waving arms as you drove by Keith's place." Dean chuckled.

"I… I was a little… nervous about coming over here." Kristy admitted.

"What? Why?" He pulled back and met her eyes.

"I didn't know what happened and whether it was good or bad." Kristy sighed.

"It doesn't matter. When you want to come here don't let anyone or anything stop you." Dean stepped back and took her hand.

"So, what happened?"

"I'm surprised with your family you don't already know." Dean laughed as they strolled toward his bunkhouse.

"Me too but none of them seemed to know or they wouldn't tell me." Kristy glanced up at the porch.

Dean's sister sat on the porch in one of the chairs. She gave Kristy a hesitant smile.

"Hannah?" Kristy glanced up at Dean.

"Hannah, you remember Kristy." Dean practically dragged Kristy up the five steps to his porch.

"I do. It's nice to see you again, Kristy. I apologize for my behavior the first time." Hannah's voice was soft and somehow sad.

"You were fine. I'm glad to see Jason was able to get you out." Kristy sat next to her.

"Me too. It's not over, but at least I'm not in that awful place." Hannah looked at Dean.

"I've got a phone here for you, Hannah. I know you're probably exhausted so if you want to call it a night, I can walk you next door to the other bunkhouse." Dean held an iPhone box out to his sister.

"Thanks, Dean. I'm going to take a long hot shower and call it an early night." Hannah stood up, and Kristy didn't miss the cringe. She was still in pain from something. "I'm sorry I don't want to be rude, but it's been a long day."

"Don't worry about that. We'll have plenty of time to talk in the future." Kristy smiled as Hannah and Dean walked toward the smaller house next to his.

When he returned a few minutes later, Kristy had curled her feet under on the large deck chair. He crouched in front of her and took her hands in his.

"What do you want to know?" Dean smiled.

"Whatever you want to tell me." Kristy squeezed his hands.

"Let's go inside. I need to switch out my phone." Dean stood up and held her hand as she stood and followed him inside.

She gave him some time to get his new phone working by making herself a cup of tea. He called out to her when he'd finished.

"So, obviously Jason got Hannah out of that dreadful place." Kristy started when she sat next to Dean.

"Yes, and according to Stewart she won't be going back." Dean sighed. "I hope he's right."

"Me too. What about…" Kristy stopped.

"The baby she gave birth to, I haven't asked her yet. I don't know how to bring it up, but I need to know. I figure I'd give her a day to get her bearings and then talk to her. It's not that it will help with who killed Ivan or Pey, but I still need to know." Dean wrapped his arm around her shoulder, and she leaned into him.

"Let's enjoy the fact that she's out of that place. I do have to mention something though." Kristy tipped her head back and looked up at him.

"What's that?" Dean ran his finger down her cheek.

"I think you need to get her to a doctor. She seems to be in pain. I've noticed the couple of times I've seen her stand she cringes." Kristy saw anger flash across his face and then he calmed.

"I noticed it too; she says she's fine and won't talk about how she got the bruise." Dean brushed his thumb across her lip.

"She could have a broken rib or something." Kristy placed her cup on the table next to the couch.

208

"I'll talk to her, but right now I want to take you into my bedroom and forget the world for a while." He kissed her cheek and moved his hand down to her shoulder.

"That sounds like heaven. I dropped Isabelle a text and told her I was coming here." Kristy closed her eyes when his lips moved to her ear.

"You should tell her not to wait up," Dean whispered as his hand slid down her forearm to her elbow.

"She already said she wouldn't expect me home." Kristy gasped when he ran his tongue around the shape of her ear.

"I knew your sister was a smart girl." Dean moaned. Probably because Kristy had slid her hand under his shirt and she was gently tugging on his piercing. She didn't know why but it turned her on when she did it, and he responded.

"It's still a little early to be going to bed." Kristy sighed as his lips moved down the side of her neck.

"I'm not planning on going to sleep." Dean slipped his arm under her knees and lifted her onto his lap. His lips moved down to her collarbone and across the top of her breast.

"What about eating?" Kristy panted as he nipped her hardened nipple through her shirt.

"I'll be eating alright," Dean growled and stood up so fast that Kristy squealed.

"Food, Dean. Food." Kristy laughed as he stomped toward his bedroom.

"You first." Dean lowered her to the bed and crawled over her.

Kristy bit her lip as he slowly raised her T-shirt up over her torso over her breasts and stop to flick his tongue over each nipple through her thin bra. He continued to push off her shirt until it was over her head but still around her arms.

"Leave that there," Dean growled and yanked his own shirt over his head.

Kristy dropped her eyes to where his erection bulged inside his jeans. He was a large man, and she wanted to release it from its confines so she could wrap her hand around it and lick him. When she tried to throw off her shirt Dean grabbed her arms and pulled it tight around them.

"Hey," She tried to pull away.

"I want to kiss and taste every fucking inch of you, but if your hands are free you're going to touch me, and I need a little control right now. You did see him trying to escape; I saw you lick your lips when you looked at it." Dean's gaze traveled down her half-naked body. "Now, let's get rid of these."

Dean unbuttoned her jeans and slipped them off her hips while his tongue, teeth, and lips did amazing things to her nipples through her bra. He'd nip one then lick the other and then gently blow across the dampness his mouth made. It drove her crazy.

"Dean, I want to touch you." Kristy panted as her jeans slipped off her feet. She didn't know where her flipflops had gone because she didn't remember kicking them off but she couldn't think at the moment because his warm hands glided slowly up her legs gently massaging as his tongue followed.

"Soon, Kitten," Dean whispered right before his tongue slid between her legs and licked her through her panties.

"Ah… Dean." Kristy moaned.

"That's it, moan for me. I want to hear your pleasure." Dean's hot breath blew across her damp underwear, and she shivered.

"Please… take them off." Kristy was desperate to feel his hot mouth on her.

"With pleasure," Dean growled and grabbed the waist of her panties and gradually slid them off her legs. Taking his time to kiss every inch from the top of her hips to her ankles. It was about to drive her right off the deep end.

Whatever he'd done with her shirt she couldn't free her hands, and when she lifted them to see what he did, he pushed them back over her head.

"You're going to torture me to death," Kristy whined.

"You don't like what I'm doing." He unhooked her bra which opened in the front.

"I want to do a little torturing myself." She grinned and dropped her gaze to his groin.

"I want to ravish you before I release you." He grinned and brushed his lips against hers and pressed his covered erection against her swollen clit.

"I need to come." Kristy groaned as she pressed up against him.

"I'll help you with that, but you need to promise to keep your hands above your head." Dean grinded harder against her.

"God, yes." Kristy moaned.

He really was driving her to the brink of insanity with the way he was grinding against her. She should have let him continue but he stopped, and she growled. When he chuckled, she wanted to kick him, but before she could, he sucked her pebbled nipple into his mouth and slipped his finger between her wet folds.

"Oh, yes." Kristy gasped and raised her hips off the bed.

He sucked gently on her nipple and switched to the other and back again. All the while he pressed the heal of his hand against her swollen clit. His finger slid forward and back between her folds but not going inside. She raised her hips again, and he pushed them back down.

"Patience, Kitten," Dean whispered against her chest.

"Dean, you're driving me… ahhh crazy." She groaned as he flicked his tongue into her belly button and continued to lick his way down to where she wanted him most.

"I never saw anything so beautiful in my life," Dean whispered, and his hot breath blew across her wetness.

He flicked his tongue quickly against her clit once, twice then on the third time he sucked it hard into his mouth and drove his fingers deep inside her. It pushed her completely over the edge, and she arched off the bed.

"Ahh … Dean. God. Yes." Kristy screamed, and her body shuddered as her orgasm shot through her body like a pleasurable wave of electricity.

Before she had a chance to come down from it, he had her trembling with pleasure again. This one was more intense. So much so when she opened her eyes, she saw stars.

He's trying to kill me.

Chapter 15

Dean's cock was about to burst through the zipper of his jeans but watching her as her release overtook her was beautiful. He could have stayed there forever making her come, but the painful ache in his groin told him he needed his own release.

"Dean, take this off my hands." Kristy panted as she struggled to release her arms from her shirt. He straddled her hips and released the knot he'd tied to keep her hands together.

It wasn't that he was into all that fifty shades shit, but some of it was interesting. Not the painful stuff but the bondage could be a real turn on, and with Kristy, it was painfully arousing.

When he released her hands, he rubbed her wrists to make sure they didn't hurt. Her aroused gaze started from his eyes and slowly moved down his body until she stopped at the waist of his jeans. She pulled her hands from his and pushed them behind his back.

"Now, I won't tie you up but keep those behind your back." Kristy wiggled until she was out from under him and knelt up on the bed in front of him. It was difficult to keep his hands behind his back, but he wanted her to feel the same control he had a few minutes before. He clasped them behind his back and watched as she pressed her lips against his bare chest and used her hands to pop the button on his jeans.

She sucked his nipple into her hot mouth and slowly lowered his zipper. Her hand slid inside, and with a quick flick her hand was wrapped around his engorged dick, and her teeth were gently biting down on his nipple.

"Holy Fuck." Dean groaned.

"Stand up," Kristy demanded as she pushed him back to the edge of the bed until he stood next to it.

His hands were starting to hurt from holding them together so tightly. Kristy moved off the bed and pushed him back still with her hand grasped tightly on his cock.

"You're so hard." She whispered and licked his bottom lip. "I'm going to do that to this." She pulled his cock out of his briefs but didn't bother to push down either his jeans or underwear.

"Fuck, Kitten. Do what you want." He growled when she fell to her knees and pumped his cock while she squeezed pre-cum out of the top of his dick.

"Someone is ready to pop." She smiled right before she slowly ran her tongue up his entire length. Then she sucked his head into her mouth and let go with a pop.

"Damn, do that again." Dean moaned.

"Like that huh?" She repeated the motion, and he could feel that tingle in the base of his spine.

"Yes, but I don't want to come yet. If you keep that up, I will." Dean tried to pull out of her grasp, but she grabbed the base of his cock and squeezed it while she repeated her motion a third time.

"Pull down your jeans, Dean." Kristy seemed to enjoy giving commands, and if he was honest, it was hot.

Dean slowly slid his jeans and briefs off his hips and down to his knees. Kristy pushed his hands back behind his back and took over the rest of the clothing removal. He stepped out of them and stood there with his cock less than an inch from her plump lips.

"Lay down on the bed." Kristy stood up.

She almost seemed worried he wouldn't comply, but it was so damn hot he sat down and flopped back on the bed. His feet were on the floor, and he spread his legs when she stepped between them.

"Now, what are you gonna do with me?" Dean grinned.

"I'm going to see how far I can suck you into my mouth." Kristy smiled.

He must have had a surprised expression because she laughed and bent over to flick her tongue against the swollen head of his cock. Dean propped himself up on his elbows and glanced behind her. His full-length mirror was in the perfect position for him to get a good look at her sexy ass as she sucked him slowly into her mouth.

"Fuck, yeah. That's it, Kitten." Dean groaned while she took him deep into her mouth. Although she wasn't able to get him all the way in, she sure as hell gave it the old college try. What she couldn't get into her mouth she was pumping slowly with her hand.

He watched her ass wiggle as her head bobbed up and down on his dick. It was getting more difficult to hold off on coming, and he knew he had to stop her before he did. He wanted to be buried inside her when he had his release.

"Baby, stop." Dean panted.

"Mmm." Kristy's moans sent vibrations shooting through his body.

"Kitten, I want to be inside you." Dean groaned as she pumped him faster.

When she finally popped off his head, he fell back on the bed. He'd been so close to exploding into her mouth. He reached toward his nightstand and pulled out a condom.

"I want to put it on." Kristy snatched it out of his hand and straddled his legs.

"I don't know if that's a good idea but fuck I love when you touch me." Dean ran his hands up her thighs and held onto her hips.

Kristy placed the condom on the head of his erection and rolled it on slowly making little strokes as she did. When she rolled it all the way on, Dean lifted her by the hips and moved her above him.

"Ride me, Kitten. I want your pussy to swallow my cock." Dean whispered as she lowered herself down over his stiff dick.

Dean almost lost his breath when she took him completely inside her. She felt so fucking amazing, as she ground against him. It was so damn hot.

"You're so hard." Kristy moaned and increased her speed.

"You make me that way." Dean moaned as he gripped her hips and pulled her back and forth. Her inside squeezed him as she leaned forward and pressed her lips against his.

Dean cupped the back of her head and drove his tongue into her mouth as she moved her hips in circular motion. He slipped his other hand between them and pressed his thumb against her clit.

Kristy groaned, and when she sucked his tongue, he was sure he could feel it in his dick. He could hear the wetness as they moved together, but he needed to go faster.

He flipped her over onto her back without breaking their kiss or slipping out of her. Kristy grabbed his ass and wrapped her legs around his hips as he slammed into her over and over. He was ready to come but he wasn't without making her scream his name.

"Come for me, Kitten." Dean pulled his lips from hers and moved his thumb against her clit as he continued to slam into her.

"Don't stop." She moaned.

"I don't think I could at this point." Dean growled.

"Dean, yes. Yeah." Her body arched off the bed, and she trembled as her pussy tightened around his cock. With her release, it only took one more thrust inside her, and he lost it.

"Fuck, baby. Yes, oh fuck." Dean shouted as he pushed deep into her and held himself there while his cock jerked inside her.

Dean's arms shook as he held himself above her and gazed down. Kristy's eyes were closed, as she seemed to try and regulate her breathing. She was so damn beautiful. Dean used the moment to study her face while her warm hands glided up and down his back.

"You're staring." She whispered without opening her beautiful eyes.

"I am." He shuddered when her pussy squeezed his sensitive cock.

"Why?" Kristy opened her eyes and met his eyes.

"Because I want to." He smiled and brushed his lips against hers.

"I'm just wondering how long you're going to be able to hold yourself up." Kristy chuckled, and he could feel it inside her.

"I'm wondering that myself, but I need to get up and get rid of this thing." Dean gave her one quick kiss and jumped to his feet.

"I can't move right now." Kristy sighed.

"Good, I don't want you to move." Dean winked and hurried to the bathroom to dispose of the condom.

He returned to find her snuggled under the blankets with her hand tucked under her cheek. She smiled as he approached the bed and pulled back the comforter so he could crawl in next to her.

"I could get used to this," Dean whispered as she snuggled into his side.

"Me too and to think if you hadn't been so stubborn we could have been doing this for years." Kristy tipped her head back to look at him.

"I'm a fucking idiot. I know." Dean chuckled. "You can remind me of that at least once a week for the rest of my life."

"I like the sound of that." Kristy rested her hand on his chest and swirled her finger around in small circles.

"Han thinks you're beautiful." Dean kissed the top of her head.

"So is she. Even with the bruised eye, you can see she's a knockout." Kristy pressed her lips against his chest.

"My sister has aged in the four months for obvious reasons, but when I was a little boy I remember two guys fighting over her on our front lawn. My dad grabbed them by the shirt collars and told them to grow up. I don't think I had started school, so I was about four. I don't know who they were, but I remember her screaming from the step telling them to stop." Dean had clung tightly to his mom that day.

"Isabelle had that happen over her at a softball game when she was in high school. The guy she was dating beat the crap out of some guy from the other team for flirting with her." Kristy laughed.

"Knowing your sister, she probably dumped the guy." Dean chuckled.

"Actually, he was killed in a motorcycle accident a couple of years later," Kristy whispered. "He was a good guy."

"Is that why she doesn't date?" Dean couldn't remember in all the years he'd been back in Newfoundland ever seeing the oldest of the O'Connor girls ever date.

"She's married to her restaurant, but no they were broken up long before that happened." Kristy yawned and draped her leg across his. "I guess she hasn't found the right guy."

Dean closed his eyes. It was the most content he'd felt in a long time and the soft sound of her even breathing lulled him into a deep sleep. He didn't know what answers he'd get the next day but the only thing he cared about at that moment was the woman next to him.

Dean's eyes flew open a short while later. He didn't even realize he'd fallen asleep. At least not until he was into the horrible nightmare where he was locked in a cage and some sadistic man tortured Kristy.

He glanced down at his chest. Kristy's long hair covered it like a silky blanket. She was turned away from him but still tucked into his side. Her soft snore proof she was still sound asleep. He didn't want to wake her, but he couldn't help but turn into her warm body and pull her against him.

She moaned a little but pushed her body into his before her breathing became deep and even again. He pressed his lips against the back of her head and then eased out of bed, so he wouldn't wake her.

A quick shower and two cups of coffee later, Kristy was still asleep, and Dean sat on the deck watching a wild rabbit feed on a tall patch of grass next to the tree line. It was a little after seven in the morning, and when he closed his eyes, he could hear the waves crash against the rocks in the distance.

"I see you still get up at the crack of dawn." Dean opened his eyes and glanced up at his sister.

"I'm surprised to see you up this early." Dean chuckled.

"It's a strange place and a new bed." She sat next to him on the bench.

"Did you sleep at all?" Dean held up his cup, and she shook her head.

"Better than I thought but still a lot of dreams." She turned away but not in time for him to miss the tears in her eyes.

"Han, I'm so sorry." Dean dropped his head.

"Dean, you did nothing wrong. I know I blamed you at first, but I know this wasn't your fault." Hannah rested her hand on his arm.

Dean covered it with his own and met her sad expression. She'd lost so much. Her husband, daughter and the last four months of her life she spent locked up.

"Han, there's something I need to ask you." Dean figured there wouldn't be a better time.

"What's that?" She appeared to study him before she sat back on the bench.

"Did you have a baby when you were fourteen?" Dean watched her face and knew the answer without her answer. Her eyes widened, and he saw the pulse in her neck increase.

"How…who…where did you hear that?" She shifted on the bench and tucked her hands under her thighs.

"Is that really important? I need to know." Dean touched her knee.

She dropped her head, and a soft sob escaped her. His heart pounded in his chest as he waited for the answer he didn't want to believe. He didn't push her to answer as she covered her face with her hands and took a deep breath.

"Yes," Hannah whispered when she raised her head and met his eyes.

"You put the baby up for adoption." Dean swallowed the lump forming in his throat.

"I was only a kid and the father… well, it wasn't a good situation." She wiped a tear from her cheek.

"It was a boy, and he was born in November." Dean wanted her to know he had an idea of who adopted the baby, but he needed her to say it.

"Yes, he was so small." Hannah blew out a shaky breath. "I couldn't care for him."

Hannah was quiet as she stared in front of her. She seemed to lost in the memory of when she gave birth. It was evident with the way the tears ran down her cheeks.

"I need to know Hannah." He didn't recognize his own voice as he tried to get to the truth.

"What?" She turned to look at him.

"Am I that child?" Dean watched her for some hint of an answer, but all she did was stare at him. "I want to know."

"Wait, you think…. Why would you think I'm your mother?" She appeared to be in a state of shock.

"It makes sense. I was born when you were fourteen in November. I know mom was supposed to have had me after years of giving up on having any more children." Dean still found it hard to wrap his head around, but it made sense.

"Dean, yes I got pregnant at fourteen and gave birth to a baby boy. He was three months early because I went into premature labor. Mom had you a week before that. I'm not your mother, Dean. My baby died three days after he was born." She sniffed. "I held him while he took his last breath."

"Han, I'm sorry." Dean was relieved, but he could feel the sorrow of losing the child radiating from his sister.

"Mom told me she'd help if I wanted to keep him, but she'd just had you. It had been a tough delivery for her." Hannah wiped another tear from her cheek. "He was born too soon."

"Can I ask who the father was?" Dean assumed it was Ivan because he and Hannah had been high school sweethearts.

"That's a whole can of worms I don't know if I should open." She whispered.

"So, it wasn't Ivan?" Dean couldn't think of any other man his sister had dated.

"No, I dated someone else for a few days before Ivan." Hannah hiccupped. "I miss him so much."

Dean stood and pulled her up from the bench. He hugged her to his chest while she wept. She probably hadn't had a chance to grieve him with everything that happened. She wasn't even able to attend his funeral. Trevor couldn't get her out for it. According to the man, it wasn't right for her to go to the funeral of the man she killed.

He didn't know how long he stood there with her soaking his shirt in tears, but she finally took a deep breath and pushed back from him.

"I miss them both." She sighed.

"I know, Han." Dean did know. He missed Peyton terribly. He tried to keep it in check until they cleared up the whole mess

"I guess if you know about the baby you should know everything." Hannah sighed. "I'll need a strong cup of coffee to dig into that buried memory."

Chapter 16

Kristy woke slowly and rolled over on her back. The other side of the bed was empty, and she felt a little disappointed, but she could hear the quiet mummers in the kitchen. The other voice was female and sounded upset.

She jumped out of bed and pulled on her clothes that she tossed on the floor. She hated to put on clothes from the day before, but she hadn't been bright enough to bring an overnight bag with her. Of course, she hadn't been sure that she was staying because she didn't know what had happened at court.

She pulled her hair into a ponytail and cringed because she knew she'd suffer later for not brushing it beforehand.

Dean sat in the kitchen across from his sister, and they were deep in conversation. It looked intense, and she hated to interrupt, but when she turned to go back into the bedroom, Dean called out to her.

"Where are you going, Kitten?" She spun back and met his smile.

"I didn't want to intrude." She shuffled into the kitchen.

"You aren't. As a matter of fact, you should know as well. I'm not Dean's mother." Hannah gave her a forced smile.

"I... okay... ummm…. Is that a good thing?" Kristy wasn't sure how to react.

"It's good that Dean knows nobody lied to him." Hannah reached across the table. "You were always my cute annoying little brother."

"I'm still cute but much less annoying." Dean grinned as he covered her hand with his.

"Sure, honey. If that helps." Hannah chuckled.

"Did you want something to eat?" Dean asked her as he pulled out the chair next to him for her to sit.

"No, I need to head home and get showered and changed." She glanced at Hannah.

"I'm gonna take Hannah to see your dad this morning but if you want we can meet for lunch at the pub." Dean offered.

"Sounds great. Hannah, I hope you can join us." Kristy stood and pushed in the chair.

"I'd like that." It was the first time in the short time she'd known Dean's sister her smile reached her eyes. It also showed how much Dean and Hannah looked alike.

"Great, I look forward to it." Kristy made her way around the table toward the front door.

"I'll walk you out." Dean stood up and grabbed her hand as they walked to the exit.

He held her hand the whole way down the steps to the driver side of her car. Giving it a little squeeze when she stopped by the vehicle.

"You seem more relaxed." Kristy turned to face him and wrapped her arms around his waist.

"It's a relief to know my parents and Hannah weren't lying to me. They did hide a pretty big thing from me, but it wasn't something that affected my life." He kissed her forehead.

"That's true." Kristy closed her eyes and allowed his lips to move down the side of her face. "I'm guessing Ivan was the baby's father."

"Actually, no but Eric was." Kristy's eyes popped open, and she pulled back from his comforting kiss.

"Isn't that Ivan's brother? The one that she said to keep away from Peyton?" Kristy had heard Dean mention the name.

"One in the same. Apparently, Han dated Eric first but she was convinced he only wanted to get her on her back. After they had sex, he stopped calling her. A couple of weeks later Ivan asked her out." Dean shook his head. "In the tiny town we lived in there wasn't a lot of choices in dating."

"You're telling someone who grew up in a town that at least a tenth of the guys were either my cousins or friends of my cousins." Kristy laughed. "And look here I am madly in love with a friend of my cousin."

"He's also head over heels for you." Dean ran his finger down the side of her face as he lowered his lips to meet hers.

Kristy's lips met his in a soft sweet kiss. It wasn't as intense as the night before. It was more of a promise of forever.

"Mmm… I'll text you when Hannah and I are on the way to the pub." Dean gave her another quick kiss before he opened the car door for her.

"I love you, Dean." She touched his cheek and stared into his hazel eyes.

"I love you too, Kitten." Dean covered her hand and pulled her palm to his lips. "With every beat of my heart."

Kristy drove to Isabelle's, and she couldn't keep the smile off her lips. For the first time, she saw a future with Dean, but she still didn't want to get her hopes up.

Kristy pulled up in front of Isabelle's and hopped out of her car. She was almost halfway up the steps when she noticed the sold sign on the house next door.

"Damn. Someone bought it. I hope they don't tear that down and build some modern thing there." Kristy mumbled to herself.

"I'm pretty sure the owner is renovating it." Kristy spun around when she heard a male voice.

"Matt, you scared the shit out of me." Kristy laughed.

"Better get inside and change then." He chuckled as he tossed something into the back of his truck.

"Keith has the contract for the renovations?" Kristy hoped so because her cousin would do everything to get the owner to stick with the general building style of the old house.

"Yes, but I'm designing the layout inside." Matt rested his arms on the front of his truck. "The new owner wants it the same as when it was first built on the outside but an open layout on the inside."

"Good, I love that old house. I think it's one of the first ones built in Hopedale." Kristy couldn't ever remember the house not there.

"What would you do with it?" Matt tucked his fist under his chin.

"I don't know. I'm not a designer or architect." She laughed.

"I know but if you were the owner what would you want to be done with it?" Matt motioned for her to come over. He propped his tablet on the bonnet of the truck and tapped the screen a few times. "This is what I've got done. What do you think?"

Kristy grabbed the tablet and studied the screen. Matt was a good artist. The front of the house was much like Isabelle's with the full covered front porch. Large bay windows jutted out on both sides of the main entrance to the house.

"This is great." Kristy thought it looked exactly the way she imagined.

He showed the layout of the inside. It was all open concept on the bottom floor. Four rooms on the bottom floor flowed together. On the front of the house next to the kitchen was a smaller place marked as the office. She thought it would give the owner a great view of the beach when he or she worked.

"It's great, Matt." She handed him back the tablet, and he grinned.

"Thanks. I'm really enjoying this part of the job." He opened the door to his truck.

"You were made to do that type of work." Kristy backed toward the house.

"I've got a meeting with the owner, so I need to run." Matt jumped into the truck and waved as he drove off.

At noon, Kristy was joking with Aaron in one of the window booths when Dean walked in with Hannah. Aaron said something to her but when she saw Dean, she completely tuned out her cousin.

"Oh yeah, you're only killing time with me until your man gets here." Aaron feigned shock.

"Isn't that what all women do with you, A.J." Dean chuckled as he slid next to Kristy.

"Bull, you have no idea what women do with me, and since I'm in the presence of a beautiful lady, I'll remain the gentleman I am." Aaron held out his hand to Hannah. "Aaron O'Connor or you can call me A.J. Either way you can call me anytime."

Kristy glanced up at Hannah who seemed in total shock as Aaron kissed her hand. She glanced between Aaron and Kristy as if she couldn't believe what she witnessed.

"Stop hitting on my sister, Ass," Dean growled, and she heard the toe of his boot hit the seat next to Aaron.

"There is no way you're related to this stunning lady." Aaron shook his head. "No, that's impossible.

"Does this stuff really work for you?" Hannah laughed, and Aaron winked at her.

"All the time." He sat back and tapped his hand on the seat next to him.

"Don't you have to go to work?" Kristy groaned.

"Not yet." He smiled.

"Okay let me save you some time, honey. If you think this kind of stuff is going to get you a date with me. You may as well leave now. First, you are a little young. Second, I'm not looking for a date, and finally, you should probably know I'm being investigated for killing my husband." Hannah crossed her arms over her chest, and Kristy pressed her lips together to keep from laughing.

What Hannah didn't know was Aaron knew all about her. When he didn't show any change in his flirtatious behavior, Hannah seemed to get uncomfortable.

"Well, Honey, I know all about your investigation because I'm one of the officers trying to figure out the screw-up. You can thank me with a little kiss on the cheek." Aaron turned his head and pointed his finger to his cheek.

Kristy glanced at Dean and laughed at his expression. He looked about ready to leap over the table and strangle her cousin.

"A.J. I'm going to rip off your head and shit down your neck," Dean growled.

"Fine, you can thank me when Mr. Grump is not around." Aaron slid out of the booth and stood up. "It is nice to meet you, Hannah. Welcome to Hopedale."

With that statement, Aaron sauntered out of the pub leaving Hannah staring after him and Dean ready to chew nails.

"Wow, well he's …. Interesting." Hannah finally stammered as she slid into the seat Aaron had left.

"He's a little full of himself sometimes but he means well, and he wasn't lying about working on your case. He's a police officer and another cousin." Kristy picked up her menu and pointed to the main counter. "That girl over there is also a police officer and my older sister. She's helping mom train a new waitress."

"Dean said your family was close." Hannah folded her hands in front of her on the table.

"Yes, and really big." Dean chuckled and nodded toward the other side of the pub.

Kristy glanced up as Ian, Sandy and their kids walked through the door. Well, Ian walked through, Sandy mostly ran as she tried to corral the four children.

Evie was Sandy's daughter from a former relationship and the oldest at ten. Lily was Ian's little girl also from a former relationship and just turned Ten in August. The two little girls were best friends as well as step-sisters.

Then there was the whirlwind that was little Grace. She was almost four and had a mind of her own. She was also Lily's full sister. Alexander was the baby of the family at two years old.

How the couple found time to do anything with all the kids was beyond her, but they were happy, and the kids were the joy of their blended family.

"Bull," Grace screamed as she broke free from Sandy's grasp and scooted right to Dean.

"Hello, Goldilocks." Dean caught her as she launched herself into his arms. The Goldilocks comment was probably because the child had incredibly curly hair.

"We got Evie's name fixed." She squealed excitedly but stopped when she noticed Hannah on the other side of the table. "Who are you?"

"Gracie, what did mommy tell you about being rude?" Sandy sighed as she handed Alexander to a smiling Ian.

"Sorry, who are you please?" Gracie tilted her head, and Sandy rolled her eyes.

"This is Hannah; she's Bull's sister." Kristy used his nickname because Grace refused to call him Dean.

"You got a little sister. You're so lucky. I only got a brudder." She sighed.

"Actually, Bull is my little brother." Hannah smiled at Grace, and everyone laughed at the adorable little girls shocked expression.

"He's not very little." Grace pointed out the obvious.

"He used to be, and he was a big pain," Hannah said with a sigh.

"Little brudders are the worst." Grace wiggled around until she was sat comfortably on Dean's lap.

"But you love them anyway, huh?" Hannah winked.

"Daddy, says I have to." Grace rolled her eyes.

The little girl lost interest in the conversation when Dean began to introduce Hannah to Ian and Sandy. Kristy glanced out through the window while the rest of them chatted. She had an eerie feeling of someone staring at her.

Harbour Street was the busiest road in the town with most of the businesses located from one end of the street to the other on one side and the harbor dock on the other. It was common to see people walking up and down or stopping to talk to other people. What she didn't see was anyone looking toward the pub or her.

"Kristy," She faintly heard Sandy's voice.

"What? Sorry." Kristy glanced up at her cousin's wife.

"I asked if you're going to continue to work at that place." Sandy had sat next to Hannah.

"Of course, I…" She started.

"Absolutely not." Dean's voice was loud enough that most of the patrons in the restaurant turned.

"Excuse me?" Kristy stared at the man next to her, but she didn't know if she was more shocked or angry.

"Yeah, I'm gonna go now." Sandy stood slowly. "Nice to meet you, Hannah."

"I know I didn't stutter." Dean glanced up as Jess placed their order in front of them.

"No, you didn't, but there was no way I heard you properly." Kristy snapped.

"Hannah, I'm Jess. Come on I'll introduce you to some of the other family here." Jess stepped back, and Hannah all but jumped out of the seat.

"You're not going out there when there could be a killer out there." Dean jabbed his fork into the potatoes on his plate.

"I've got a job out there, and I made a commitment to Sophia to finish out the month until her other nurse returns." Kristy tried to keep her voice from raising, but it wasn't easy when Dean sat next to her as if he made the rule and that was that.

"I'm sure she will understand when you don't return." Dean picked up his sandwich and took a huge bite.

"Wait a minute. Who gave you the authority to tell me what to do?" Kristy snapped.

"I'm not telling you what to do. I said you aren't going back there." Dean shrugged his shoulders as he continued to eat.

"Do you hear yourself? Listen, here, nobody tells me what I can or can not do." Kristy pushed him to try and get up from the table, but he had her on the inside. It made it very difficult to stomp away.

"Your dad did." Dean chuckled.

Kristy didn't see anything but red. She grabbed the edge of his plate and tipped it into his lap. Dean jumped to his feet which gave her the space to get up from the booth.

"What did you do that for?" Dean grabbed a handful of napkins and wiped the front of his shirt.

"You're lucky I didn't dump it over your head. It's no fun when the food will only slide off your bald head." Kristy stomped away from him about ten steps and spun around. "If you want to get together later, Hannah. Jess will give you my number."

She spun back around and left the restaurant. She was so pissed she didn't even take her car. She walked back to Isabelle's house the whole way complaining about men and their Neanderthal ways.

Kristy loved Dean, but she was raised to be a strong independent woman, and no man was going to tell her what to do. The comment he made about her father was probably right, but she was also taught to respect her elders.

The truth was if she'd really wanted to stay in her apartment, her father wouldn't have changed her mind. She wanted to come back to Hopedale. Even though she'd only been there for a couple of weeks, the place was crawling with mice, and she missed her family.

By the time she got back to Isabelle's, she'd calmed a little but not enough for her to go back to the pub. She'd go back later to get her car, but now she was going to sit on Isabelle's porch and watch the waves crash on the beach. Dean Nash could kiss her ass.

Chapter 17

Dean thanked Alice as she helped him clean up the food from the floor where Kristy had dumped it over him. He still didn't know what the hell happened or why she lost her mind. It was so unlike her. She was usually so in control.

"I'm sorry about this, Alice." Dean tossed the last of the napkins in the garbage.

"It's not me you should be apologizing to, Dean." She raised her eyebrow, turned and disappeared into the kitchen.

"What the fuck am I apologizing for?" Dean mumbled to himself.

"Are you kidding me right now?" Sandy stepped in front of him with her fists on her hips.

"No, I'm not." He knew what he'd said to Kristy, but he honestly didn't mean it in a bad way. He didn't want her to be out there without him to keep her safe.

"Is the sun too hot on that Chrome Dome of yours?" Sandy pointed to his head.

"No, all I said was she wasn't going back there." Dean rolled his eyes.

"Oh, so you've been together what? A week? Give or take a day." Sandy had a way of making you feel about two feet tall.

"What does that have to do with anything?" Dean shrugged his shoulders.

"Why are men so stupid? Bull, she's been in love with you for years and probably had this fantasy of you supporting her in everything she wanted to do in her life. Then all this terrible stuff happens, and she's there for you. This job obviously means a lot to her, and I guess she thought, oh I don't know, you'd support her. You can't tell her what to do." Sandy glared up at him.

"There could be a killer out there." Dean shook his head. "I can't let anything happen to her. I can't lose her."

He hated the crack in his voice especially around so many people. Kristy seemed to bring out an emotional side of him that he couldn't hide when it came to her.

"You will lose her if you try to control her." Sandy touched his arm. "Talk to her, not at her."

"Sandy is right." Dean turned when his sister linked into his arm. "I know you love her, Dean. Don't waste time with petty arguments. Life's way too short."

If there was anything, he knew it was how quick a life could change in the blink of an eye. It's also the reason he didn't want

Kristy near that place until they knew for sure what happened to Peyton.

"You should know by now, Bull. The women in the O'Connor family are strong, stubborn and independent." Ian chuckled from where he sat with the kids.

"Yeah, remember we were all raised with Nan in our lives." Jess laughed.

"Jesus, with my luck she's probably calling your grandmother to come kick my ass." Dean chuckled.

"Don't let Nanny Kathleen hear you say bad words, Bull." Grace stared at him. "She got the pepper."

It seemed that Kathleen O'Connor threatened pepper on the tongue if any of the kids used curse words. It seemed to work because all the kids always reminded the adults about it.

"Han, I'll bring you back to the compound. I need to go talk to… I mean apologize to Kristy." Dean sighed.

"She can stay and finish her lunch. We'll bring her back, or she can come to the house for a bit." Sandy offered.

"Is that okay with you, Han?" Dean asked because the truth was his sister didn't know these people and he wasn't sure how comfortable she was with a new crowd of people.

"I'd like that." Hannah smiled at Sandy.

"I want to warn you that all the kids are going to be going back with us. The older two don't have school today." Sandy chuckled.

"That sounds great." Hannah walked back to the table, and Grace quickly moved from her spot and sat next to his sister.

"Was Bull really a big pain?" He heard the little girl ask as he made his way out of the pub. Hannah could probably keep little Gracie entertained for hours with stories of his behavior as a little boy.

He spotted Kristy's car as soon as he got outside. Panic started to rise in his gut, but he tamed it down by reasoning that she probably walked home to calm down. He hoped he was right but in case he wasn't he quickly spun his truck out of the lot and sped down Harbour Street to Beach Street.

Kristy was on the front porch gazing across the street at the beach. He pulled his truck into the driveway and watched her for a moment. She had to have seen him drive up but the fact that she ignored his presence made him chuckle. That was his girl.

"Is it safe to come up there?" Dean asked as he closed the door to his truck.

"I don't have a bat, or a gun if that's what you're asking." Kristy deadpanned.

"Good to know." Dean shuffled up the steps to the porch. He glanced toward the house next door at the workers. Matt had told

243

him they were starting on the outside that afternoon and that he'd run into Kristy as he left.

"The house got sold." He heard the disappointment in her voice and was tempted to tell her he'd bought it.

"Looks like they're renovating." Dean braced himself against the railing of the deck.

"What are you doing here, Dean?" Kristy didn't look at him.

"I wanted to apologize." He admitted.

"Okay," She was still pissed.

"Just okay?" Dean pushed himself off the rail and walked toward her.

"What else am I supposed to say?" She glanced at him as he crouched in front of her.

"You forgive me? You know I'm an overbearing ass, but you understand that I didn't want anything to happen to you." He reached for her hand.

"I know you're an overbearing ass." Kristy pulled her hand away.

Dean sighed and dropped his head. He placed his hands on his knees and pushed himself to a standing position.

"I'm sorry, Kitten. I wasn't thinking." She looked up at him, and he held out his hand.

Kristy put her hand in his and stood up. He wanted to pull her into his arms and kiss her until she gave in, but he knew that wouldn't work with Kristy.

"I need to go back there. I love working there, and I can't leave them short staffed." Kristy's voice was soft.

"I understand but is it still okay that I don't like the idea of you being there?" Dean pulled her closer, and to his relief, she didn't pull away.

"It's okay you're concerned." Kristy lay her hands on his chest and played with the button on his shirt.

"So, you're going to drive back and forth for your three shifts?" Dean asked.

"It's night shifts for me this round." Kristy tipped her head back and stared up him.

She had to have felt his body stiffen. Night shifts meant a couple of things. Less staff at the facility during those hours, worrying about her driving back in the morning after being up all night and not being able to have her sleep in his arms for three nights.

"I could drive you back and forth," Dean suggested.

"So, you want to drive out there come home and then drive out to pick me up. That would be an awful waste of gas." Kristy slid her arms up and around his shoulders.

"I could stay out there." Dean knew it sounded stupid.

"What are you going to do sleep in the parking lot?" Kristy smiled. "Besides, you need to be here for Hannah."

"As much as I don't like it, I know you're right. I need to find out when we can put Pey to rest." The tightening in his chest made it hard to breathe for a second, but when Kristy touched his cheek, the pressure eased.

"You might want to talk to Hannah and see what she wants to do. I mean… Peyton was her daughter." Kristy was right.

He may have been responsible for Peyton for a short time, but Hannah was her mother. Plus, his sister still wasn't really out of trouble. Jason was able to get her released because of the poor representation she'd had to begin with and the fact that there were significant screw-ups in the investigation.

"So, tonight?" Dean pulled her tightly against him.

"Tonight, what?" She grinned.

"You go back to work tomorrow evening don't you?" Dean lifted her off the ground, and she wrapped her legs around his waist.

"Yes, I do." Kristy nipped his lower lip with her teeth, and it went straight to his dick.

"Kitten, don't play with me." He growled.

"That's what kitten's do." She nipped him again.

"Then come to my place tonight, I'll cook supper, and you can repay me by showing me how much kitten's like to play." Before she could answer, he covered her mouth with his and plunged his tongue into her mouth. His hands cupped her sweet ass as he held her in his arms.

"Do I need to get a hose on you two?" John shouted from his front yard.

"This is why we need to go to my bunkhouse. I can keep most of your family out of there." Dean whispered as he lowered Kristy to the ground.

"I know. They're a virus that keeps growing." Kristy laughed.

"Hey, John," Dean wrapped his arm around Kristy's shoulder because he really didn't want to let her go.

"I heard your sister got released. That's great news." John sauntered over to the fence that divided Isabelle's property and John's.

"Yeah, I'm hoping it's permanent," Dean admitted.

"You have an awesome legal team helping her." John nodded.

Before Dean could answer a loud squeal came from the side of the house. When they looked in the direction, a little girl came running around the house being chased by a golden Labrador retriever puppy.

"You got her a dog." Kristy laughed.

"No, no. My mother was kind enough to get her a dog." John grumbled as Olivia ran directly to him and clung on to his leg.

"Daddy, Tippy's chasing me." Olivia giggled as the dog caught up with the little girl and frantically began to wag his tail.

"That's because you have ice cream all over your face." John lifted the four-year-old up into his arms as the dog bounced and jumped around his legs.

"See my puppy, Bull." Olivia smiled.

"I do, Livy. He's got almost as much energy as you do." Dean laughed.

"No, the dog actually naps." Stephanie appeared with little Brendan in her arms.

"You need a nap, Mommy." Olivia hugged her father, and for the first time in his life, Dean wanted what they had.

Having kids was always something in the back of his mind but it never happened. Now, a little piece of him could see a possibility of being a father.

"I think you may be right, little girl." John smiled at his wife, and even a blind man on a galloping horse could see the love he had for her.

"Yep, cause that's possible." She nodded towards the little girl.

"I'll take care of little missy here. Brendan is ready for a nap so why don't you take him to bed and get some rest." John offered.

"This is why I love this man." Stephanie kissed his cheek. "Will you be a good girl for daddy?" She said to the little girl who clung to her father.

"Yes, mommy." Olivia leaned toward her mother and gave her a sloppy kiss.

A short while later Dean gave Kristy a quick kiss and made his way to the compound. He checked in with Hannah who was apparently enjoying her time with Sandy and the kids. He was glad because it gave him a chance to check in with Vince.

Dean and Keith shared an office in what they called the main building on Keith's property. Technically it was a huge gym with a large room on one side. All the guys that worked for Newfoundland Security Services, the O'Connor men, and women, as well as the guys from O.K. Construction, would work out there all the time.

He and Doug Kelly had combined their companies because Doug wanted to retire. He was Marina and Stephanie's father and in his late fifties. About six months earlier he offered Keith the partnership and Keith jumped at the chance.

Now the office was the center for two businesses. Dean was in denial that technically he was running Decker Corp from there as well. Vince was running it from Decker Tower, and that was fine with Dean.

"Vincent Day's office. Harper speaking" It seemed that Vince had kept the same office assistant that Ivan had hired.

"Can I speak with Vince please, it's Dean." Dean plopped down in the chair behind his desk and turned on his computer.

"Oh hello, Mr. Decker. I'll transfer your call." Harper still called him Decker no matter how many times he corrected her. Dean figured they hired her because she looked pretty behind the reception desk. She certainly wasn't the sharpest knife in the drawer.

"Dean, glad you called." Vince answered a few seconds later.

"What's up?" Dean wanted to groan because that usually meant he would have to take a trip to town.

"I know nobody has been at the house since... well, you know." Vince stammered over mentioning Ivan's murder.

"No, I haven't been able to go there, and Hannah hasn't been able to go back there. I doubt she'd want to either." His sister wouldn't want to go anywhere near the house where her husband died.

"I don't blame her but here's the thing. I've had some calls on the property." Vince seemed hesitant.

"What kind of calls?"

"People that want to purchase it." Vince sighed. "I know what your thinking. What kind of people would want to buy a place where something like that happened? There are some weirdo's out there, but the truth is you can make a bundle on this sale."

Dean took a deep breath and let it out. Could he sell the house that held so many memories? Not all of them were bad. Before his mother died, they had some wonderful family celebrations there.

"I can email you the offers. There are three that I'm sure are serious offers. I can mark the one that I think would get you the best profit. Of course, you need to check with your sister." Vince was a smart guy, and Dean knew if Vince was bringing it up then it was something he and Hannah should consider.

"Email it to me, but I need to see what Hannah wants to do. Give me a week or so." Dean picked up a pen and spun it between his fingers. "Is there anything else going on I should know about?"

"I've got some papers that need to be signed, but I'll courier them over on Monday as usual. Nothing is urgent." Vince seemed to be on top of things.

"Great. Thanks, buddy. I'll check in with you on Monday, and I'll go over the offers with Hannah and let you know. Have a good weekend." Dean ended the call and tossed his phone on the desk.

His computer booted to the login screen, and he logged in and opened his email. As usual, there were several from Keith with updates on clients and possible contracts. Not something that was urgent because Keith had told him not to worry about N.S.S business until things settled down.

The email from Vince popped up seconds after he opened his email. Curiosity made him click on it because he really wanted to know what kind of person would want to purchase a house that had such a brutal murder happen inside it.

He scrolled through the first offer and was surprised that it was more than a quarter over the appraised value of the property. The second was a little less, but the third was more than the first.

"Bunch of sick people if you ask me," Dean mumbled to himself, but it would probably take a lot of weight off his shoulders as well as Hannah's if they did get rid of it.

"Who's sick?" Dean glanced up from his computer; Trunk stood in the doorway obviously at the end of an intense workout. He used the towel around his neck to wipe the sweat from his forehead.

"Someone wants to buy the family house." Dean sent the email to print at his bunkhouse.

"Are you selling it?" Trunk plopped down on one of the chairs along the wall next to the door.

"I hadn't thought about it, but I just found out about the offers." Dean felt a lot better now that he was able to talk to his friends about his family crap. He'd kept it close to the vest for so long, but now it was a weight off his shoulders.

"How's your sister doing?" Trunk popped the top of a bottle of water and gulped it down.

"I think she's a little overwhelmed right now and doesn't know what to do with herself because before all this happened, Pey was her life. She took care of her all the time and now…" Dean swallowed that annoying lump in his throat that appeared every time he thought about his niece.

"I can't imagine. Let her know we're all here for her and for you. Remember that, Bull. Don't fucking shut us out anymore." Trunk stood up and headed out through the door. Before he disappeared, he turned around. "Hey,"

"Yeah?"

"It's good to see you and Kristy are together." Trunk gave him a huge smile.

"Yeah, I finally got my head out of my ass." Dean smiled.

"Was wondering when you were going to realize your ass wasn't a hat." Trunk laughed.

"Asshole. By the way, when are you going to do that and make a move on Abbie?" Dean laughed when Trunk gave him the middle finger and stomped out of the office.

After he signed a few papers, Keith had put on his desk. Dean dropped them in Keith's box and headed back to his bunkhouse. He'd received a text from Hannah to let him know she was back at her place and Jason was stopping by with some news.

Please, God let it be good.

Chapter 18

Kristy managed to wash her scrubs, so they were ready for her three night shifts. The last thing she wanted to do after twelve hours was drive home and do laundry.

She received a few texts from the family that were at the pub during her tantrum. She did feel kind of childish for acting so foolish, but after waiting for so long to be with Dean, she didn't want to end up with a man that tried to order her around.

Kristy should have realized that he was concerned about her safety, but the truth was she wanted to go back to see if she could get any information. She'd figured out a long time ago that people will talk more when police aren't around, but Dean didn't need to know she would be doing her own little investigation.

Kristy had finished getting dressed when her phone beeped, and someone knocked on the door almost simultaneously. She grabbed her phone and hurried to the front door. There was a text from Jess and as she opened it she pulled open the front door.

"Are you out of your mind, young lady?" Her father growled as he stormed into the door and slammed it behind him.

255

Kristy glanced down at the text on her phone and inwardly groaned. Jess had sent a text to warn her that her father was on his way and he was pissed.

"Hi, Dad. It's nice to see you too." Kristy smiled but quickly lost it when he glared at her.

"You're not going back to that place." He snapped.

"Dad, I love you. I really do, and I didn't complain when you moved me out of the apartment without even getting my opinion, but I'm putting my foot down with this. I'm going back to work tomorrow." Her father's face started to turn red, and if he'd been a cartoon character at that moment, his head would have exploded.

"Bull is letting you do this. This is his idea of not letting you get hurt." Her father flailed his hands in the air.

"Dad, first, Dean doesn't tell me what to do. We just started seeing each other, and even if we were together for years, he wouldn't be able to tell me what to do no more than you can tell mom what to do." Kristy knew her mother's independent attitude frustrated her father every day.

"Do you see all this grey hair? I swear the older you girls get, the more shows up." Her father paced back and forth the foyer.

"I think that's called getting old, Dad." Kristy chuckled.

"Between you girls and Sean's boys, I'm gonna end up in a mental hospital." He stopped and blew out a huge breath.

"Nah, we wouldn't let that happen to you." Kristy wrapped her arms around his waist and kissed his cheek.

"I worry about you. You're my baby girl." Her dad kissed the top of her head and hugged her.

"I know, but I had the best father in the world who taught his daughters that they are strong enough to make their way in the world and protect themselves from all the creeps out there." Kristy tipped her head back and looked up at the man that had raised her. He'd always been her hero and still was.

"That's not fair." He finally smiled.

"I'm sorry, Dad. You raised us." She hugged him again.

"I did, and I'm so proud of all three of you." He squeezed her a little hard, but she didn't mind.

"So, since you're rampage is subsided, do you want a cup of coffee or something?" She laughed when he rolled his eyes.

"You know, you and your mother are so much alike it's scary." He chuckled. "As hard as it is to see you fall in love, I almost feel bad for Bull because your mother probably gave me most of these grey hairs. Don't tell her that though." He warned.

"I can't promise I won't tell her. I might use that as future leverage." Kristy moved into the kitchen laughing.

While her father complained about how he wished her mother would start taking some days off from the pub, Kristy reminded him he hadn't taken a vacation for a long time either. She laughed when he narrowed his eyes and was about to respond, but he was interrupted by the phone.

"I'm not done with this conversation, little girl. Hello." He smiled as he answered but that smile vanished when he jumped up and ran to the living room.

Kristy followed in time to see him turn on the television and change the channel to the local news. Her heart dropped when a picture of Hannah flashed on the screen. Her father turned up the volume.

"Reports say that Hannah Decker-Humphrey fired her previous lawyer Trevor Poole and hired the firm of Stewart Michaels. She was released from custody yesterday after her new lawyer Jason Brenton, had her released on her own recognizance. He also got special permission for her to leave the city to stay with her brother in Hopedale." The pretty reporter continued.

"Well the arse is gone right out of er'," Her father grumbled the old Newfoundland expression meaning things were now a whole lot worse.

"There has been no other information received from the family of Mrs. Decker-Humphrey, but we did have a chance to speak with her brother-in-law, Eric Humphrey." The video of a man Kristy didn't recognize appeared on the screen.

"What is your thoughts on the release of your sister-in-law, Mr. Humphrey?" The reporter asked the man.

"Please call me Eric, I'm shocked that our justice system would allow a person to be released who committed such a horrific murder." The man stopped and dropped his head as if he was trying to compose himself. *"Especially, since I found out that my niece, my brother's child also passed away. The worst thing is they suspect murder."* He dropped his head again.

Kristy couldn't hear the reporter's response over her father's cursing and anger.

"How the fuck did he find out about that? It was supposed to be kept under wraps until we knew for sure." Kristy glanced at him to answer but realized he was talking to someone on the phone.

"They didn't even bother to contact me to let me know she'd passed." Eric sniffed and wiped his finger under his eye as if he were crying but she didn't see any tears.

"I'm so sorry for your loss, Eric." The report turned back to the camera. *"Up to the time we went on the air, requests for a statement from the Newfoundland Police Department, Stewart Michaels, Jason Brenton or the Decker family went unanswered."* The reporter continued, but her father had muted the television as he paced and ranted to someone on the phone.

Kristy ran to the kitchen to grab her phone from the counter. She got to it as it began to ring. Dean's picture popped on her screen.

"Hey, I saw it." Kristy held the phone to her ear.

"Hopedale is about to get a lot smaller." Dean groaned.

"What do you mean?" Kristy couldn't see how the town could get any smaller.

"Reporters, Kitten. They are going to swarm here now." He sighed.

"They aren't going to get inside Keith's compound." Kristy knew her cousin would never let them inside his property.

"Sweetheart, they will camp out and follow anyone that comes out of there." He cursed.

"I'm coming over." Kristy headed toward the door but stopped when her father grabbed her arm.

"You can't go over there, honey." He told her as he shoved his phone into his jacket pocket.

"Dad, I'm going to be with Dean and his sister." Kristy yanked her arm from his grasp.

"There's no point arguing with you is it?" He sighed.

"No," She already had the door opened.

"Fine, I'm driving you." Her dad followed, and they practically ran to his truck.

It had been a total of fifteen minutes since the report aired, and already there was a line up of reporters in front of Keith's gate. They did move to the side when her father drove up to the gate.

Many of them were shouting questions at her father, but he ignored them as Crunch and Trunk stood outside the gate to allow her father to drive through and make sure none of the reporters got through the entrance.

"Fucking vultures." Her father grumbled.

"This is going to get worse, isn't it?" Kristy wasn't asking.

"You've got no idea. I don't know if you remember when Mr. Decker died but it was all over the news for months. That family couldn't fart without something showing up on the news. I can honestly understand why Bull wanted to separate himself from the family name." Her father made his way past Keith's house to the bunkhouses.

Dean was on the couch as Hannah sobbed in his arms. Although, the sounds coming from her sounded more like a wail. The poor woman was in a terrible hell that Kristy wasn't sure anyone could ever come back from it.

"Han, it will be ok," Dean whispered, but when Kristy caught his gaze, nothing about his expression said he believed that.

"How… he…" Hannah gasped. "He… can't believe this."

"He's looking for publicity." Her father interjected.

"He… hates me." Hannah took a deep inhale of air and started to wail again.

"Nobody that knows and loves you would believe a word he says." Kristy crouched in front of her.

"Thank you, but people still believe my dad killed himself because he made some corrupt investments." She said through tears.

"People will believe the worst of others because it makes them feel good about themselves." Kristy took Hannah's hands. "We believe you."

"You don't know me." Hannah stared at her.

"Dean does, and I trust him." Kristy smiled.

"My daughter is a smart cookie. I trust her judgment too." Her father placed his hand on her shoulder.

An hour later Dean's place was busting at the seams. The entire O'Connor family had congregated with support and of course tons of food. Emily, Marina, and Stephanie had taken all the kids to Keith's house, so they wouldn't be in the way or catch something they didn't need to hear.

"Keithy, if yar gonna have yar by's livin' here, maybe ya should build houses big enough fer everyone to visit." Nanny Betty scurried around the kitchen making due with the tiny room.

"Nan, these weren't exactly built for our family to be squeezed into them." Keith rolled his eyes as he squeezed by Kristy and Jess.

"Bull, ya need to get a bigger house." She called from where she stirred a pot of soup on the stove.

"I'm sorry, but I can't help but be awed by your family." Hannah had stopped crying when everyone started to file into the area.

"They are great." Kristy smiled as she glanced around the house.

Aaron wasn't there or Mike because they were at work. Her mother was still at the pub and Isabelle was at her restaurant. The rest of the family showed up as supportive as ever. Most of the security staff of Newfoundland Security Services were away on jobs except Trunk, Rex, and Crunch. Rex stood outside as if he was on guard and the other two were still at the gate.

"Are you okay?" Kristy found Dean on the front of the house leaning against one of the trucks.

"This was why I didn't want to involve your family." Dean linked his hands and rested them on the top of his head.

Kristy stood in front of him and wrapped her arms around his waist. He was tense, and every bit of him was trembling. As long as she'd known Dean, it was the first time he seemed terrified.

"It's your family too." She stood on her toes and gave him a quick kiss on the cheek.

"I think they'll disown me after all this." He wrapped his arms around her and hugged her tightly against him.

It seemed to calm him a little, but she could hear his heart thud as she rested her head against his chest. If it weren't such a crazy situation, it would have been romantic to be so close to him.

"Bull," Kristy turned as John joined them.

"What now?" Dean groaned.

"We were talking inside, and we agree, we should get Jason to make a statement. At least it will give them the bone their digging for." John glanced at Kristy and then back to Dean.

It was a good idea, but she'd seen enough news programs to know that the media could put their own spin on things.

"No, if anyone is going to make a statement…" Dean paused. "I'll do it."

"Bull, it's better…" Dean stopped John before he could continue.

"I've been staying below the radar with my family for far too long. I need to let people see I'm not hiding from being one of them. The Humphreys may not be as well known as the Deckers, but they do have pull. Eric is the only one of them left, and he declared war on my family." Dean stood up to his full height.

"Well, let us at least prep you for this." John motioned for them to go inside. "Uncle Kurt is an old pro at handling the media."

John slapped his hand on Dean's back as Kristy followed behind them. She wasn't sure this was such a great plan but what other alternative did they have. She was starting to regret the thought of going back to work the next day when the proverbial shit was about to hit the fan.

Chapter 19

Kristy adjusted his tie as he buttoned his jacket. He hated wearing suits and hadn't done it in a long time. He was starting to doubt his decision, but he knew he had to.

"Jason will be outside when you go out there. He will shut down questions that pertain to the case. We've told the vultures out there that you will be making a statement at three so that will give them enough time to call more of their friends." Kurt held up a couple of sheets of paper. "Stick to this."

"I'm not supposed to answer any questions or only the ones that have to do with the cases?" Dean turned but kept his arm wrapped around Kristy because at that moment she was the only thing keeping him calm.

"Trust me, all the questions they throw at you will be about the case. Anyway, they are going to refer to you by Augustus Decker." Kurt informed him.

"Why?" Dean couldn't understand why he had to go by his given name.

"How do you think it will look when Dean Nash talks to the press? The first thing they'll say is you're trying to distance yourself from the Decker name." Kurt glanced at his watch and then back up to Dean.

Dean gave Kristy a quick kiss and followed Kurt out of his bedroom. Most of the family had left to go home or to crowd in front of the gate for support. Nanny Betty, Kathleen, and Jess stayed at the bunkhouse with Hannah.

He'd tried to convince Kristy to stay with them, but she told him she was going to be there with him for support. He didn't argue because the truth was he was glad she would be close.

As soon as he walked through the gate, Jason stood next to him on one side while Kurt stood on the other. John, Kristy, Trunk, and Crunch were behind him. He also noticed Aaron, Nick, and James at the back of the crowd with some other uniformed police officers. Keith, Sandy, and Ian were to the side of the group.

Before he even got a chance to speak, questions came at him from all sides of the reporters. Kurt told him to read straight from the paper and ignore anything they asked.

"If you could all settle down, Mr. Decker will make his statement," Kurt shouted.

It wasn't completely hushed; he was able to start. After a quick glance back at Kristy he turned back to the reporters and began.

"Thank you for being here today. Although I can't give you any information about the cases of my sister or niece, I will let you know that the Newfoundland Police Department is running a full investigation." He tried to continue, but a voice from the back of the crowd interrupted.

"Is it true your niece was murdered as well?" The female voice shouted.

"Please let Mr. Decker continue," Kurt warned.

Dean took another deep breath and continued.

"I can not comment on that. I ask for some privacy for our family while we grieve her. She had been ill for a long time and although it is difficult for us…" Dean paused to swallow the lump in his throat. "she's not suffering anymore."

Kristy's hand touched his back, and it gave him the strength to finish his statement before he lost it but a voice from the crowd had him tense.

"She wouldn't have suffered if her mother hadn't murdered her father." Eric pushed through the crowd and stood in front of the reporters.

"This isn't the time or place, Eric." Dean tried to keep his voice calm.

"When is the time? She lied to me, and the fucking Deckers kept me from family and the people I loved. What did I do to

268

deserve it? I didn't even get a choice to see the child grow up." He shouted as reporters recorded and clicked pictures.

"I was told by your brother that you were a danger to my sister and niece. I did what he wanted." Dean raised his voice but still tried to keep his composure.

"Liar," Eric shouted but it got lost in the sound of a loud pop, and Eric's eyes grew wide as he dropped to the ground.

"Gun," Dean didn't know who called out the warning, but the crowd ducked, and Dean turned to cover Kristy with his body.

He raised his head enough to see most people laying on the ground except Aaron, Nick and a man with his head covered by a hooded sweatshirt.

"Drop it now," Nick shouted.

"Stay down," Dean whispered to Kristy as he started to rise off of her.

"I had to do it." The familiar voice shouted from where Nick and Aaron, stood with their weapons drawn on the man.

"Drop the gun, and we can talk about it." Dean hadn't noticed James off to the side of the man.

"Talk about what, I'm ruined. My life, my career its all over." Dean finally recognized the voice.

"Trevor," The man spun around and pointed his gun at Dean.

"Drop it now," Aaron shouted.

"It's okay, A.J. I know this guy." Dean stepped toward the man that once represented his sister.

"It's all his fault. He made me do this." Trevor shouted.

"Your job was to defend my sister not to listen to the man that was convinced she killed his brother." Dean took another step forward.

"Don't come any closer." Trevor shook the gun at Dean.

"Bull," James' voice was calm with a hint of warning. One that said he was walking a thin line.

"Okay, why did you listen to him? Tell me and why kill him now?" Dean didn't move any closer, and he did keep a close eye on Trevor's trigger finger.

"He helped me. He was like a father to me, but I didn't have a choice. He needed to die. Love sucks." Trevor glanced around as if he saw for the first time his situation. "She... God what have I done."

Before anybody could move Trevor put the gun in his mouth and then there was a loud pop. Dean watched his body flop to the ground, and the guy skittered across the road.

"Dean," Kristy shouted from behind him, and he spun around to stop her before she could see the man on the ground with his hood soaked in blood.

"Kitten, stop." He stood in front of her.

"For God's sake Dean, I'm a nurse." She tried to move around him, but he wouldn't let her.

"It's too late for him." Dean turned her and walked her away from the body.

"Eric's dead." Kristy motioned to where Crunch covered the other body.

"That was a huge cluster fuck," Kurt growled.

"I'll get the scene secured," James had his phone to his ear while the other officers helped the reporters to leave the area that was being closed off.

"What was he talking about?" Kurt asked.

"I've no idea. All I know was when Hannah got arrested, he showed up hired by Decker Corp." Dean squeezed through the gate his arm tightly around Kristy.

"This is a whole lot more fucked up now." Kurt sighed. "You two go back to the house because the chances are that went live, and your sister just watched what happened."

Keith pulled up next to them in his jeep and threw open the door. It wasn't that far to his bunkhouse, but Kristy trembled next to him. He helped her in and hopped in next to her.

"That didn't exactly go well," Kristy mumbled probably to herself.

"I wonder if that bullet was meant for you." Keith looked at him but before Dean could respond Kristy slapped her cousin across the arm.

"Really? Did you have to put that thought in my head?" Kristy snapped.

"Kitten, calm down. He was thinking out loud." Dean pulled her to his side and kissed the top of her head.

"He should learn to keep his stupid thoughts to himself." Kristy sighed and turned her face into his chest.

Kurt wasn't wrong. As they pulled up in front of the bunkhouse, the door flew open, and Hannah ran through the door followed by Kathleen and Nanny Betty.

"Dean, my God. Are you okay?" Hannah almost bowled him over as he stepped out of the jeep. She wrapped her arms around him and held tight.

"I'm fine, Han but Eric…" Dean took a deep breath.

"I know we saw it on the news." She hugged him tightly.

"Did they get the shooter?" Kathleen asked.

"Yes," Dean nodded as they made their way into the bunkhouse.

"Who was it?" Kathleen sat next to Kristy on the couch.

"Trevor Poole." Dean glanced down at Hannah.

Her body stiffened, and she slowly tipped her head back to look up at him. Her hazel eyes were as wide as saucers, and the color had drained from her face.

"My old lawyer?" It was as if she didn't have enough air to get the words out.

"Yes." Dean grabbed her before her legs gave out and helped her to a chair.

"I don't understand." She shook her head.

Hannah wasn't the only one that didn't get it. Eric and Trevor both died with the reason all this happened. What the hell were they supposed to do because right now they had no way to prove that Eric had something to do with the start of all this.

After a night of hell, Dean managed to get less than an hour of sleep. Kristy didn't get much either as she slept next to him. She clung to him all night. He was glad he didn't have to be concerned with Hannah being up all night because Ian dropped by and gave her something to help her relax and get some rest. It was the only way she settled down.

Dean pulled on a pair of track pants and tiptoed out of the bedroom. Kristy was asleep, and he didn't want to wake her. He walked by the couch where Hannah was turned into the back of it still resting.

He walked into the kitchen and jumped back when he saw Kurt and Keith sat at the table. Keith nodded toward the coffee pot as they sat in silence.

"When did you get here?" Dean asked as he sat at the table.

"About an hour ago." Kurt yawned. "Not that I slept at all."

"Me either," Dean admitted.

"Emily spent the night clinging to me with Noah tucked between us." Keith sighed. "She didn't want to be separated from either of us."

"How did Kristy sleep?" Kurt looked him straight in the eyes.

"Not much," Dean didn't look away, but it felt weird to talk with him about sleeping next to his daughter.

"Is she still going back to work today?" Keith asked.

"As far as I know but I wish she wouldn't." Dean sighed.

"You don't have to worry about that now." Kristy appeared in the doorway.

"You changed your mind?" Keith turned around to look at her.

"Sophia called me. They've had to move all the patients to other facilities." Kristy sat in the chair next to her father.

"Why?" Dean could see something was wrong.

274

"Someone broke in last night and set the place on fire." Kristy took a deep breath. "They were barely able to get the residents out before the place went up. There are also a couple of staff missing."

"Who?" Dean didn't like the sound of this.

"Leah and Gemma." Kristy's eyes filled with tears.

"Jesus," Dean growled.

"When did this happen?" Kurt seemed to be in the same mindset as Dean.

"It was after two in the morning." Kristy pulled up the news report on her phone and showed Dean.

"Why would Leah be there at that hour? Wasn't she on your rotation?" Dean glanced through the news story.

"That's what I'm wondering, and Gemma shouldn't be there at night. She works all days. She's management." Kristy reminded him.

"It obviously wasn't Eric or even Trevor that started it." Keith reminded them.

"So, either one has nothing to do with the other, or there is someone else involved with all this. I don't get the reason to burn down that facility." Kurt plowed his fingers through his grey hair.

"But if they are connected, who the hell is doing this?" Dean sighed.

"Considering the rumors that I've heard about your dad's business practices before he died. It could be anyone that he may have screwed over." Keith shrugged.

"Seriously, Keith. Could you be any more heartless?" Kristy snapped.

"No, Kitten. He's right. Ivan, Vince or I have never been able to find anything on what the media reported about dad undercutting people on the property, but that doesn't mean it didn't happen." Dean hated to believe his father would ever do something illegal.

Chapter 20

Kristy spent the next three days checking in with Sophia for any news on Leah or Gemma. Her heart went out to the woman because not only did she lose the business she and her husband built from the ground up, but two of her employees vanished.

As much of a bitch as Gemma was, Kristy found it hard to believe that the girl would set fire to the building. She definitely didn't strike her as that crazy.

Leah didn't either, but something had her stressed the last time Kristy spoke with her outside of Comfort Life Care. She said something about needing money which was why she worked extra hours.

"The fire chief said that as soon as all the hot spots are gone, they can investigate and search for any…" Sofia's voice cracked.

"Don't think like that, Sophia. We have to stay positive." Even as she said it Kristy knew it was a stupid thing to say.

"It's been three days. Both their phones are off, and neither of them has gone home." Sophia sighed. "I've got a sick feeling they got stuck inside the building and couldn't get out."

"I pray they didn't." Kristy's stomach turned every time Leah or Gemma entered her thoughts. "Keep in touch please and call if you hear anything. Dean's going to talk to my cousin because the coroner report on Peyton is back."

"Oh dear, please let me know the outcome." Sophia didn't have that quiet confidence that Kristy first admired about the woman. Who could blame her?

"I will. Take care, Sophia and give my best to Graham." Kristy ended the call and snatched her purse off the table.

She headed out through the door in time to see Dean pull up in front of the house. He'd dropped her off earlier, so she could get a change of clothes while he and Hannah grabbed a bite to eat.

"Hey," Kristy kissed his cheek as he met her at the passenger side to open her door.

"Hi," He looked exhausted, and Kristy hadn't missed his tossing and turning the previous night.

Kristy got in, and Hannah gave her a weak smile from the back seat of the truck. The woman had gotten extremely quiet over the last couple of days, and Kristy was worried she was sinking into a depression.

"I just got off the phone with Sophia." Kristy told them as she pulled on her seatbelt.

"Still no word on the girls?" Dean pulled out onto the road and made a quick U-turn.

"No, and she thinks they got stuck inside." Kristy watched the houses as they drove toward the police department.

"It's got to be connected." Dean whispered but mostly to himself.

"Sandy's looking into any potential links, but I don't think she's come up with anything." Kristy reached across and rested her hand on his leg. "We'll get this figured out."

"I know, Kitten." He covered her hand with his.

"Why do you call her Kitten?" Hannah spoke as they pulled into the parking lot in front of the station.

"I can't remember him ever calling me anything else." Kristy smiled back at her.

"Keith told me to watch out for you because you would scratch my eyes out if I pissed you off." Dean chuckled when her mouth dropped open in shock.

"He's such an ass." Kristy opened the door and hopped out of the truck. "When this is all over, remind me to scratch his eyes out."

"As long as I can watch." Dean took her hand as soon as he turned the front of the truck.

Hannah walked next to him on the other side and the closer they got to the door the slower she moved.

"I'm not sure I want to know." Hannah's voice cracked.

"Yes, you do, Han. We both need to know." Dean wrapped his free arm around her shoulders, and they entered the building.

John was waiting in his office for them with Kurt and Aaron. From their grim appearances, things were about to get a whole lot worse.

Aaron closed the door as they all entered, and John motioned for them to sit. Dean helped Hannah into a chair, and he sat next to her. Kristy stood behind them with her hands on both his and Hannah's shoulders. Hannah grabbed her hand and held it tightly.

"So, thanks for coming in." John began and glanced up from the papers on his desk.

Dean nodded but didn't say anything. He glanced at Kurt and then back to John. Hannah squeezed Kristy's hand.

"We have the coroner report on Peyton." John glanced up at them and then back to the paper. "He said she had a high amount of Propofol in her system."

"What's that?" Dean sat up straight.

"It's a drug they use for general anesthesia," Kristy answered his question.

"The same as they use for surgery?" Dean glanced at her, and she nodded.

"I understand she hasn't had any recent surgical procedures." John continued.

"No, she wouldn't have made it through surgery in her condition." Kristy cringed when she realized she blurted that out so matter of fact.

"That's what killed her?" Dean's body slouched in the chair.

"Not exactly," John glanced at Kristy.

"What do you mean?" Hannah's voice cracked.

"The coroner believes the medication was used to put her to sleep, but there were fibers in her nose and throat." John handed the report to Dean.

"Someone smothered her." Dean's body trembled, and Hannah gasped as she started to sob.

"Yes," John folded his hands in front of him and steepled his index fingers. "I'm so sorry, Bull, but it appears to be a homicide."

"Fuck. Fuck. Fuck," Dean growled and jumped to his feet.

"We'll figure out who did this." It was the first time her father spoke since they'd entered the room.

"How are you going to do that? You still can't figure out who killed my husband." Hannah shouted. "Someone is slowly killing off my family and getting away with it."

"John, someone is knocking people off left and right. Han is right. To make it worse, the one I thought did all this shit is dead." Dean had his fists pressed against the window next to John's desk.

"You mean Eric Humphrey?" Aaron met Kristy's eyes.

"He was the only person we knew that hated me enough to set me up for Ivan's…." Hannah couldn't continue as she started to hyperventilate.

Kristy pushed her head down between her legs and urged Hannah to take slow breaths. It was hard to see because Kristy knew if she was in the same situation she'd probably be freaking out too.

"Where do we go from here?" Dean sighed as he sat next to his sister.

"Sandy found some information on Trevor Poole and that nurse Leah." Aaron handed a paper to Dean.

"They were both in foster care," Dean said after he'd glanced through the paper.

"Yeah, but that's not it. Eric was involved in the big brother program for years. Trevor was one of the kids he mentored."

"You're saying Leah had something to do with Peyton's death?" Kristy spun around.

"She's the only one from that place that's connected to Eric and Trevor." John looked almost apologetic.

"I know I only knew her a couple of weeks, but she's been there for years," Kristy remembered the conversation she had with the girl about her years working at Comfort Life Care.

"We know, but right now that's all we have to go on." John sat back in his chair.

"No, I don't believe Leah did that." Kristy shook her head.

"I don't either." Dean shook his head. "That girl is sweet, and Sophia thinks the world of her."

"That doesn't explain what happened to my husband either." Hannah pulled her head up from her legs and wiped her face with her hands. "I didn't kill him. I couldn't, but someone did."

"That's the other thing we wanted to talk about." Her father dropped a folder he had under his arm.

Her father explained that the folder contained all the notes on the investigation into Ivan's death. By the furrowed brows and the straight line of his lips, her dad didn't like what he'd read.

"I don't need to look at that to know the fucking thing got screwed from the beginning." Dean didn't bother to touch it.

"You're right." Her father's voice was firm. "The thing is, that house has been closed off since that night, correct?"

Dean nodded.

"I wanted to send forensics over there to go over that room again," John explained, but there was something in the expression on his face that told her something else was about to go wrong.

"So, do that." Dean appeared to be ready to lose his patience.

"It's been four months, Bull." Aaron glanced at her again.

"Nobody has been in that house since this happened. I couldn't go in there." Dean sat back in the chair.

"Someone was," John told him.

"I'm sorry? What?" Dean leaned forward.

"Nothing appears to be taken, but we wouldn't know that. You'd have to check that out." John stood up.

"Then why do you think someone was in there?" Dean didn't move from the chair.

"The police seal was broken. They checked it out but didn't find anyone inside." Her father turned toward the door. "We have a team on the way there now to go through it with a fine-tooth comb."

"So, more waiting." Hannah sighed as she stood up.

"I'm sorry, Hannah but I promise you, my nephews and I will not rest until we know what happened." Kristy couldn't help but smile at her father when he wrapped his arm around Hannah's shoulder.

"Thank you." Hannah nodded, but the look on her face said she didn't believe any of this would be solved.

The short drive back to Dean's bunkhouse was quiet except for the soft sniffle from Hannah in the back seat. Dean's hands clamped on the steering wheel so tight that his knuckles were white. The worst thing was Kristy felt useless. There was nothing she could do to help either of them.

"Do you want to pick up some supper before we go back to the compound?" Dean asked as they stopped at the one stop light in Hopedale.

"I'm not feeling very hungry. I want to go to the other bunkhouse and lay down." Hannah's quiet voice cracked several times as she spoke.

"Kitten?" Dean glanced at her.

"I'll make something at your place." Kristy wasn't that hungry either.

As they pulled onto Main Road, Dean spat out a string of curse words. The media set up camp in front of the entrance to Keith's property.

"They'll give up eventually." Kristy tried to sound positive but just because they were in Newfoundland didn't mean that the local reporters couldn't be as aggressive as the national media.

"Well, I don't give a fuck what they do. They better not step in front of this jeep, or I'll knock them the fuck over." Dean growled as he turned into the driveway.

Like a swarm of bees, men and women ran toward the truck holding out recorders as they shouted questions. They did seem to know it wasn't a good idea to step in front of Dean's vehicle. There were four security guards stationed in front of the gate only two of which Kristy recognized.

Dean lowered his window as he pulled up next to Trunk. Crunch stepped to the other side of the Jeep, and the two that Kristy didn't know walked to the back of the vehicle.

"They are a persistent bunch of nosey bastards." Trunk shook his head as he stepped up to the window.

"That they are." Dean sighed.

The gate clicked and started to open while Dean moved his jeep slowly between them. Kristy turned around and watched as the four security men spread out in front of the closing gate to keep any of the reporters from getting inside.

"How do famous people live with that every single day?" Kristy turned back around.

"My dad always said as long as they are talking about you then you're not dead," Hannah whispered.

"He was wrong there." Dean scoffed.

"Yeah," Hannah signed.

Dean didn't say much for the rest of the evening. He spent most of the time reading the files that John had copied for him. Data that he wasn't supposed to have because John had warned him not to show them to anyone or tell anyone he had them.

He only told Kristy because Dean knew she would never do anything to jeopardize John's job. Plus, her father was probably the one that gave John the okay to sneak them to Dean.

She sat next to him and watched a marathon of friends' episodes on one of the cable channels. There were containers in Dean's fridge that had been left by her grandmother with a note to make sure they eat. Dean had smiled when he read it and told Kristy how lucky she was to have such a great family.

Kristy cleared the dirty dishes and put them in the dishwasher. When she went to wipe down the counter, Dean stepped behind her and wrapped his arms around her waist.

"Thank you," Dean whispered into her ear.

"For what?" She turned her head to look up at him.

"For being you." He smiled and kissed her temple.

"I don't know who else to be." Kristy smiled.

Dean turned her around and cupped her face in his hands. He didn't say a word, but he studied her face as if she would disappear.

"Kitten, you are the one thing in my life that keeps me from flying off the handle. When I feel the urge to punch someone, I think or look at you, and this wave of tranquility comes over me, and I can breathe again." She watched him swallow hard as his eyes glistened.

"I love you, Dean. There is nowhere else I want to be but by your side." Kristy raised her hand to cup his cheek.

"The word love doesn't seem strong enough to explain how much you mean to me. I love you, yes but I adore you, worship you, I cherish you, and even with all that, it still doesn't seem like a strong enough statement of how I feel about you." Dean stared into her eyes, and she could swear she could feel it down to the depth of her soul.

"Then show me," Kristy whispered as her lips met his.

Dean's fingers threaded through her hair, and he tilted her head to the side as his mouth covered hers. The only way to describe the way he kissed her was to say he devoured her and plunged his tongue into her mouth.

Kristy slid her hands under his shirt and up his back to the most extensive part. His muscles rippled as she dragged her nails across and pulled him closer.

He pushed her back against the counter and pressed his hips into her. He crouched a little, so his erection was in line with the aching junction of her thighs. He groaned into her mouth and dropped his hands to her waist without breaking the kiss.

Kristy moaned as he lifted her into his arms and spun around. He broke the kiss long enough to make sure he didn't trip on the way to his bedroom. Kristy didn't have to watch because she was too busy nipping and kissing up and down both sides of his neck

She only stopped when she heard the click of the bedroom door closing. Dean lowered her onto the bed as he resumed the mind-blowing kiss he'd stopped seconds earlier.

Kristy wanted nothing between them as she frantically tried to rid him of the t-shirt he wore. The problem was he didn't seem to want to break their kiss again.

"Dean," Kristy moaned against his lips as he thrust his covered erection against her again.

"Hmmm." He moaned against her mouth.

"Clothes," She gasped when he nipped her lower lip.

"You want me naked, Kitten." He whispered in her ear and then sucked the lobe into his hot mouth.

"Fuck," Kristy groaned.

"I know you don't say that word very often but when you do, God it turns me on." Dean sucked on her earlobe again.

"Well, you're about to explode in a minute." Kristy wiggled under him. "Get out of those fucking clothes."

"Grrr," Dean growled and knelt between her legs as he ripped his T-shirt over his head. Kristy managed to unbuckle his belt and open his jeans before he ripped open the front of her blouse. The buttons clicked as they flew across the room.

"You will be sewing all those back on." Kristy giggled when he tried to do the same to her bra, but since it opened in the front with a little clip, it simply unfastened.

"I'll buy you a new one." He stood up long enough to drop his jeans and boxer briefs while she wiggled out of the rest of her clothes.

As she lay naked on his bed, Dean stood at the foot of the bed; his gaze ran up the entire length of her body. It was highly arousing, and he hadn't even touched her. When his eyes met hers he grabbed her ankles and pulled her to the edge of the bed and knelt on the floor between her thighs.

He gently placed each of her legs over his shoulders as he turned his face into each thigh and placed light kisses slowly up one then the other. For a moment he stopped, and she could feel his hot breath against her wet folds.

"So fucking wet." Dean blew against her clit and quickly flicked his tongue between her folds.

"Ohhh, yesss." Kristy panted and squeezed her thighs together around his head.

"I love the taste of you." Dean started from the bottom of her opening and slowly licked between until he reached her throbbing clit.

"Dean, yes." Kristy fisted the sheets next to her as he did it a second time and then a third.

"My cock is aching to be inside you right now." He groaned as he spread her swollen lips apart and licked her again, but this time stopped before he reached her clit. "I want you to come before I drive deep inside you. I want to watch you come undone as my mouth devours this sweet pussy."

"You are driving me insane, Dean. Please make me come." Kristy moaned and raised her hips off the bed to get closer to his mouth.

Dean didn't make her beg, he sucked her hard nub into his mouth as he slowly slid a finger inside her. She gasped as he slid it in and pulled it out slowly while he sucked and nibbled on her sensitive clit.

"Dean, yes. Don't stop." Kristy panted as the pressure of his suction increased, and he slid a second digit inside her. She couldn't hold it in and shouted his name every time he pushed his fingers deep inside her.

"Come, Kitten." Dean released her clit long enough to say the words but quickly took up where he stopped.

His fingers swirled inside her, and he fluttered his tongue against her clit still covered with his hot mouth. The orgasm slammed through her body with such intensity that the muscles in her legs tensed and squeezed around Dean's head.

She squeezed her eyes shut as her body shuddered and twitched. Dean continued to stimulate her sensitive nub, and his fingers turned inside her. She didn't think another would hit her so fast, but when he pressed against the inner wall of her core, she screamed his name.

"Kitten, that was the most beautiful thing I've ever fucking seen," Dean growled.

He pushed her up so that her legs were now resting on the bed instead of on his shoulders. Dean knelt between them, and she slowly opened her eyes to look at the beautiful specimen of a man before her.

The dark colorful pair of wings tattooed across his chest from one shoulder to the other. The color spread down both arms into beautiful sleeves on each arm. Then there was his body. Broad muscled chest with defined abdominal muscles. He didn't have any body hair except for the beard that he continued to grow which made him look sexier if that was even possible.

"Are you done staring yet?" Dean smiled showing straight white teeth.

"I could stare at you all day, but I want to get a taste of that gorgeous piece of equipment pointing to the ceiling." Kristy pushed herself up on her elbows and grazed her knee against his stiff cock.

"Not tonight, Kitten." Dean reached for the nightstand.

"Why not?" Kristy grinned when she used her foot to rub against his balls.

"Damn, one because I want to be inside you and two if I let you put that sweet mouth around my cock now, I'll lose what little control I've got." Dean rolled the condom onto his erection.

He guided it to her opening as he locked his gaze with hers. It took everything she had not to close her eyes as he filled her. Dean groaned when he was fully seated inside her.

"I love you, Kitten," Dean whispered against her lips as he slowly began to thrust in and out of her.

"I love you too, Dean. So much." Kristy wrapped her legs around his thighs and met his thrust with her own.

She's always dreamed of making love to him, but nothing in her fantasies could ever compare to the real thing. As sexy and handsome as Dean Nash was, he was much more to her. He was her heart, her soul. Dean was her life.

"Nobody has ever made me feel the way you do, Kitten," Dean whispered against her lips and quickened his thrusts.

"I've never wanted anyone as I want you. I've never loved anyone the way I love you." Kristy moaned as he plunged into her.

"Yes, baby. I'm gonna… ahhh." Dean slammed into her, and his muscles tightened against her. His body trembled as he roared out her name.

Dean dropped his head to the nape of her neck while they both tried to catch their breath. Dean's body made several involuntary spasms as he came down from his orgasm.

"Do you know the only time you say my name is when you come." Kristy chuckled.

"Probably because it's all I can manage to vocalize when I come." Dean laughed and pressed his lips against her chest.

He lifted his head and smiled down at her. She loved this man with every fiber of her being, and she knew he was the only man she would ever love. The sudden thought of someone was out there that wanted to harm his family and possibly kill him made her vision blur with tears.

"Kitten, what's wrong?" Dean's concerned face made her want to kick herself.

"I don't want to lose you." Kristy sniffed and tried to hold back the tears.

"I'm not going anywhere." Dean rolled off her. "The only place I need to go is get rid of this condom, and I'll be right back. Then we'll talk about these unnecessary tears."

It was no more than a minute, and he was crawling into the bed next to her. He pulled her against him and kissed the top of her head as she tried to compose herself.

"I love you." She whispered.

"I love you, too but why the tears?" Dean tipped her face up, so she had to look at him.

"With everything going on, it seems like someone wants to hurt you …. Or worse." Kristy swallowed.

"Kitten, I'm going to be fine." Dean kissed her lips, but something in his eyes told her he was concerned too.

"Promise me, you won't take chances with your life." Kristy cupped his cheek.

"The only way that would happen is if someone tried to hurt the people I love." Dean covered her hand with his.

"Someone is doing that now." Kristy swallowed the lump in her throat.

"I know but can we forget that for tonight. I want to spend the rest of the night making love to you, over and over." Dean rolled her onto her back and covered her mouth with his.

How could she argue with that? She could forget about the danger for a night and simply be with the man she loved until they were so exhausted they couldn't do anything but fall asleep in each other's arms.

Chapter 21

Dean dropped the weights to the floor after the last set of squats for the day. His quads were aching, and sweat rolled down his face. Mornings were always the best time for him to work out but he wasn't alone in the gym. Keith was working on his back and shoulders on the other side of the room, while Hulk was pounding the shit out of a punching bag.

They'd gotten through the first week of October, but they were no closer to figuring out anything. The team that was sent over to his house had found some hair and fingerprints that the idiots missed before and a piece of chocolate under the sofa. It was a small piece, but they were having it tested anyway. Basically, there was more waiting.

"Bull, I'm heading out for that new client in the morning. Is there anything you need before I go?" Hulk asked between blows to the bag.

"Nah, it's not much anyone can do right now." Dean grabbed a bottle of water from the cooler and gulped it down.

"John let it slip that you've got a copy of the files on both cases," Keith grunted as he let the weights on the shoulder press drop.

"Yeah, keep that under your hat." Dean wiped his head and face with the towel around his neck.

"You know when my brothers, you and I work together we get things figured out. Why don't I get them over tonight for a guy's night?" Keith walked toward him.

"I've had it for almost two weeks, and the truth is, I don't see anything." Dean plopped down on one of the benches.

"Sandy's checking into the connection between Eric, Leah and Trevor but the only thing she can find is what I already told you. She did manage to get that adoption record open." Keith raised an eyebrow, and Dean knew what he was about to say.

"I know. Hannah told me all about it. Eric was the baby's father which was why he probably hated his brother and Hannah so much." She'd told him about being with Eric before dating Ivan.

"That's not what the record says, Bull." Keith sat next to him.

"What does it say?"

"It doesn't have the father's name, but Hannah's listed as the mother." Keith opened the email on his phone.

"Hannah told me Eric was the kid's father. I guess when the baby died, she didn't bother to put the father's name on the birth... Wait, you said adoption records? The baby died." Dean glanced from Keith to the phone his friend had in his hand.

"This doesn't say the baby died, Bull." Keith handed Dean the phone so that he could read the email from Sandy.

"Hannah told me the baby died in her arms three days after he was born." Dean couldn't believe what he read.

"Then where is the death certificate?" Keith was asking a relevant question.

The email stated that a baby boy born to Hannah Decker was adopted, but the adoptive parent's names were blacked out. The birthdate that Hannah had given him was correct, but the adoption date was the date the baby was supposed to have died.

"This doesn't make sense." Dean tapped the phone and forwarded the email to himself.

He needed to talk to Hannah about this. Had she lied to him about the baby and if so why? It's not like it would change anything.

"You know I figured when the O'Connor girls started to date that it would be nice, quiet and fun to tease them. What is it with your family?" Hulk sighed.

"Never a dull moment." Keith chuckled.

Dean left the gym and ran back to his bunkhouse. Hannah sat with Jason going over all the evidence that would be presented in her case when and if they went to court.

It was a little after eleven when Jason stood up from the table with a satisfied smile on his face. He'd made several comments about things being circumstantial or bullshit. The only thing Dean understood from it was that it didn't look like Hannah could have killed Ivan.

"He seems pretty positive that I won't have to go to trial." Hannah poured a cup of coffee for herself and Dean.

"I hate to bring this up now but Han, this doesn't make any sense." Dean pulled out his phone and opened the email from Keith.

Hannah read through it, and he could see the very minute she saw the contradiction to what she'd told him a few days earlier. She shook her head as she read it.

"No, I know my baby died. He's buried in Jersey Harbour next to Dad's parents. I named him after Dad, and there is a small headstone with his name on it." Tears streamed down her cheeks.

"You had a funeral for him?" Dean asked.

"Not really, the priest came to the gravesite and did a small service there." Hannah sighed as she wiped her eyes. "I don't understand what baby Aiden's death has to do with any of this. I've lost two children, Dean. Two. One of them because I went into premature labor, but I'd resigned myself that it was meant to be.

299

Now I think my kids were taken away from me because I'm a bad person." She was sobbing so hard that it was hard to understand some of what she said.

"Hannah, you're not a bad person." Dean pulled her into his arms.

"I was wild back then, Dean. The truth was Eric was in love with me, but I didn't care. I slept with him and then went on to the next guy. He didn't sleep around like I said before. I didn't want you to think badly of me." Hannah continued.

"The next guy turned out to be his brother." Dean could see where she was going with this, but it was crazy to think that her kids died as some sort of Karma for her wild behavior.

"Yeah, and to be honest, I had no intention of staying with Ivan either, but something happened between us. When he kissed me the first time, it was like a light came on in my life, and I couldn't see myself with anyone else." She'd calmed a little, but she still clung to Dean.

"None of this is your fault, Han." Dean kissed the top of her head.

"I should have been honest with Eric from the beginning. I should never have hidden the fact that he was the baby's father and maybe he wouldn't have set all this up." Hannah sighed.

"Eric was unstable." Dean walked her to the sofa and sat her down.

"He wasn't always like that. He used to be fun, and it didn't seem to bother him when I started seeing Ivan, or even after we got married, but when we moved to St. John's, he snapped." Hannah covered her face.

Hannah seemed to be filling in little missing pieces of the puzzle. Maybe it was after they moved that he found out he had been the baby's father. There was no way to find that out now. Eric was dead and unless he told someone there was no way to know.

"He and Ivan were so close when we were teenagers." Hannah smiled. "When I slept with Eric, it was after a night of drinking, and you know how teenagers are. Everything is about hormones. I guess it was cruel of me because I knew how he felt about me." Hannah shook her head. "The past really comes back to haunt you doesn't it. It's why I want you to know. The bruise I had on my face, and the sore ribs were because I wouldn't bow down to my cellmate."

It made him proud that she stood up for herself but then again Dean always looked up to his sister. The truth was he didn't know what she was like as a teenager, but he couldn't blame her for being wild. He was no angel growing up. It was hard to believe the same sister that gave him shit about running around did it because she'd learned from experience.

For the next few hours, Dean read through the files again and again. Keith had come by to help, and they made a list of things that didn't add up. Such as there not being any gunshot residue anywhere on Hannah when they arrested her. The only blood on her nightshirt was under her. The gun was in her left hand, but it would have been hard for her to shoot him in that position.

They were still huddled over the table when Kristy arrived. She'd gotten a call from the hospital earlier in the day with the offer of a permanent position in the emergency department.

"How did it go?" Dean asked when she came through the door.

"Awesome, I start in two weeks." Kristy's excited expression made him smile.

"I'm happy for you, Kitten." He kissed her cheek when she stood behind him and wrapped her arms around his neck.

"Congrats, cuz. You deserve it." Keith stood up.

"I'm so glad. It's only a couple of months until Christmas, and I don't want to have to work at the mall to make extra money this year." Kristy chuckled. "I hate shoppers."

"You don't hate shopping though." Keith laughed.

"Nope." Kristy gave Dean a quick kiss on the cheek and moved away from him. "I also saw Zoey there."

"Zoey?" Keith glanced at Dean.

"She was one of the nurses that worked at Comfort Life Care," Kristy told him.

"She's working there?" Dean asked.

"No, she's a patient. She got hurt during the fire." Kristy plopped down on one of the chairs.

"Bad?" Keith asked.

"A couple of small burns on her leg and hand. She got stuck by something falling on her. She'll have some scars, but she'll be okay." Kristy sighed.

"What's wrong?" Dean knew by her expression she wasn't telling them everything.

"Zoey said that the night of the fire Leah and Gemma had a huge argument in Gemma's office. Something about a guy Gemma was sleeping with. Zoey said she never got a chance to talk to Leah about it, but she said Leah ran into the staff room crying." Kristy propped her elbows on the table and rested her chin on her fists. "They fought the night Peyton died too."

"I'm pretty sure James questioned both of those women. At least I think it was them. He said he'd got an odd feeling about an intense argument between two of the staff and he questioned them." Keith flipped through the files on the table.

"If it's the argument they had that night then, it was over Gemma being in the staff room when she's not supposed to be." Kristy sighed. "Now that I say it out loud, it doesn't sound very believable."

"According to this, James wasn't convinced either. It says Leah seemed nervous and Gemma got angry." Keith turned the paper so that he could read it.

"It was a stressful day. Maybe they both had enough and didn't like to be questioned." Dean sighed.

"Or maybe they had something to hide. Add that to the list, Bull." Keith raised an eyebrow. "It may not mean anything, but it's still a little odd."

"I thought your brothers were coming over as well?" Dean remembered Keith mentioning a guy's night.

"John will be over when the kids go to bed, James is pulling up as we speak, Mike and Ian are with him, A.J. and Nick will be here at the end of their shift." Keith didn't bother to look up as he scrolled through his phone.

"That's my cue to leave." Kristy stood up, but before she had a chance to move away from the table, Dean grabbed her around the waist and pulled her onto his lap.

"You don't have to leave." Dean brushed his lips against her cheek.

"Me, you and all my cousins. Ummm…. No. I'll run over and spend some time with Hannah. Maybe I'll get Pam, Jess and Isabelle to come over and have a mini girl's night if Hannah is up to it." Kristy gently caressed the top of his head with her hand.

"Kitten, don't do that." He growled into her ear.

"Did you two need a minute?" James chuckled as he, Mike and Ian clomped into the bunkhouse.

"I'm chaperoning, so no they don't." Keith laughed.

Kristy slowly ran her hand across the top of his head one more time before she jumped to her feet and wiggled her fingers in a flirty wave as she made her way around her cousins and out through the door. The woman was going to drive him to the brink of insanity, but it would be worth it. He stared at the door long after she disappeared through it.

"Can you stop mooning after her and pay attention?" Keith had papers spread out on the table in separate piles. James had plopped another bunch of files on the table as well.

"What's all this?" Dean asked.

"Reports on the fire at Comfort Life Care, the investigation on the evidence collection last week, everything Sandy dug up on Humphrey, Poole, and the two nurses as well as any staff at CLC that even said hi to your niece." James had one more file in his hand. "This one is the report on what happened to your sister in jail. One of the guards caught an inmate pounding on her in her cell. It seems she was hired to put a beating on your sister from someone on the outside. The inmate died of an overdose a couple of days later. So that's all the information on that. Unless you can get more from Hannah."

"She told me about that, but she thinks it was because she didn't bow down to them." Dean scanned the report.

James took a deep breath and plopped down on the kitchen chair that Kristy had vacated. He smiled at Dean and nodded toward the door when Kristy had left.

"Things going well?" James rested his arms on the table.

"Considering the situation, very well." Dean glanced up as Ian dropped a couple of boxes of beer in the center of the table.

"These situations make you stronger." Ian opened the box and held a bottle of beer out to Dean.

"And nobody knows that like the O'Connors." Mike chuckled.

"That's for sure." Keith popped the top of a bottle he grabbed out of the case.

"If I forget to tell you later, thanks for all this." Dean waved his hand over the table.

"No need to thank us, you're family." Mike slapped him on the back.

"Yeah, there's no escaping it now." James chuckled.

Over the next few hours, he and the O'Connor brothers set out to figure out who was messing with his family.

Chapter 22

Her cousins were terrific men, and she loved them dearly but to spend an entire evening with them as they tried to sift through all the information they had was not her idea of a fun evening.

Kristy knocked lightly on the door of the small bunkhouse next to Dean's place. At first, nobody answered, and she knocked once more. She was about to leave when the door opened, and Hannah gave her a forced smile.

"Hey, did I wake you?" Kristy hoped Hannah wasn't ignoring her.

"No, not at all. I was in the bathroom, but I guess you didn't hear me call for you to come in." Hannah stepped back so Kristy could enter.

"I'm sorry to drop by unannounced, but my cousins are …" Kristy stopped when Hannah held up her hand.

"It's okay, Dean told me you were coming over." Hannah motioned to the small kitchen where she had two glasses waiting.

"I mean I love them, but I can't take all of them together with no other females to even out the testosterone." Kristy sat next to the small island and picked up the glass filled with wine.

"I can understand that. I only grew up with Dean, and I was practically an adult by the time he came around." Hannah didn't sit she stood on the other side of the counter and sipped her own glass of wine.

"Would you mind if I called my sisters and cousin to come over and have a mini girl's night?" Kristy didn't want to call them without asking.

"I don't mind. It might be nice to have some other company to get my mind off things." Hannah sighed, and Kristy's heart went out to her. The woman was only a few years younger than Kristy's mother, but she appeared to have aged quickly.

Kristy sent a text to her sisters and wasn't surprised to get a *'hell yeah'* from Jess and a *'grabbing a few bottles of wine from the restaurant'* from Isabelle. It took a few minutes before Pam answered, but she was on board as well.

So she didn't end up in the doghouse with her cousin's wives, she did text all them as well. Stephanie was not up for it, and Marina's youngest was sick. Emily declined as well because she'd been up all night with baby Noah and Billie wasn't feeling well. Sandy on the other hand, informed Kristy that she would be over as soon as the babysitter arrived.

In less than an hour, Sandy had the five women that arrived laughing hysterically at the antics her two younger children caused.

"I swear, Gracie has some sort of power over Alex. He's easily manipulated and at four years old Gracie knows that." Sandy pointed her finger at each one of them. "You four have no idea."

"I wouldn't know either." Hannah smiled. "Peyton was a pretty quiet little girl and because of her illness didn't run around a lot."

"I can't imagine going through that." Sandy's eyes filled with tears.

"No, don't cry. Peyton did have a great life considering but now that I think about it, she was very manipulative as a little girl. If she wanted something, she could really put on a show. Especially with my dad." Hannah smiled.

"See, they know who they can fool." Sandy laughed.

"Oh, come on. That's not a kid thing. That's a female thing." Pam laughed.

"This is true." Isabelle refilled all the glasses.

"So now that we have Kristy marinated a little, it's time to hear all the dirty details." Jess rested her elbows on the counter and propped her chin on her fists.

"Oh God, yes." Pam mirrored Jess's pose.

"What are you talking about?" Kristy feigned confusion.

"Oh no, you don't, Kitten," Sandy emphasized the nickname that only Dean used.

"I swear I melt a little more every time I hear him call her that." Pam fanned herself.

"Do you really think Hannah wants to hear about her brother and me?" Kristy glanced at Dean's sister.

"You have no idea how much I want to hear about this. You have to understand growing up Dean didn't talk to anyone about his girlfriends. At least nobody in the family. There was a time I questioned his sexual orientation." Hannah smiled. "I guess to him it was like talking to a parent about such."

"I think it's a guy thing," Sandy interjected.

"It certainly isn't a Sandy thing." Isabelle nudged Sandy with her elbow.

"Hey, I'm not about to hide the fact that Ian rocks my world." Sandy grinned.

"Oh Jesus, Stop." Jess gagged.

Kristy was glad they hadn't noticed their focus had momentarily shifted away from her. It wasn't that Dean didn't blow her mind, but their relationship was new, and she'd waited so long for him she still wasn't entirely confident that he wouldn't turn tail and run.

"Come on, Jess; you can't tell me Jason still doesn't make you want to lick him from head to toe." Sandy was at the point in her wine drinking where her mouth lost all its filter.

"Jason? As in my lawyer?" Hannah's surprised expression had the girls laughing.

"Yes. Jess and Jason used to date a while back." Pam looked at Kristy as if to ask how bad a topic it was. Pam had been away for years and wasn't around for Jess's relations with the cute lawyer.

"Look, Jas and I were over long ago and yes he is attractive, but the truth is, it wasn't meant to work out. We were both on different paths, and I wish him luck on his. I'm pretty sure he's seeing another lawyer from his firm." For the first time in a long while, Kristy could see that her sister was over Jason.

"So, are you going to tell us why you two broke up in the first place?" Sandy asked.

"I don't know why you all think it was such a big secret." Jess laughed. "He told me if I joined the police academy we were over, and I told him to go to hell."

"But you didn't join right after that." Isabelle reminded Jess.

"I know, but that had nothing to do with him. It was something Dad said a couple of days later." Jess swirled her glass in her fingers.

"Dad?" Kristy couldn't see her father ever saying anything to prevent Jess from becoming a police officer.

"I wanted to surprise him with my application for the academy, and I dropped by the department. He was talking to a guy about how he'd never have his daughter put in a dangerous situation while on duty. He laughed but said he would keep them on desk duty." Jess glanced at Kristy and Isabelle.

"Kurt said that?" Even Sandy was speechless.

"Yeah, I left and never went back. Billie was the one to convince me to go for it. When I told Dad, he was so embarrassed that every time he sees me he apologizes that I'd heard him say such a thing. The truth was it was a joke between him and his old academy buddy." Jess chuckled.

"That's what you get for eavesdropping." Sandy laughed.

"Hey, I don't know if anyone else noticed, but the subject got changed from what we originally wanted to know, Kristy." Pam tapped her finger on the counter.

Fuck!

"Oh yeah, you sneaky bitch." Sandy pushed Kristy's shoulder.

"What?" Kristy laughed.

"Spill it," Pam ordered.

"God, you guys are nosey." Kristy shook her head and rolled her eyes.

"We never said we weren't. Now dish." Isabelle leaned closer.

"Things are good. He's not running away anymore." Kristy laughed.

"And?" Jess smiled.

"He's sweet and makes me feel beautiful." Kristy rested her chin on her palm.

"And?" Pam waved her hand in a rolling motion apparently telling Kristy to continue.

"He said he's sorry he fought it for so long." Kristy knew what the women wanted to hear, but she wasn't giving it very easy.

"For fuck sake, woman. The sex. How is the sex?" Sandy practically shouted.

"You know for a woman that says she gets so much sex; you're awfully concerned about other's sex lives." Kristy laughed.

"Maybe she wants to make sure nobody gets more than her. I for one am not getting any." Hannah laughed, and for the first time since she met Dean's sister, it was a real one.

"We can fix that if you like younger men." Sandy laughed.

"Are you offering your husband to Hannah?" Pam asked, and the shocked expression on Hannah's face had all six women laughing hysterically.

"Nobody is getting my Doc, but there are some pretty hot to trot men in this town." Sandy reminded everyone.

"True, too bad I'm related to most or might as well be." Jess sighed.

"So, the sex?" Sandy's statement had all five sets of eyes back on Kristy.

"You are not going to give up, are you?" Kristy laughed.

"No." Sandy laughed.

"Fine, he's gentle and tender…" Kristy felt a hand cover her mouth.

"The screams I heard last night didn't sound gentle or tender." Hannah laughed as she released Kristy.

"Screams?" Jess raised an eyebrow.

"Yeah, screams don't constitute gentle. Screams mean ecstasy and getting pounded hard…." Jess and Pam both slapped their hands over Sandy's mouth.

"You're like a freaking sailor." Isabelle laughed.

"I work with all men," Sandy mumbled under their hands that still covered her mouth.

"I work with mostly men too, and I don't sound like you." Jess dropped her hand from Sandy's mouth.

"Oh, trust me that will change." Sandy laughed. "Sex?" Sandy swung her attention back to Kristy.

"Dear Lord, woman." Kristy laughed. "It's hot, awesome; he makes me come so hard I see stars. Are you happy now?"

"Okay, not what a girl wants to hear about her little brother but good for both of you." Hannah laughed.

Kristy was so glad that she'd invited the girls and particularly Sandy. She seemed to make everyone forget for a few hours. Hannah really seemed to enjoy herself, and by the time they were all ready to leave, she looked relaxed.

"We have to do this again, soon. Jess said as she followed Sandy through the door.

"Yeah, but next time all the girls should get together." Isabelle agreed.

"We have to get Abbie next time. She's worse than Sandy." Kristy laughed.

"Hey. Nobody is worse than me." Sandy pointed her finger toward Kristy.

"I want to thank you for all this tonight. I enjoyed myself." Hannah stood on the step next to Kristy as the girls walked away.

"We will do this again. See you all later." Kristy wrapped her arm around Hannah's shoulder as she waved to her sisters and Sandy.

Once Kristy had helped Hannah tidy up from their girl's night, she headed back to Dean's place. She could still hear her cousins inside, but it was almost midnight, and she was a little tipsy from the wine.

"Here you go. Kristy can tell you." Dean held out the paper he was holding as Kristy entered through the door.

"I'm a doctor, and you think a nurse can tell you more about a drug than a doctor." Ian shook his head.

"No, you idiot. I'm talking about how long it was from the time I left her room until I went back." Dean rolled his eyes.

"We were talking about the drug traces they found in that chocolate piece." Ian threw his hands up in the air.

"Asshat, we already determined that the amount of … what was the name of it again?" Mike sifted through some papers.

"Temazepam." Ian groaned.

"Yeah, that. We know it would have knocked her out cold. You said she probably would have been out for hours if the amount in that small piece was any indication of what was in the whole thing." Mike glanced at Kristy.

"So?" Eight pairs of eyes turned toward her, and she didn't have a clue as to why.

"So, what?" Kristy shrugged her shoulders.

"Do you know how long it was between the time Dean left Peyton's room and when he returned?" Nick asked as if he was annoyed she didn't know.

"I don't know. I only saw him on his way back." Kristy shrugged, "but I remember Graham saying that he'd been in the lunch room with him at least an hour or more."

"So the drug could have been before or after you left." James tossed a paper on the table.

"What are you talking about?" Kristy stepped behind Dean.

"I was telling them that Pey had slept a lot that evening and they said she could have been administered the drug to put her asleep earlier in the day." Dean looked up at her.

"What was in her system again?" Kristy looked at Ian because she knew the rest wouldn't remember the name of the drug.

"Propofol." Ian raised an eyebrow because he knew it wasn't a drug they typically used in places like Comfort Life Care. It was a drug that was used in assisted suicide situations though.

"It would have taken effect pretty fast so I'd say it all happened after Dean left the room. Whoever it was had plenty of time." Ian sat back in the chair. "Is Sandy gone home?"

"Yes, and if you hurry, you may get some before she passes out." Kristy smiled.

"I'm starting to think she drinks a lot." Aaron laughed.

"Nah, but when she does… Let's say; I'm glad I don't have to get up to work tomorrow." Ian stood up with a grin on his face.

"I think we should call it a night." Dean leaned back in the chair and wrapped his arms around the back of him embracing Kristy in his arms.

"Yeah. Besides, Nick needs to find some other excuse as to why he's dropping by the pub tomorrow on his day off." Aaron chuckled and jumped to barely avoid Nick's fist.

"Why does he need an excuse to go to the pub?" Kristy glanced around the room, obviously missing the inside joke between the men.

"Nothing, A.J. is an idiot." Nick glared at his younger brother.

"Your cousin has a little crush on the new waitress at your mom's restaurant," Dean whispered when her cousins were out of earshot.

"Really?" Kristy smiled.

"Don't say I told you." Dean watched as John and Keith put the pile of papers and files into a box.

"I won't." Kristy kissed his cheek.

"I'm going to show this to uncle Kurt and the guys in charge of the investigations and see what they think. Maybe between all of us, we can figure this out sooner rather than later, but I would think about getting the security turned back on in that house, Bull." John tucked the box under his arm.

"Yeah, I'll give Vince a call tomorrow and have him get on that." Dean yawned.

Kristy stood next to Dean with her arms wrapped around his waist as her cousins piled into Nick's truck. He was dropping all of them off but Keith who walked the short distance to his house.

"I don't know if we accomplished anything tonight, but I do feel a little better about things." Dean kissed the top of her head as the tail lights of Nick's truck disappeared.

"Good." Kristy tipped her head up to gaze up at him.

"How did you enjoy your evening?" Dean closed the door and pulled her into his embrace.

"It was fun, and Hannah really had a great time." Kristy moaned when Dean kissed his way down the side of her face.

"Good, but I've spent the last few hours with your cousins and right now all I want is you in my bed naked, and moaning."

"I like that idea." Kristy allowed him to tug her towards the bedroom.

She had a couple of glasses of wine to relax her, but she was definitely up for a hot night with the man she loved.

Chapter 23

Two weeks passed, and all the investigations were at a standstill. They did manage to put to rest the fact that Hannah's baby boy did die, and he wasn't put up for adoption.

Sandy figured out the record she did find was entered into the system only a few years earlier. It raised red flags as to why someone would try to put a fake adoption document on government files.

Eric didn't have the skills to do such a thing, and neither did Trevor. They had figured that much out as well. According to people that knew Eric personally, he was barely able to use his smartphone. Trevor had a little more experience but not the skills that he would need get into a secure system and insert a fake record without getting noticed.

The good news, the charges against Hannah got dropped thanks to Jason and Stewart. When they were digging through her arrest and processing, they found out she'd been brought to the hospital because the nurse at the department said she wasn't lucid.

Another one of the many things missing from the report. The blood showed a high dosage of Temazepam in her system. According to tests, there was no way Hannah would have been lucid enough to do anything. He didn't understand that part of the investigation but when Kristy and Ian explained that Hannah was lucky she didn't die that night because of the amount of the drug in her system. All he cared about was that Hannah was cleared.

He also asked Vince to drop by the house and take a walk through it to see if he noticed anything missing or different from the night that Ivan died. When he called Dean back a few hours later, he made a point of saying he would not be going inside the house again. It was creepy and felt as if someone was watching him.

Vince did have the security system checked and turned on because of Dean's concerns. He also said that the company wouldn't bother Dean with any issues and if there were any Vince would contact him right away.

"So, what about the interested buyers?" Vince asked him.

"I haven't even mentioned it to Hannah, but maybe I should because the truth is, she said she wants to stay in Hopedale." Dean leaned back in his office chair.

"What is it about that town?" Vince laughed.

"It's Heaven." Dean smiled as his angel walked into the office.

"Maybe I should come out there again and look around." Vince laughed.

"Let me know; I'll give you the grand tour." Dean grinned when Kristy closed and locked the office door behind her.

She'd started her new job at the hospital and finished her first round of shifts. It was her day off, and she wasn't happy that he left her in bed alone that morning. Dean hadn't wanted to leave her naked and wanting either, but he needed to get some contracts signed, and Keith didn't understand the words 'wait until later.'

"Well keep in touch, Vince. I'll get those papers signed and email them back." Dean smiled when Kristy spun his chair around and pushed his legs apart.

"Sure, I'll make sure everything gets done." Vince's voice trailed off in his ear when Kristy unhooked his belt and popped the button on his jeans.

"Yeah, everything." Dean tried to keep his voice steady, but she'd opened the wrap around dress she wore to reveal she had nothing on under it.

"I'll let you know if ..." It was the last thing he heard from Vince because he had to end the call once Kristy wrapped her mouth around his cock.

"Jesus, Kitten." Dean groaned. "I don't know if this is a good idea here."

It didn't matter if it was or not because right at that moment he was in Paradise. Kristy knew how to drive him wild with her lips, tongue, and teeth.

"It's okay; I might have jammed something against the door so nobody could get into this part of the building," Kristy whispered when she popped her mouth off his swollen head.

"Fuck," His eyes rolled up in his head as she covered his dick again and took it as deep into the back of her throat as she could.

Dean was aware he was bigger than some men, and nobody had ever been able to get him entirely into their mouth, but Kristy made a good effort and what she wasn't able to swallow she gripped with her hand.

"Kitten, that feels so fucking good," Dean growled as he pushed her soft hair back from her face.

Kristy was incredibly beautiful, and he focused on her naked body between his legs. He knew every inch of her luscious curves and had learned where she liked to be kissed, sucked and touched.

Kristy pulled him out of her mouth slowly making sure with every inch of him she released from her mouth she covered with her hands. She twisted them together as she sucked the head of his cock hard. He was about to explode inside her mouth, and he had no way to stop it.

"I'm…. fuck…. Kitten…. Come." Dean gripped her hair with one hand and the arm of his chair with the other.

Dean closed his eyes and shook as she swallowed every last ounce of semen that shot from him. She didn't stop her torture but moved her hand to his sack and gently massaged it while his body jerked with his dick.

"Kitten... Jesus." Dean almost didn't recognize his own voice as he spoke. "You need... fuck... you have to stop."

It felt so good, but after coming so hard, he was sensitive and weak as a newborn baby. He didn't even have the strength to pull away.

"I'm not done with you yet, big boy." Kristy slowly rose to her feet and unbuttoned his shirt.

If anyone walked into his office to see him overpowered by a tiny naked woman they'd never hire him to do any kind of security, but the truth was Kristy always made him weak in the knees, and now that they were together, he'd let her do anything she wanted to him.

"I fucking love you." Dean sighed as she straddled his legs and rubbed her wetness against his still half hard cock.

"I love you too, but I've gone three whole days without you, and I want you to fuck me." Kristy purred into his ear and his cock was at full staff again.

Dean was on his feet and Kristy on hers. He spun her around and braced her hands on his desk. If she wanted to get fucked he was going to make it as good for her as she did for him.

324

"You want me to fuck that sweet pussy," Dean whispered into her ear as he slid his hand down over her stomach and cupped her wetness.

"Ahh.. yes." She moaned and pushed her hips back against his erection.

"You're so wet, Kitten." He slid his fingers between her folds and rubbed it against her swollen clit.

"Three freaking days, Dean." Kristy groaned.

"I know because I slept alone for three freaking days." Dean nibbled on her ear lobe and pushed his finger inside her opening.

"Dean, I want your cock inside me." She gasped when he curled his finger and pressed his thumb against her clit.

"I know you do, but I don't have condoms here at the office, Kitten." As much as he would love to see Kristy swollen with his child, he wasn't ready to do that until the house was finished. The way things were going that was going to be February.

"Oh, silly boy." Kristy bent over and pressed her ass against his crotch as she reached for the dress she'd dropped.

To his utter delight, she pulled out a strip of condoms and tossed them on the desk.

"Exactly how long are we going to be here?" Dean laughed, but he didn't hesitate to grab one and rip it open.

"I figure you should be prepared if you're going to leave me every time I finish my last night shift." She pulled open the drawer and tossed the rest inside. "Now shut up and fuck me."

"Woman, you're getting bossy." He growled as he pulled her ass back against him.

"You don't like it?" Kristy turned her head and gave him the most seductive smile he'd ever seen.

"I fucking love it." Dean positioned his throbbing cock against her opening and moaned. He could feel her heat and he didn't think it was possible, but she was even wetter.

Dean pushed into her with one quick thrust making her gasp. He stopped when he was fully seated inside her and let her squirm for a few seconds as he kept her tightly pressed between him and the desk.

"I need you to move, Dean. Please." Kristy begged as her hips wiggled against him.

He slid his hand around her and cupped both of her firm breasts in his hand making sure he gave her sensitive nipples extra attention. He squeezed and pinched them while she begged him to move. Dean loved the feeling of being deep inside Kristy, but he was a man and could only hold himself for so long.

When he pulled out slowly, he gave each of her breasts a gentle squeeze, and slammed back into her, as he pinched her nipples. Then he would stop for a couple of seconds and repeat.

"Dean, faster." Kristy panted, and he gazed over her shoulder to see her finger pressed against her clit.

"That's it, Kitten. Play with that clit for me." He growled into her ear and increased his thrusts.

Dean released her breasts and grabbed her hips as he felt that familiar tingle in the tip of his dick that told him he was about to explode.

"Kitten, come for me. Now." Dean dropped his head into the nape of her neck as he pumped in and out. He felt her body tense, and she clenched around him.

"Dean," His name came out in a hiss as her body shivered and her pussy clamped around him.

He couldn't hold back and exploded after two more thrusts.

"Fuck, yeah." Dean pulled her tight against his body as his eyes rolled into his head.

How they ended up in his chair her still with her back to him and him still inside, he didn't know, but for a few minutes, he basked in the scent of her.

"Do you think anyone is trying to get into this part of the building?" Kristy chuckled, and the vibration had him slipping from her.

"I'm sure if someone were they would have called by now. Plus, Keith is in St. John's and the only other people that come into the office is Trunk and Hulk. Their both out of town." Dean turned her around on his lap and pressed his lips against hers.

"So you're saying anytime I want an office quickie all I have to do is make sure those three are out of town?" Kristy nipped on his lower lip.

"Oh yeah," Dean growled and covered her mouth with his.

"Hmm.... I wonder how many prank calls can I make before they catch on." Kristy giggled when Dean grabbed her by the ribs.

"Let me say two names. Sandy and Smash." Dean referred to both the computer analysts that worked for Newfoundland Security Services.

"Enough said. I guess I'll have to be satisfied with sex at your place." Kristy stood up and grabbed her dress from the floor.

"So love me and leave me, huh?" Dean pulled off the condom and knotted the end. He tucked himself back into his pants and refastened his clothes.

"Well, duh." Kristy wrapped the dress around her waist and tied it.

"I feel so used." Dean tucked his shirt into his jeans.

"Poor big boy." Kristy wrapped her arms around his neck and stretched up so she could kiss his cheek.

"You can use me anytime, Kitten." Dean pulled her into his arms and kissed her softly. It was a kiss that showed how much he loved her and cared for her.

"Mmmm… I'll remember that." Kristy whispered against his lips.

"Please do."

Dean gazed into her eyes. She took his breath away every time he did, and all the reasons he'd had for keeping his distance from her made no sense anymore. He loved her, and the one thing he knew for sure the rest of his life he'd spend loving Kristy O'Connor.

"What's that face?" Kristy smiled as she cupped his cheek in her hands.

"It's the only face I have." He chuckled.

"Smart ass. I mean you're looking at me like I'm about to vanish." Kristy met his eyes, and he swallowed hard.

"I… I don't know… sometimes…I think I don't deserve you and someone is going to pop out and rip you away from me." It was hard to finish the words because the lump in his throat had grown bigger at the thought of losing her.

"I'm not going anywhere and come on, who'd put up with my bossiness." She winked.

"You're right; nobody would ever be able to deal with that." Dean hugged her against his body and tucked her head under his chin. "I love you, Kitten. Never forget that."

"I love you too, Dean. Forever and Always."

Chapter 24

Kristy spent her three days off either at the pub with her family and friends, spending time with Dean or helping Hannah redecorate her new house.

Dean's sister bought a small house at the end of Hope Road. It was a little bungalow that had recently been put up for sale because the woman that lived there had moved into a nursing home. It was close to Keith's compound, and if any reporters were hanging around, Dean or Keith would send over one of the guys to deal with it.

They'd had a service for Peyton the week before Kristy started her new job and Dean had made sure it was a private service for family and close friends. Peyton was cremated and laid to rest with her brother in Jersey Harbour.

Hannah had also insisted that they have a service for Eric as well. Regardless of what he'd done or didn't do, he was still Ivan's brother and deserved a proper burial.

If it weren't for all the unanswered questions, things would be going pretty well. There was still no sign of Leah or Gemma, and

331

both had been all over the news reports as missing. Since they didn't find any remains in the rubble of Comfort Life Care, there was still a chance they were alive.

Sophia told Kristy that Leah's dad was beside himself over his daughter's disappearance. It was also the first time that Kristy had known Leah had a little boy. She'd felt so awful for the man and the little boy that she asked Sandy to find where they lived so she could check on them.

The idea didn't sit well with Dean, but Kristy still didn't believe that Leah had anything to do with Peyton's death or that she was involved in any of the events afterward.

When Hannah offered to go with Kristy, Dean almost lost his mind. He only agreed they could go if he went to meet the man as well. Kristy wanted to argue, but what choice did she have. Dean would only follow her anyway.

Kristy knocked on the quaint little two story in the downtown area of St. John's. It appeared to be an older home but upgraded. When she knocked the second time, she heard Dean grumble from behind her but before she could say anything Hannah turned and glared at him.

"Grow up," Hannah whispered.

The door opened, and a tall, muscular man stood in a firefighter's uniform. The only difference this guy wasn't a regular firefighter. Kristy had seen enough of them to know that this guy was probably a supervisor or possibly the Chief.

"I'm sorry, but I don't have time to listen to anything about your church." The man gave them a weak smile and started to close the door.

"I worked with Leah." Kristy practically shouted before the man closed the door.

He pulled the door slowly open and glanced over her head at Dean and then at Hannah. She could see the doubt in his eyes, but at least he didn't slam the door.

"Where?" He asked

"At Comfort Life Care." Kristy's words came out in a whisper.

"What's your name?" He still seemed skeptical.

"I'm Kristy O'Connor, and this is my boyfriend Dean Nash and his sister Hannah Humphrey." She introduced the two.

"I know who those two are. They've been on the news quite a bit. I'm sorry for your loss by the way." The man still didn't move from the doorway.

"Look, Mr. Sellers. Kristy wanted to come by to see if you and the little boy were okay." Dean sounded pissed. "No agenda. That's the way she is."

"She said you were very sweet." He glanced at Hannah for what seemed like the tenth time. "The girl that died, she was your daughter?"

"Yes. Leah was one of her nurses." Hannah folded her hands in front of her.

"She didn't hurt your daughter." His voice stayed calm, but his eyes flashed with anger.

"We don't believe she did." The way Dean spoke must have affected him because the man stepped back and motioned for them to come in.

"I won't be staying. I've got a couple of things I need to do but call me if you need something." Dean kissed Kristy's cheek and then Hannah.

"I promise they are safe with me." Mr. Sellers nodded.

"I don't doubt that." Dean turned and walked back to the truck.

The house inside was decorated modern and masculine with a hint of femininity in the kitchen. He led them into the kitchen and offered them something to drink.

"I'm sorry I only have coffee. Outside of that we only have water or juice. We're a coffee bunch here." He gave them a half smile and set the coffee pot to brew.

"Coffee is fine," Kristy said.

"My name is Garrett, by the way." He pulled three cups from the cupboard. "Liam is in school until two then he goes to daycare until five. The bus drops him off here."

"I didn't know Leah that long. I wasn't aware she had a child until recently." Kristy glanced at Hannah.

"Leah had a rough start to life." His voice was sad.

"She has done well though." Hannah's eyes hadn't left the back of the man, and Kristy couldn't blame her.

"Yes, she worked hard to get her life together." He filled the three cups and then brought them to the table. His big hands carried all three in one hand and cream and sugar in the other.

"She was in foster care for a while?" Kristy accepted the cup and poured in some milk.

"Yeah, I never knew about Leah until she showed up on my step at twenty-six with a one-year-old in her arms." He sat at the table and curled his hands around the cup.

"Her mother didn't tell you she was pregnant?" Hannah's voice cracked probably because the story was similar to her own.

"I met her at a bar when I was in my early twenties. We had a good time for a couple of weeks, but I went to the west coast of Newfoundland to become a firefighter." He raised his head, and Kristy saw the same eyes that Leah had. Green with flecks of gold.

"You took her in." Kristy took a sip of her coffee.

"She didn't want anything from me only to introduce herself and Liam. She'd started nursing school, and Liam's dad had flown the coop." He smiled. "That kid wrapped me around his finger the minute he smiled at me."

"Kids tend to do that." Hannah's sad smile broke Kristy's heart.

"I was never married and never expected to have any children of my own. I got this house after my parents died and I moved in. I didn't even use the second floor until Liam and Leah…" he dropped his head, and as if it was second nature to her, Hannah reached across the table and touched his arm.

"They'll find her." Hannah's voice cracked.

"That's what I keep telling myself." He lifted his head and wiped his face with his hands.

"For what it's worth, we don't think Leah had anything to do with what happened to Peyton or the fire." Kristy wanted to make sure he understood that.

"She wouldn't do anything to jeopardize Liam's well being," Hannah interjected.

"I know that, but the truth is something was up with her for the few weeks after your daughter died." He sighed. "She said it was that assistant to her boss."

"Gemma?" Kristy wanted to make sure, but she already knew the answer.

"Yeah, she gave Leah a hard time from the day my daughter started working there." Garrett sat back in the chair.

"Have the police talked to you?" Kristy asked.

"One guy dropped by and asked if I'd heard from her. He was by a couple of times, but now that I think about it, he never showed me his identification." Garrett glanced between Kristy and Hannah.

"Was he in uniform?" Hannah asked.

"No, he was dressed in a suit."

Kristy knew it was a long shot, but she sent a message to Sandy and asked her to send pictures of Eric and Trevor. While they waited, Garrett showed her pictures of Liam and Leah on his phone.

"I might not have known about her until she was an adult, but I love her and that little boy with all my heart. I don't know what I'll do if…" he stopped when Hannah grabbed his hand.

"You can't think that." Her eyes filled with tears because Hannah knew more than anyone how it felt to lose a child.

A few seconds later Kristy's phone dinged with a message from Sandy. She tapped the screen and brought up the picture of Eric Humphrey first.

"Is this the man that was here?" Kristy inwardly rolled her eyes because she sounded like some television detective.

"No, but I know who that guy is." He took the phone and stared at it for a moment.

"That's the guy that was shot on television a few weeks back." He glanced at Hannah. "Isn't he your late husband's brother?"

"Yes," Hannah dropped her head.

"What about this guy?" Kristy swiped to the picture of Trevor.

"No, but he was here once. He was in foster care with Leah, and she wasn't happy about him coming by here." He handed Kristy back the phone.

"Did you know why?" Kristy didn't know what she was doing, but something told her to keep probing.

"She said he was trouble but nothing more." He sighed.

"I'm sorry, I don't mean to throw questions at you, Mr. Sellers but I'm hoping something will help find Leah." Kristy smiled at him, and he returned it.

"Call me Garrett, please, and I understand. I wish I could help because the truth is I don't know how much longer Liam can take not knowing where his mommy is." He glanced at his watch.

"I hope we aren't keeping you." Kristy stood up.

"No, I find I'm watching time more and more every day." He stood up and offered them more coffee.

Hannah's phone vibrated, and she picked it up. Something in the way her facial expression changed to confusion had the hair on the back of Kristy's neck stand on end.

"Has he lost his mind." Hannah handed her the phone. It was a text from Dean.

Dean: Hannah, I need you to come to your house. I found something here that you need to see.

"How does he expect us to get there." Hannah sighed. "I really don't want to go back to that house."

"Let me see what he's up to." Kristy pulled out her phone.

Kristy: Hey, you do know we came to town with you, right? How are we supposed to get there? What's up?

She waited for a few seconds and then saw him typing a response. He seemed to be typing forever, and she groaned when the bubble disappeared and reappeared a few times.

"Is everything okay?" Garrett asked.

"Besides my brother forgetting he took our transportation and wanting us to go halfway across town to go to my old house, yep." Hannah smiled when Garrett chuckled.

"What the hell is he typing? A book?" Kristy was getting frustrated.

"If you need a drive, I can drop you off. Liam won't be home for a couple of hours." Garrett offered.

Dean: Kristy, I found the proof that Eric killed Ivan and Peyton. Get a cab if you have to. Just get here.

Kristy: Call John and my dad. Garrett is going to drive us over there. Don't touch anything.

Dean: I already called them. hurry.

Kristy, Hannah, and Garrett hurried outside and hopped in Garrett's car. He pulled out of the driveway and Hannah gave him directions to her house.

Something was bothering Kristy. It was as if something was tapping at the back of her head telling her to think. When they got stuck in traffic behind a construction detour, she touched her cousin's number.

"Hey, Kristy," John answered on the second ring.

"Did Dean call you?" She didn't have time for pleasantries.

"No," John chuckled. "Did he run away on you already?"

"He never called to tell you he found proof that Eric killed his brother and niece?" Kristy continued

"What? Shit? No." She could hear John running across a hard floor.

"I'll send you the texts he sent Hannah and me. Something's wrong. You need to get to that house." Her father said to listen to her gut, and she wasn't questioning it this time.

"Where are you?" She heard a car door and an engine starting.

"I'm on the way there with Hannah, and Leah's dad." Kristy pulled the phone away from her ear when John shouted.

"Are you out of your fucking mind? Do not go near that place, Kristy. I'm warning you." She heard the siren blaring, and he cursed.

"Don't worry about me." Kristy ended the call.

She read over the message Dean sent her over and over. When she finally saw it, she tapped Hannah on the shoulder and asked to see the text Dean sent her.

Again the same thing popped out.

"He called you Hannah," Kristy said a little louder than she probably should have.

"Isn't that her name?" Garrett glanced at Dean's sister and then at Kristy in the rearview mirror.

"Yeah, but he calls her Han not Hannah. He doesn't call me Kristy either." She held up her phone to Hannah.

"What does he call you?" Garrett seemed to be catching on.

"Kitten," Hannah and Kristy said together.

Garrett did a u-turn in the middle of Elizabeth Avenue and hit the gas again.

"What are you doing?" Kristy shouted as she grabbed on to the seat in front of her.

"I'm not taking you somewhere you could get hurt." Garrett turned again and headed toward Parade street.

"Please, Garrett. I need to go there now." Kristy pulled herself up close to the back of the seat.

"Garrett, it's my brother and the man she loves." Hannah seemed to want to go there as much as Kristy did now.

He stopped his car almost in front of the St. John's division of the Newfoundland Police Department. It was as if he was trying to choose whether he should listen to Hannah or not.

"My cousins are police officers. My dad is the Chief. I promise you I'll be safe." Kristy was begging.

"Kurt O'Connor's your father?" Garrett spun around in his seat.

"Yes," Kristy sighed.

"If anything happens to you he will beat me to death. I've known him for a long time." Garrett turned to Hannah. "You both stay in the car."

"Sure," Kristy shook the seat. "Please, let's go."

"I know I'm going to regret this, but God help me if it helps me find Leah it will be worth it." Garrett slammed on his gas and Kristy flew back in the seat.

Please, God let him be okay.

Chapter 25

Dean was pissed, and the fact that his head hurt like a son of a bitch wasn't helping his mood. His arms and legs were duct taped to a fucking chair, and the smell in the room made him gag.

He didn't have to look to know what the smell was. There was a decomposing body in the corner of the room covered with an old blanket. The only thing he could see was the feet. Small feet that told him he was probably looking at Leah's body.

Dean came to the house because of a text from a possible buyer for the house. Vince told him about three who were extremely interested, and Dean told Vince to have them call to set up a time to view the house.

When he walked inside, the smell hit him right away, but it was faint. At first, he thought it was a dead animal that had gotten inside and died. He sent a text to the buyer to rearrange the viewing. The guy returned a message to say he would reschedule.

Dean checked upstairs for the smell, but it wasn't as strong. As he made his way down to the basement something hit him from behind and the next thing he knew he was duct taped to a chair with a decaying body not twenty feet from him.

"Hey, whoever you are, when I get out of this chair, I'm going to beat you to death with it," Dean shouted and then gagged because he could actually taste the foul odor.

He heard feet shuffle around over his head and tried to move the chair, but it wouldn't budge. He glanced down at the floor and cursed because the bastard secured the chair to the floor.

Dean squirmed, pulled and tugged at his arms but as able-bodied, as he was the duct tape seemed to be stronger. He dropped his head back and roared in frustration.

He was thankful the girls hadn't come with him because that would have made things a hell of a lot worse. The shuffling again and then a whimper. He listened. Quiet. Dean almost convinced himself he imagined it when he heard a female cry out.

"Please, let me go back to my son." The female cried. "I promise I won't say anything."

Dean listened, but he didn't hear the other person, but the voice sounded familiar, and he let out a huge breath when he realized it was Leah. There was one problem. He couldn't do a thing to help.

"I did everything you asked. I helped you put her downstairs, and you said you would let me go." Leah's voice was frantic. "No. No, please. Don't bring me down there."

Dean saw the light from the top of the basement stairs, but he couldn't turn to see who was coming down. He was facing the wall, and he wasn't able to see that far.

"Please, don't do this." Leah's voice was more of a screech than a cry.

"Leave her alone," Dean shouted and rocked violently in the chair which was no use.

"Oh, I'm not going to hurt her. I'm going to leave her here to die. Just like you." The voice didn't sound familiar, but it did sound purposely altered so Dean wouldn't recognize it.

"Who the fuck are you?" Dean shouted.

"You open your mouth and tell him who I am I will make your last few days on this earth pure hell. Remember, I can get your kid like that." Dcan hcard fingers snapping and Leah whimper.

For a few minutes all he heard was the sound of Leah crying and what he figured was more duct tape securing Leah to something.

"Now I have company coming so do be quiet, or I'll have to use this on your mouths." Dean heard the clomp of the man stomping up the stairs and then the door close.

Dean lived in the house long enough to know exactly where the guy was when he walked around upstairs. He closed his eyes and tried to visualize each room above him and concentrate on the guy's feet stomping across the floor. He listened for the creaky click of the front door knob.

Leah softly sobbed while Dean listened to the movements of the unknown man upstairs. The man seemed to know the house well enough that he was not hurrying around.

"I'm sorry," Leah whispered.

"Shhh," Dean warned because for all he knew the guy was waiting for them to start talking.

Then he heard it. The familiar text tone of his phone and it was the one that he used for Kristy. Hopefully, this guy didn't pay attention to it but when Dean heard the sinister chuckle from him, he knew. The second ping had his heart racing and his blood about to boil.

The clomping continued toward the front door and then the click. Thank God for old houses. Dean waited, but it was completely quiet. The guy was gone, but Dean wasn't about to sit in the basement and let this guy hurt Kristy.

"Who is he?" Dean demanded.

"Vinnie, we were in foster care together." Leah's voice sounded defeated.

"What are you doing with him?" Dean lifted his wrists to stretch the tape, but it wasn't budging.

"He came to the center a few weeks before your niece. He said his grandmother was sick and he was looking for the best place to put her." Leah stopped.

"He called you?" Dean asked as he continued to listen for the return of who she called Vinnie.

"No, Gemma actually…" Leah burst into tears again, and her breath came in choppy pants.

"Calm down, Leah. I need you to stay calm so we can get out of this." Dean heard her take a few short, shaky breaths.

"He kept us locked up in his van until the police left here then he killed her. In front of me. He tossed her body into that corner. She was nothing to him." Leah took another couple of breaths and continued. "He was fooling around with Gemma, and he strangled her right in front of me."

"This guy's crazy, Leah but I need you to continue." Even if it didn't help, keeping her talking would give him information.

"The night that your niece died…. I'm sorry… I saw him leave the building. When I saw him, he said he'd been with Gemma in her office." Leah sniffed.

"Are you saying he wasn't?" Dean's body shook because he knew what she was about to say.

"Gemma and I fought that night because I told her I was going to report her for screwing him when his grandmother was a potential resident. She called me a liar and told me I was jealous of her and Vinnie. She also said he wasn't there that night, but I talked to him. He was there." Leah seemed a little calmer.

"Did Gemma confront him?"

"I called him and told him what happened. He said that she didn't want to get in trouble. He asked me to meet him the night of the fire, and he would give me the money to pay the debts my ex-boyfriend left me to pay. It's why I work so many hours. When I went to meet him, he said he had to come to his house to get the money." Leah sighed. "He said this was his house and when I got in here he wouldn't let me go."

"How did Gemma get here?" Dean had actually forgotten about the odor until he mentioned the woman's name.

"He called her and told her he wanted to talk to her. I was tied up down here, and they got into a huge fight. I heard her scream something about a video, and he wasn't going to dump her." Leah sighed. "I don't know what happened at that point. All I know a few minutes later I heard a thud, and he ran down here. He dragged me up the steps and out to the van in the back and chained me to a seat. A few minutes later he opened the van and dropped Gemma on the floor. I thought she was dead, but she woke up a little while later. I'll never forget the look in her eyes." Leah stopped when something upstairs crashed.

"Shhh..." Dean listened for a moment then he heard the voice that made his blood run cold.

"Dean, are you here?" Kristy shouted.

"I'm sure I told you to stay in the truck." Dean was sure that was Leah's father, and Leah's gasp confirmed it.

"Dad. Dad." Leah shouted.

"We're down in the basement." Dean shouted.

"Where's the basement, Hannah?" Kristy shouted, and he heard Hannah's muffled voice.

The heavy stomping of people running to the kitchen and the basement door opening was the best sound he'd heard in a long time.

"Fuck, Kristy, stay here," Garrett ordered, and Dean knew as a firefighter the man probably knew what the putrid smell was.

"I'm not staying here; Dean is downstairs." Dean rolled his eyes because that was his girl stubborn and beautiful.

"Now I see why your father said girls were hell." Garrett sounded pissed.

He was the first one down the basement stairs from the sound of the heavy footsteps. Leah cried louder when she saw him, and Dean heard him softly try to soothe her.

"Dean. Oh God, Dean, are you okay?" Kristy was touching his face, head, arms but he didn't care. "Your head is bleeding."

She ran her hands over part of his head, and he flinched from the sting. He hadn't realized he was hurt at all but chances were he probably tumbled down the stairs when Vinnie knocked him out.

"Get this shit off me." Dean yanked at his arms.

"Here, I've got a knife." Kristy stepped back while Garrett cut through the tape on Dean's arms and legs.

Kristy enveloped Leah in her arms while Garrett released Dean from the chair. When he stood first, he knew for sure he'd taken a tumble because his muscles ached. Nothing appeared broken, but he wasn't about to let Kristy realize he hurt all over. Dean stood up and the four of them made their way to the stairs.

As they made it to the main level, Hannah stood stiffly in the living room, but her face was hard to read. She looked scared but also a little pissed all at the same time.

"He's not hurt, Hannah and we found Leah… what the…" Kristy spun around when she heard the front door slam shut.

"So now we have the whole family together." Dean's head snapped toward the voice. The first thing he saw was his brother in law. Ivan Humphrey stood in the hallway of the house with a huge smile, and a gun pointed toward Hannah. Next to him was Vincent Day.

"What the fuck?" Dean started toward him, but Ivan held the gun higher and wiggled his finger over the trigger.

"Ah...ah...ah… Dean, my brother. Your sister over there is right in my good friend Vince's sites. You remember Vincent?" Ivan laughed and sauntered to the couch in the living room.

Dean's body shook with anger, but when Kristy nudged him, his attention focused on Hannah. Tears streamed down her cheeks, but she was perfectly still with her back to Ivan.

351

"You know if your father hadn't gone and gotten himself killed, none of this would have been necessary." Ivan crossed his long legs and rested the butt of the gun on his thigh.

"Why?" Hannah spat, but she didn't turn around to look at the man she'd loved for so many years and thought was dead.

"Why she askes?" Ivan laughed and glanced at Vince. "Why don't I start and then Vince can tell you his part."

"No matter what you tell us, nothing is terrible enough for what you've done." Dean pushed Kristy behind him and noticed Garrett do the same with Leah.

"Really, I loved your sister, but she betrayed me with my brother. Not once, but twice. Isn't that right, honey?" Ivan glanced toward Hannah.

"What is he talking about?" Dean asked his sister, but he kept his gaze focused on Ivan and the gun. Dean could see Garrett glare at Vince.

"Tell him, sweetheart. Tell him how you fucked my brother and got knocked up with a little boy that died. Karma number one. Then tell him how you fucked him again and had a little girl who drained both of us physically because of her illness."

Dean stared at his sister. Her eyes were closed, but tears streamed down her cheeks. Was Eric Peyton's father? There was no way.

"Tell him," Ivan shouted.

"I won't tell him that because it isn't true. Peyton is your daughter." Hannah spun around and shouted.

"Was, darling. She's dead remember. I do have a question for you. If she was my child, why did my brother show me proof he was her father?" He jumped to his feet and frantically swung around his arms.

"You're a liar." Hannah never raised her voice, but it was so high pitched at that moment, Dean was sure only dogs could hear her.

Ivan reached into his pocket and pulled out a sheet of paper. He tossed it on the coffee table in front of him and pointed at it. Hannah didn't move as he backed away and eased on to the couch.

"There's your proof." He growled.

Hannah moved slowly toward the table and snatched the paper from the table. After a few minutes, she dropped it on the table and with her head high walked toward Ivan.

"I don't care what that paper says, Peyton is your daughter. I slept with Eric once. The night you're talking about is the night he begged me to leave you for him. I was already pregnant with Peyton. That piece of paper is a fake, and there is no way he gave that to you." Hannah was dangerously close to Ivan, and it made Dean very nervous. Garrett didn't seem comfortable either.

"Oh well, you caught me. I figured I'd try to have this big dramatic climax but hey. I got tired of being second fiddle to all of

353

you. Hell, even Peyton was ahead of me in the lineup, and we all know she was as good as dead. Thanks to old Vince here, we got that part out of the way. So that you know, she went quickly." Ivan stood up, and Hannah backed away.

"How are you not dead?" Kristy poked her head around Dean to ask the same question Dean had running around in his brain.

"Well, Ms. O'Connor, yes I do know who you are. Thanks to dirty cops who love money, and drugs that make people sleep through anything, it was possible." Ivan pointed to Vince, and he glanced out through the window next to the front door. When he moved back, he shook his head.

"You paid off cops to botch the investigation." Dean kept his tone calm but inside he was raging.

"Well the ones that you spoke with weren't police, and right now they're on a beach somewhere in South America. The real police I paid off were ready to retire and didn't mind fucking over the department in exchange for a hefty retirement package from Decker Corp." Ivan grinned. "You see anyone can be bought, isn't that right, Leah."

Dean and Garrett turned, but Leah shook her head as she trembled next to Kristy. It was apparent she had no idea what she'd been involved with until it was too late.

"I never agreed to hurt people or kill people. I only agreed to help Vinnie get his grandmother into Comfort Life Care. Pull a few strings for an old friend." Leah continued to shake her head. "I never would have agreed to this."

"Isn't your son soon going to be dropped off by the daycare?" Vince or Vinnie laughed. Dean wasn't sure what to call him. Except for a dead man when Dean got a chance.

"You keep your fucking hands off my grandson, or I swear I'll kill you with my bare hands." Garrett's voice vibrated through the room like an earthquake.

"I'm sure you could, Mr. Sellers but you see we're holding the weapons and I can shoot your daughter a lot faster than you can get to me." Vince chuckled.

"How could you do this? I loved you?" Hannah sounded off, and Dean wasn't sure what his sister was about to do.

"You never loved me, Hannah. You loved the idea of me. The idea of the man you thought I was. I spent years putting a plan into motion where I could take this company places. You see, Vince here lost his father when your family took his house and business away. He killed himself, and Vince ended up in foster care with Leah and Trevor." Ivan stood up and walked toward the door.

"Trevor, why did he kill Eric?" Dean wasn't letting them get away so easily.

"Can I fill them in?" Vince laughed.

"Sure," Ivan leaned against the wall.

"I kept my dear friend Trevor supplied with all the drugs he would ever want. He did me a favor, and I gave him what he wanted." Vince sighed. "It was too bad he snapped and figured it all out, or he thought he did. He actually thought Eric was behind all this."

"You two are crazy." Kristy stepped out from behind Dean.

"Kitten, no." Dean tried to step in front of her, but she moved.

"Just so you know, the police, the real ones who can't be bought are on their way and this…" Kristy held up her phone. "Has both of your recorded confessions on it."

"She's cute." Ivan laughed.

"It's almost a shame we have to kill her." Vince moved toward her with a sinister scowl on his face.

"Don't fucking touch her." Dean stepped in front of her.

"I wasn't going to, but I don't know. With that body, I might have to get a taste of that before I blow off her pretty little head." Vince moved closer.

"I don't think you could actually get it up because you know that big gun says you might be overcompensating for something." Kristy pointed to the gun.

Dean stared at Kristy. He couldn't believe what she said to a man with a gun pointed at her.

"You see, real men don't need guns to please a lady." Kristy linked her arm into Dean's, and he noticed her hand. She'd typed a message and turned so he could read it.

Kristy: I'll get him close enough for you to grab the gun. James texted me. He has Ivan as soon as you grab this guy.

Dean had to scan the text twice, and he had no idea how Vince didn't see the screen from how close he stood, but when he glanced down at Kristy, her blouse was open enough that her bra was visible.

Fuck.

"What's wrong, Vincent? That is your name, right?" Kristy traced her finger between her breasts. She put on a brave front, but Dean could feel her tremble as Vince stepped closer.

"I go by Vince or Vinnie." He growled.

"Okay, so am I right or are you going to show me what kind of gun you have hidden away?" Kristy's purr was pissing Dean off because he could see the arousal in Vince's eyes as the man scanned Kristy's body.

"We don't have time for this shit, Vince." Ivan groaned from the front door.

"I'm taking the fucking time," Vince reached for Kristy and the hand he held the gun with dropped enough for Dean to spin around and grab it while pushing Kristy out of the guy's reach. In the same second, Garrett lunged for Hannah and covered her with his body. Kristy had Leah on the floor behind Dean.

Vince's scream muted a loud pop, the crash of a window breaking and the thud of Ivan hitting the floor. Probably because Dean snapped the man's arm like a twig the second he got the chance.

"Don't move," Nick shouted as Vince rocked back and forth on the floor holding his arm.

"He broke my arm." Vince cried.

"I'll fucking break your other one if you don't stop moving." Nick rolled his eyes.

Dean didn't know what happened after that because he was on the floor pulling Kristy into his arms. She clung to him and as brave as she was he could hear the heavy sobs from her as she tucked her head into his neck.

Dean saw Leah clinging to her father. He scanned the room for his sister and wasn't surprised to see Hannah stood over her dead husband.

"Hannah, I need you to step back from him," John spoke calmly as he pulled her back from Ivan.

"I loved you. How could you do this?" Hannah collapsed into John's arms, but before he got a chance to pick her up, Garrett was next to him helping her to the couch.

All though they didn't have all the answers, it was over. Hannah had definitely not killed Ivan, Vince confessed to killing Peyton and starting the fire. The only problem was, would Hannah be able to deal with the betrayal as well as the loss.

Something told Dean his sister was about to find out how strong of a person she really was.

Chapter 26

Kristy probably annoyed everyone in the waiting room with her constant pacing back and forth. They'd taken Dean, Leah, and Hannah to the hospital emergency room as a precaution when everyone was finally permitted to leave the house.

Garrett sent one of the other firefighters to be there for when the bus dropped his grandson off. According to him, Liam loved all his brothers at the fire department. The little boy adored the attention, and since none of the guys had kids of their own, he was spoiled by them.

She knew she'd taken a crazy risk with what she'd done earlier, but since Dean stood in front of her, Kristy took a chance and sent a text to James. Before she'd received an answer, she made sure her phone didn't vibrate at any incoming text or calls.

James sent a text back, and the plan got put in place. It took her a while to build up the courage to lure Vince closer, and she didn't think it would work.

Kristy was about to ask the nurse for the fourth time how much longer it would be before she could see Hannah or Dean but as she glanced down the corridor, all she saw was two arms that pulled her into a familiar embrace.

"Jesus Christ, Kristy. What on earth were you thinking?" Her father held her against him, but she didn't care. His hug was comforting and safe like when she was a little girl.

"I needed to get to him, Dad. I knew he was in danger." Kristy rested her cheek against his chest and closed her eyes. "I just knew."

"Is he okay?" Kristy opened her eyes to see her mother next to them.

"He seemed to be, but he had a cut on his head, and I think he may have hurt his wrist. I'm waiting for someone to tell me something." Kristy lifted her head and glared at the nurse behind the desk.

"Honey, you know what it is to be on the other side of that counter. Have patience." Her mother reminded her of how often people snapped at her for news on their loved ones.

"I know, but it's not just Dean. Hannah seemed in a fog." Of course, she knew shock had set in. It was a wonder Hannah was even able to walk out of the house considering what she'd found out.

"I'll see what I can find out." Her uncle Sean squeezed by them. Kristy hadn't seen the rest of the family behind her parents, but as she leaned around her father's arm, she saw the most beautiful sight.

Uncles, Aunts, Cousins, sisters, and friends all gathered inside the waiting room. It was the most beautiful thing she ever saw and her eyes filled with tears. She shouldn't have been surprised because her family and friends were the best in the world.

"I heard they found your friend and the other girl," Jess said as Kristy sat next to her.

"Yeah, Leah seemed okay physically but Gemma… she didn't make it." Kristy glanced at Garrett on the other side of the room. He sat with his elbows on his knees and his hands folded in front of him. His head dropped as if he was in the middle of a prayer.

"I can't believe you walked right into that." Isabelle wrapped her arm around Kristy's shoulder.

"All I could think about was that he was hurt or … I had to get to him." Kristy sighed. "That's Leah's dad." She nodded toward Garrett.

"Do you need anything, Mr. Sellers?" Jess asked.

"I want to make sure Leah and the rest are okay, but thanks and please call me Garrett." He smiled at Kristy.

"Leah's tough, Garrett. Look who her dad is." Kristy winked.

Kristy began pacing again because she was sure they'd been there ten hours at least but according to her cousin Mike, it had only been a little over an hour.

"Why is it hospitals make time move so fucking slow?" Keith arrived and looked about ready to kill.

Before anyone answered his question, a face popped into the waiting room. Adam Carter was an emergency room doctor, but Kristy's family was very familiar with him. He always seemed to be there when one of the family ended up in the emergency room.

"Well if it isn't my favorite family." He sauntered in.

"Unless you have news about Bull, Hannah or Leah, we don't want to see you." Ian chuckled.

"I guess I'm in luck then. Mr. Sellers, Leah is going to be fine. She's a little dehydrated and malnourished, but there are no physical injuries other than a few bruises. Physically she'll be good, but she will probably need to see someone to deal with the trauma over what happened." Adam shook Garrett's hand.

"Are they keeping her here?" Garrett stood up, and Kristy almost laughed when Isabelle gasped.

For a man over fifty, he was hot and built like a man half his age. Her sisters noticed, and so did some of her cousins' wives. Even her mother took a double take.

"I'd feel better if we kept her overnight to make sure she's fully hydrated and eating. She did say her captor didn't feed her very much." Adam tried to sound calm, but Kristy knew him well enough to know that he was angry about Leah's treatment by Vince.

"Thank you, Doctor. Can I go see her?" Garrett was practically out the door before Adam finished saying yes.

"What about Bull and Hannah?" Keith snapped.

"I see your sparkling personality hasn't changed." Adam laughed.

"No, it hasn't." Keith growled but there was a slight twitch in the corner of his mouth.

"I was told to give all the information to Kristy," Adam turned to her.

"Is Dean okay?" Kristy couldn't control the panic in her voice.

"He'll be fine. He's not too happy about needing a cast on his wrist or having stitches put in the cut on his head but other than that he's peachy." Adam winked at her.

"Thank God. What about Hannah?" Kristy glanced around the room then back to Adam.

"She does have a couple of bruised ribs, but I was told it was because someone threw her to the floor to keep her from being hurt by flying glass." Adam sighed before he continued. "We did have to sedate her because she began crying hysterically and tried to leave. I understand she's had quite a shock, and I don't need to know all the details, but I talked to her brother and got the short version."

Adam sat on the chair next to Isabelle and crossed his ankles in front of him. It was as if he was trying to find the right words to explain what Hannah was about to face.

"Is she going to come out of this?" Her father asked before Kristy could.

"I think she will. From what I understand she's got lots of help since she got in with one of the best families in the province." Adam grinned. "But she's going to need a lot of therapy, and if she's as strong as I believe she is, I think she'll come through this even stronger."

"Thanks so much, Adam." Kristy practically jumped on the man to hug him.

"Hey, I didn't do anything. Your family keeps me busy." He stood up. "You can go see Dean now. Hannah's resting, but if you feel the need to check on her, she's in the next room to Dean. He forcefully insisted on that." Adam chuckled as he said a few words to almost everyone as he made his way out of the waiting room.

Kristy pulled the curtain back to enter the room. Dean appeared to be asleep. A white bandage about six inches long was secured to the top of his head and there was a black fiberglass cast on his right hand. He was shirtless and covered to his thigh with a thin white sheet. It was the most beautiful thing she'd ever seen in her life. He was alive and that's all that mattered.

Kristy quietly moved to the side of his bed and pulled back the curtain between him and Hannah. Dean's sister looked peaceful in her sedated state.

"She's going to get through this." Kristy snapped her head back to Dean when she heard his voice.

"I'm sorry I didn't want to wake you." Kristy grabbed his uninjured hand and sat on the edge of the bed.

"You didn't. I was trying to get my head around all this and it gave me a huge headache." Dean smiled. "Or maybe it was the crack to the head."

"I'm so happy you're not badly hurt." Kristy pulled his hand up to her lips and kissed his fingers.

"You can't keep a bull down with a knock on the head." He winked.

"It's not funny, but it sure is fucked up." Kristy sighed.

"I can't believe that cocksucker. He made us all believe that Eric was the danger and it was him all along." Dean closed his eyes.

"He's gone, and Vince is in custody. The rest we can figure out when we go back home." Kristy held the palm of his hand against her cheek.

"You put yourself in danger." Dean growled.

"I had to get to you." She met his intense gaze.

"You could have been taken away from me." It was when she saw the tear escape the corner of his eye. "I wouldn't have survived that."

"I wasn't, and I'm okay." Kristy wiped the tear from the side of his face.

"Kitten, I love you so fucking much but don't ever put yourself in a situation like that ever, ever again." Dean cupped the back of her head and pulled her down so that her face was an inch from his. "Never." He covered her mouth with his and kissed her as if he needed her to breathe.

She didn't care because the truth was, she wouldn't have survived if something happened to him. She knew that. Dean was her life, her breath, and her heart.

"I love you too." Kristy whispered as she pulled back from the kiss and pressed her forehead against his.

Chapter 27

Kurt stood next to Dean as they watched through the window into the interrogation room where John and Steve questioned Vincent Day.

Kristy's father was a little more than pissed when he found out which officers helped Ivan fake his own death. They'd had his ashes exhumed but discovered that they weren't human remains at all.

Dean watched a furious Vince slouched over in the chair staring at the window where Dean and Kurt stood. Of course, he couldn't see them, but it sure looked as if he could see Dean through the glass.

"So, here's what we know, Vincent old pal." Steve sat in the chair across from Vince and propped his ankle upon his knee.

"Vince or Vinnie and I'm not your fucking pal." He snapped.

"Fine, Vinnie." Steve sighed. "The confession on the recording we got from Ms. O'Connor tells us you killed Peyton Humphrey and set fire to Comfort Life Care. That's two pretty big charges there. Technically, we don't need anything else, but maybe we can swing a deal if you tell us everything."

"Fuck you," Vince growled.

"I don't swing on that side of the fence, but I'm sure you can find someone your type inside." Steve pulled his phone out of his pocket and started to scroll through something on the screen.

"Since you declined a lawyer, there's nothing more to do here. Steve lets call it a night and call the Crown Attorney. This is open and shut." John sauntered across the floor to the door leading out of the room.

"Your right, he'll be put in with all the crazies anyway. I'm sure when they find out he killed a terminally ill woman for shits and giggles, they'll want to discuss that with him." Steve stood up and stretched his arms over his head.

Dean knew they were trying to freak Vince out. The man had never been in jail before or even arrested, so the fact that they were giving him the worst case that could happen was amusing.

He watched Vince wince as he moved the arm Dean had broken, and it made Dean grin. The fucker deserved a lot worse but knowing he hurt helped.

"His broken arm seems pretty painful." Kurt chuckled.

"Good," Dean watched Steve pick up the file folder from the table and follow John to the exit.

Before the door was open, Vince was on his feet.

"Wait," He shouted.

"Why?" Steve sighed.

"If I tell you everything can you keep me out of the general population?" Vince asked with an unsteady voice.

"I can see what the Crown Attorney can do, but I can't make promises. You're still entitled to a lawyer if you want one." Steve didn't move toward the table yet.

"I don't want a fucking lawyer. I'll tell you everything." Vince plopped down in the chair and closed his eyes.

"I guess it's going to be a long night after all." John sighed and moved back to the other chair next to Steve.

"Start from the beginning." Steve turned the camera toward Vince and sat back.

"I met Ivan when he came to our foster home with his brother Eric. I thought he was a good guy, but I found out pretty fast he didn't give a shit about Eric or his family." Vince dropped his head and then lifted it up again.

"How old were you?" John asked.

"It was my second month in foster care; I just turned fourteen. I was pissed with the Decker family because it was their fault that my father killed himself. Aiden Decker took everything

370

from my father and didn't even blink an eye." Vince's eyes were cold, and his face was tight with anger.

"Eric was Trevor's big brother, and I got stuck with Ivan. He was pretty good for a while until I found out that he was married to that Decker bitch." Vince shifted in his chair.

"You mean, Hannah Decker-Humphrey." Dean figured Steve was trying to make sure they had all the names proper in the video.

"Yes." Vince snapped.

"What happened after that?" John asked.

"Nothing at first but we went on some camping trip with the Big Brothers program, and those idiots came along. Trevor was having a woman crisis and went to Eric for some advice. It's how I found out all about that first kid and how he felt about his brother's wife. I thought when I mentioned it to Ivan he'd be pissed and there would be a huge fight. Instead, he smiled and said he knew the whole thing. He was the one that told Eric that he was the dead kid's father and they'd had a huge fight about it." Vince smiled for the first time since they'd been in the room.

"He already had a plan in motion?" John asked.

"Oh yeah, and when I told him who my father was it made him even happier. He's the one that put me through college and made sure I had a job when I needed it. Ivan planned this for years to get back at his brother and his wife, but I was fully willing to help him." Vince sat back in the chair and rested his injured arm on his stomach.

"You didn't suspect anything with Ivan?" Kurt turned to Dean.

"No, and neither did Hannah." How could he be such an idiot to trust Ivan so much and not see what a bastard his brother-in-law truly was.

"I guess you were a kid when he entered your life." Kurt looked back into the room.

"I wasn't even born when Hannah started dating, Ivan. Hell, I didn't even know she'd been with Eric. All I ever knew was Ivan's brother was crazy." Dean said after a few minutes. Ivan had been around his entire life.

Dean had been their ring bearer when they got married, and Ivan had given him a money clip with his name on it. He'd been so happy with it that he asked his father for some money to put into it. He used it for years.

"The old man's death kind of fucked things up. Ivan had been trying to set him up to have him arrested for illegal business activities. There was even a motorcycle club that thought they were backed by Aiden Decker. Technically they were, but the bastard didn't know it." Vince continued, and Dean's anger grew.

"So, Ivan hatched a new plan. He met with a couple of cops taking kickbacks from the motorcycle club and offered them one hell of a deal to help him pull off his own murder." Vince laughed. "It was truly a beautiful plan, and it went off without a hitch. Well, until Trevor lost his fucking mind."

"I can't listen to this anymore." Dean stepped back from the window.

"Look, Bull, know this, the assholes that Ivan hired to help him are already in custody, and they won't be well liked in prison. That guy in there is going away for a long time. He's not going to go to trial; he knows he's fucked. Your family's name will be cleared, and your niece will get the justice she deserves." Kurt dropped his hands on Dean's shoulders.

"Thanks, Kurt. I appreciate this so much, and so does Hannah. I feel like a fucking idiot." Dean sighed.

"Don't blame yourself." Kurt squeezed Dean's shoulder. "How's Hannah doing?"

"Better than I expected. She's meeting with a therapist a couple of times a week but now and then I see her drift off into a daze and she starts to shake." Dean hated to see her so broken.

"She could have PTSD. I've seen men and women go through things and seem fine but then something triggers them, and they lose it." Kurt shook his head. "I have some of those times myself. When you're involved with law enforcement as long as I have, you see a lot of pretty bad shit."

"Kristy said the same thing." Dean peered through the window to see a smug grin on Vince's face, and it was everything he had not to stomp into the room and beat it off him.

Dean left the station relieved it was all over. Also, surprised Kurt didn't beat him to death for putting Kristy in danger. Not that he didn't want to kick his own ass for that very thing. The one thing Dean knew for sure was he loved her more than his own life and he was going to marry that woman.

****

Dean never spent a Christmas day with the O'Connor family but the day before Christmas Eve was the first big party of the holiday season. Newfoundlanders called it Tibb's Eve, and it was apparently the best day to get drunk.

This year was special for him though because not only did he get to put his own ornament on the Family tree set up in Sean and Kathleen's home but Hannah received one from Kristy to put on the tree as well.

Then there was their memory tree. It was a separate tree set up in the pub where the family placed memory ornaments for those who passed away.

Nanny Betty walked into the pub with a box under her arm, and her ever-present black purse hung over her arm. She made a straight line for Hannah and Dean as soon as she removed her coat.

"Dere ye two are. Now, ya know it's time ta put da memory ornaments on da tree. Since yer part a' da family and ya have loved ones who are happy in heaven, I got ya some ta put on da tree." She carefully placed the box on the table in front of Dean.

Hannah smiled up at him and shook her head. She was in awe of Kristy's family and how welcoming they were to her. It still shocked him sometimes.

"Okay, dere are six in here. Kristy gave me da names." She pulled out the first one and handed it to Dean.

He looked at the name and smiled. His mother's name was etched on the shiny gold heart with mom on the back. Dean swallowed the lump in his throat as Hannah's eyes filled with tears.

"Thank you, Nan." Dean kissed the older woman's cheek.

"No need ta tank me. Now dis is da next one." She pulled out a silver drum with their father's name on one side and Dad on the back. She placed it in front of Hannah on the table.

One by one she pulled out four more. One was a red ball with Hannah's baby boy's name, then there was an angel with Peyton's name. The other two were plain silver balls, but Nanny Betty almost seemed worried to hand them over.

"Dese two I struggled wit. I know one a dem was a bad man and da udder ya taut was bad until recently. I got dem done anyway 'cause bad or not, dey were family. Do wat ya want wit dem." She

375

kissed Hannah's cheek and then Dean. "To heal yerself, sometimes ya need ta forgive."

She scurried away, and Dean watched Hannah pick up one of the ornaments. She cupped it in her hands as a tear ran down her cheek.

"He was the one I should have married." She held the bulb carefully.

"Eric wasn't the monster we thought he was and he did truly love you." Dean picked up the other bulb and read the name to Hannah. "Ivan, a child of God that lost his way."

"She really knows how to make someone not seem so bad." Hannah smiled.

"We don't have to hang his." Dean offered.

"I want to. Regardless of his actions, we did have good times, and hopefully, on the other side he'll find peace." Hannah stood up and gathered the six ornaments in her hands. Dean followed and helped her hang them on the memory tree.

"Look who finally got here." Kristy wrapped her arms around Dean's waist and nodded toward the door.

Garrett, Leah, and little Liam walked in full of smiles and shaking off the snow. Dean didn't miss how Garrett's eyes immediately found Hannah. He had a feeling about those two, but he knew it would be a while before his sister was ready for a relationship.

Still, she and Garrett had become fast friends, and he was glad of that. Garrett was a good man with a huge heart.

"It's about time ya got here." Nanny Betty hustled over and grabbed their coats. "Kids are over dere, and if ya want a hot toddy, da pub is da place ta be."

Liam ran directly to where all the O'Connor kids and their friends gathered around a table full of cookies and cake. Leah made her way toward them with Garrett behind her.

"This place is amazing." Leah hugged Kristy and Hannah, and Dean kissed her on the cheek.

"This family is amazing." Hannah waved her hand around the restaurant.

"They certainly are." Garrett nodded.

Dean enjoyed the gathering but the one person he needed to speak with privately was constantly surrounded by one person or another. He needed to talk to him and fast before he made any plans.

"You look about ready to jump out of your skin." Keith laughed as he sat next to Dean in the booth.

"I've been trying to talk to Kurt alone since I got here but he's hard to get away from everyone." Dean watched Alice and Cora tug Kurt into the pub.

"Uncle Kurt, come here for a sec," Keith shouted.

"Really?" Dean shook his head.

"Sometimes the obvious works." Keith laughed.

Kurt plopped down in the seat across from Dean and Keith. He had a grin from ear to ear, and Dean figured he was about to wipe that off his face if the man didn't want to hear what Dean was about to ask.

"Bull needs to chat with ya." Keith winked at his uncle and left them alone.

"What's up?" Kurt slouched back in the seat.

"I need to talk to you, but I don't want anyone to hear our conversation." Dean winced when Kurt's brow furrowed.

"Outside," he pointed to the entrance and grabbed his jacket from the coat check.

"Where are you two going?" Alice asked as she grabbed a glass from behind the counter.

"I need to show Bull my early Christmas gift." Kurt winked at his wife and practically pushed Dean through the front door.

Outside the snow slowed but most vehicles in the lot were snow covered. Kurt stomped down the stairs and made his way to the truck on the other side of the lot.

Dean followed and felt like a boy about to be sent to bed without supper. Kurt looked pissed, and Dean prayed it wasn't because Kurt figured out what Dean was about to ask. If that was the case, it wasn't going to end the way he wanted.

"Should you really be getting behind the wheel of the truck?" Dean asked as he jumped into the passenger side.

"Do you see me driving?" Kurt snapped. "If Alice asks, you think my new remote starter is great. Now what the fuck is going on?" Kurt turned in the seat and glared at Dean

"It's nothing bad, honestly. At least I don't think it's bad but …" Dean swallowed hard.

"Spit it out for Christ's sake," Kurt growled.

"I want to ask Kristy to marry me." Dean practically shouted.

Kurt's expression didn't change as he stared at Dean. It was so quiet inside the truck that Dean could hear the snow clicking against the windshield. He wanted to look away from Kurt's glare, but his father always said never be the first to break a staring contest.

"She's my baby girl." Kurt finally said.

"I know." Dean nodded.

"She's the one that's most like her mother." Kurt didn't look away.

"That's a good thing. Alice is an amazing lady." Dean smiled but lost it when Kurt didn't react.

Kurt didn't speak for a few seconds, but he did turn in the seat and looked away from Dean. He stared through the windshield and Dean did the same.

"You better not break her heart." Kurt's voice was barely above a whisper.

"I won't." Dean glanced toward Kurt the man was like a stone.

"I'll kick your fucking ass if you do." Kurt tapped his fingers on the steering wheel.

"I wouldn't expect you not to." Dean did his best not to smile, but it was hard.

"I knew she'd be the first one." Kurt shifted in the seat. "Let's see the ring and don't say you don't have it because I really will kick your ass."

Dean reached into his pocket and pulled out the small red velvet box he'd been carrying around for the last week. He placed it in Kurt's hand and watched him open the box.

"A red heart." Kurt took the ring out of the box.

"Yeah," Dean didn't want to give Kristy the traditional diamond ring. It had to be as special as she was.

"When are you going to ask her?" Kurt put the ring back in the box and gave it back to Dean.

"When do you think I should?" Dean valued Kurt's opinions, and Kurt knew his daughters very well.

"Her birthday is February fifteenth." Kurt smiled for the first time since they walked out of Jack's Place.

"You don't think I should ask her over Christmas?" Dean had initially planned to ask her on Christmas morning.

"No, I think you should ask her on her birthday at one minute past midnight." Kurt smiled.

"Why would you be so specific?" Dean chuckled.

"Because that was the time she was born." Kurt smiled. "We thought she would be a Valentine's baby, but she didn't quite make it."

"That's perfect. Especially since the house will be finished by the first week of February." Dean's plan might have changed, but it became a whole lot better.

"Are you going to do it alone or with the family?" Kurt asked as they walked back across the lot.

"Do you want to be there, Kurt?" Dean laughed.

"I was there the day she was born. You're fucking right I do but if you'd rather not I understand." Dean didn't mind because he wanted the whole world to know he wanted to marry her.

"Then you'll be there with the family." Dean wrapped his arm around Kurt's shoulder.

"I hope she doesn't say no." Kurt laughed.

Dean hoped so too.

Chapter 28

Kristy stood on the front porch of Isabelle's house and watched the snow fall to the ground. Christmas had come and gone, and it was the start of a brand-new year.

She wrapped the blanket tighter around her shoulders and watched the swirl of flakes blow across the steps. She sipped on the glass of wine and listened to the gabbing women inside her sister's house.

They finally got the chance to have a full-on girl's night. A crowd that included, her sisters, cousin, cousin-in-laws, friends, mothers, and even her grandmother.

Kristy was in pure heaven and for the first time in her life she was content in everything. Well, almost.

She looked at the house next to Isabelle's and sighed. The new owners were almost finished with the inside, but the entire outside looked terrific. They'd even installed a porch swing that was currently not there, but she'd seen Matt install the hooks just before Christmas.

"It looks really good doesn't it." Kristy turned around to see Billie huddled under a blanket and a hat pulled down over her ears.

"It does." Kristy tried not to sound disappointed.

"How's that hot man of yours doing?" Billie linked into Kristy's arm and smiled.

"Dean is amazing." Kristy couldn't help the sigh.

"I remember that feeling." Billie laughed. "Hell, I still have that feeling."

"I would hope, so you're not even married a year." Kristy laughed.

"I know. Can I tell you a secret?" Billie whispered.

"Of course." Kristy loved secrets.

"You can't tell anyone because Mike has this thing about telling everyone at the family dinner, but I'm busting to tell someone." Billie wiggled back and forth.

"I promise my lips are sealed." Kristy grinned as Billie glanced behind her to make sure nobody had come outside.

"I'm pregnant," Billie whispered.

"Oh my god!" Kristy whispered and hugged her.

"I know. We're so happy." Billie laughed.

"I guess that's why you volunteered to be the Driver of drunks tonight." Kristy laughed.

"Yeah,"

Their private conversation was interrupted when Sandy shouted for them to come in and watch Nanny Betty drink a shot of tequila.

"Jesus, she's trying to kill my grandmother." Kristy laughed as they moved back into the house.

She stopped for a moment and took one long look at the house again. With a heavy sigh, she closed the door not only to her sister's house but to ever owning the home of her dreams.

Kristy spent the next few weeks avoiding any talk about her birthday. She was about to turn thirty in two days, and for some reason, it bothered her. She didn't know why but the last thing she wanted to do was celebrate becoming the big three o as her sister kept reminding her.

When she stepped out of the shower and wrapped herself in a huge fluffy towel, she stared at herself in the mirror. She didn't look thirty or feel it. Well maybe sometimes after a hard shift but she didn't feel any different than she did at twenty.

So why did the thought of it make her stomach turn? She was happy with her life. She had a man that she loved, and he loved her. She loved her new job. She had a great family and awesome friends. She didn't want to turn thirty. It was so stupid.

"Kitten, I need to show you something tomorrow night." Dean pulled her out of her funk as he wrapped his arms around her waist.

"Can you show me now?" Kristy turned into his embrace and rubbed her hands against his bare chest.

"I can show you something now, but I still need to show you something tomorrow." Dean grinned.

"Please don't tell me were going to that Valentine's dinner at Isabelle's restaurant." Kristy groaned.

"Okay, I might as well tell you because you're going to be a big baby about this. Your family has a surprise party planned for your birthday. They are having it tomorrow because they said you'd expect it on your birthday. Please don't tell them I told you." Dean sighed.

"I warned them," Kristy growled.

"I'm supposed to blindfold you and bring you to the restaurant by midnight." Dean laughed.

"Midnight on Valentine's day? They think that wouldn't give me a hint." Kristy sighed and faked a cough. "I think I'm coming down with the flu."

"Cute but I'm not getting in trouble with your mother and sisters, Kitten. They scare me almost as much as your grandmother does." Dean started to back out of the bathroom pulling her with him. "But if you agree to be a good girl I'll fuck you until you do that eye roll thing and then make you scream."

He really knew how to get her motor running and get her to do something she didn't want to do.

"Fine but you have to do that tomorrow night too." Kristy dropped the towel she had around her and followed the man she loved.

Chapter 29

Dean was seriously about to throw up. He'd glanced at his watch so often that he was sure it stopped a couple of times. Kristy dressed for her surprise party which wasn't a birthday party at all, but she didn't know that.

She looked sexy as hell with her red dress that clung to her every curve. It didn't reveal a lot of skin because of the long sleeves and high neckline but it fit her like a glove. The sight of her walking out of his room with that dress and high heeled boots that went up to just below her knee had him painfully hard.

"You look incredible, Kitten." Dean grinned when she narrowed her eyes and glared at him.

"Thank you, but I'd rather stay here and forget this whole charade." Kristy huffed as she plopped down on the couch.

"Come on, they love you and want to celebrate that." Dean grabbed her hands and pulled her to her feet. "Besides, think about what I have to do when we get home."

"We could do that now." She ran her fingernail down the center of his chest where his shirt was open.

"I love you, Kitten but I'm not pissing off any of the O'Connor women." Dean chuckled.

"I'm an O'Connor woman, and you're pissing me off." She pouted.

"Yeah, but I can change that pout by doing this." Dean pulled her against him and dropped his head so he could suck her earlobe into his mouth.

"Not fair." Kristy gasped.

Before he could do anything else the alarm on his phone beeped. It was time to put his plan into action. He pulled the blindfold out of his pocket and held it up.

"Do we have to do that?" She groaned.

"If you're good I'll let you use it on me later," Dean whispered into her ear.

He managed to guide her out to his truck and get her inside with no issues. Well, except for her mumbling about her sisters and family but other than that he was on the right track.

He'd spent two days timing himself on how long it would take him to get to the house and walk her up to the door of their new home. Jess had been a stand in the day before as he went through it one last time. He had a total of five minutes to get to the house and two minutes to walk her up to the front porch. Once he removed the blindfold and showed her the house, his alarm would sound to let him know it was time to propose.

God, let this work.

Right on time, he pulled up into the driveway of their new home. Kristy grumbled as he helped her out of the truck and walked her up to the front of the house.

"Where are you taking me?" Kristy sighed.

"Just a couple more steps." He chuckled

Dean watched Jess and Isabelle through the enormous windows at the front of the house. They pulled the drapes closed so Kristy didn't see them until he was ready to propose.

"Okay, are you ready?" Dean whispered in her ear and turned her, so she faced the beach.

"Yes, honey." He smiled at her sarcasm.

Dean untied the blindfold and dropped it to the ground. In his hand, he had the key to the front door, and he dangled it in front of her face.

"What? Where are we?" Kristy spun around once and then again.

"Surprise." Dean shook the key in front of her.

"What?" Kristy took the key, but he didn't miss her shaking hand.

"This house is ours." Dean smiled down at her.

"Ours? Seriously?" Kristy stared at him as if he didn't speak English.

"Yes," He cupped her cheek in his hand. "I bought it for you."

"It's ours? Really?" She couldn't look more beautiful if she tried because her smile lit up the whole front of the house.

"If you want it." Dean laughed.

"Are you kidding me right now? Of course, I want it and …" Kristy stopped when the alarm on his phone beeped, and he pushed the doorbell. His cue to let her family know to open the drapes.

Kristy jumped back when both windows filled with the grinning faces of her family, but when she turned to Dean, he'd already dropped to his knee.

"Oh my God." Kristy covered her mouth with both her hands.

"Kitten, I bought this house for you because I wanted to see that face light up the way it just did. You came into my life, and for the longest time I kept you at a distance but when I finally let you close you climbed inside this scarred up heart and healed it. I bought this place because I love you more than I could ever tell you and the only thing that would make it better is if we could live here together with you as my wife." Dean pulled out the box and opened it.

"Kristy Elizabeth O'Connor, would you make me the happiest man in the world and say you'll be my wife? Kitten, will you marry me?"

"Oh my God." Kristy gasped and wrapped her arms around his neck. "Oh my God."

"You keep saying that, but I need you to say a little three letter word." Dean chuckled when she started to stomp her feet but didn't release the hold she had around his neck.

"Oh my God, Yes. Of course, yes. Are you serious?" Kristy pulled back and stared into his eyes.

"I'm very serious." Dean stood up and took her hand in his.

"Really? Oh my God, Really?" Kristy shook as he slipped the ring on her finger.

"Really. Happy Birthday, Kitten. It's not my birthday, but you gave me the most amazing present any man could ask for." Dean pulled her into his arms and pressed his lips against hers.

The sound of cheering from inside the house slowly disappeared as she melted into his kiss. The love of an incredible woman healed Dean Nash. His love. His heart. His Kitten.

Epilogue

Nick O'Connor was glad his shift was over. He'd spent his entire shift pouring over coroner reports for the latest of the murdered women found outside the city limits. His brother had put him and three other officers on a task force to find out who the hell killed these women.

The worst part was the four victims had similar features to not only his cousins and his brother Keith's wife but a striking resemblance to the cute waitress that worked at his aunt Alice's pub. The one that made his heart race every time he saw her.

His shift was over, and now he was ready to brighten up his day with a visit to Jack's Place. He wasn't even going to go home to change because he might miss a few minutes with her. She didn't know he was there to see her because Lora Norris wasn't even aware he existed beyond one of her boss's annoying nephews. No, she wasn't like most women he met.

Nick wasn't arrogant, but he never had trouble with the ladies. He knew he was attractive and used it to his advantage. It's why his older brothers called him and the youngest of the O'Connor brothers man whores. Nick preferred to call it enjoying the beauty that was a woman.

He pulled open the heavy oak door to the pub and sighed at the cool air-conditioned foyer. June in Newfoundland was usually not hot, but over the last three days, it had hit in the mid-twenties. Of course, that would seem cold to some people, but since the temperature was in Celsius, it was pretty hot. It also didn't help when you had to walk up to a crime scene with a body that had been there at least a few days.

Nick pulled off his cap and walked into the quaint pub that was divided into a cozy eat in restaurant and an old-fashioned Irish pub. His aunt and uncle owned it, but his aunt Alice ran Jack's pub. His uncle Kurt was the chief of police and a silent owner. The only input he had was the name. Jack's Place. Named after Jack O'Connor Nick's grandfather. He'd passed away years before but was still missed by everyone.

Nick scanned the bar, but to his disappointment, she wasn't there. Instead his cousin Kristy poured a cup of coffee for her fiancé who sat on the other side of the bar.

"I don't want a huge wedding, Kitten." Dean 'Bull' Nash groaned as she set the cup down in front of him.

"Honey, my family is a huge wedding." Kristy smiled.

"Your cousins have got to stop procreating." He chuckled.

"I think it's going to stop with Mike." Nick laughed as he straddled the stool next to the big bald man.

"It may, but your brother's wives are popping them out like Pez dispensers." Dean laughed.

"Oh, stop it." Kristy shook her head.

"Tell them to stop. Let's add this up, John has a boy, and girl and they are trying again. So that's two and possibly more on the way. James and Marina have three boys and found out they are having a girl. That's six. Ian and Sandy have three girls and a boy, but they may be done with having kids. That's what?" Dean glanced at Nick.

"Ten," Nick answered as he counted along.

"Right, ten. Keith and Emily have a boy and another boy on the way. That's twelve. Right?" Dean glanced at Nick again.

"Yep." Nick chuckled.

"Mike and Billie's baby girl isn't due for another couple of weeks, and they are already talking about having more before the baby is too old." Dean rolled his eyes. "Too old, the kid is not born yet. Anyway, that's thirteen."

"What's your point, Dean?" Kristy rested her elbows on the bar and leaned closer to her fiancé.

"My point is…" Dean stopped when Kristy ran one of her hands over the top of his bald head. "It's …."

"It's what?" Kristy grinned.

Nick felt a little uncomfortable with the way his cousin gazed at her soon to be husband. It was as if he was witnessing some kind of intimate secret.

"Kitten, stop doing that." The clenched teeth gave it away.

"Yeah, I'm gonna go over and get my own coffee. I don't want to know what that is all about." Nick pointed to Dean's head, and Kristy laughed as he hopped off the stool.

"I'll meet you at home, Kitten. Be prepared when you get there." Dean growled as Nick walked behind the bar.

He'd poured himself a cup of steaming coffee and was about to exit behind the bar when he was almost bowled over by the curvy auburn haired with the big sapphire blue eyes.

Lora.

About the Author

What does someone say to describe themselves? You could start with giving what others say about you. Scratch that. It doesn't really matter what others think about you. It matters what you think of yourself. So here we go.

First of all, I'm a wife and mother. I'm also a grandmother. That alone would fulfil any woman's life and to be honest it does. But.....

I'm also a writer. Someone who loves to tell stories of love, suspense, heartache and of course happily ever after. For most of my life, I've written those stories for myself. A type of therapy, I suppose. I love the characters I create. They become part of who I am because there's part of me in them.

So.... Now that you know this about me. I hope when you read my books, you fall in love with them.

You should also know that I'm a Newfoundlander. What is that you ask? Well we're a proud people who live on an island, off the east coast of Canada. Some people believe Canada ends with Nova Scotia. It doesn't. If you keep going east, there is a beautiful island full of amazing people and magnificent scenery. That is where my stories are set because let's face it. The best stories always come from the places you know and love.

If there is anything else you would like to know about me. Ask me!

Coming Soon

O'Connor Brothers

Book 6

Available May 30, 2018

Can he keep her out of the clutches

Of a sadistic stalker?

O'Connor Brother Series

Read about the sexy O'Connor Brothers

In Books 1, 2, 3, 4, and 5

Available on

Amazon and

Kindle Unlimited.

Also Available

Dangerous Therapy

Book 1

Officer John O'Connor is giving up on life after a terrible accident. His family are at their wits end when he refuses any kind of therapy. The only thing keeping him sane is his dreams of a beautiful woman he pulled in for a traffic violation months before.

Physical Therapist Stephanie Kelly is healing from a broken heart. When she is hired by Nightingale's personal care and physical therapy, she's ecstatic, but she's shocked when her boss asks her to take on a new patient. Shocked because the patient is her boss's nephew and he's not exactly keen on therapy. He's also the cop who's been heating up her dreams.

As Stephanie helps John get back on his feet, they grow closer, but someone is out to hurt Stephanie, or worse. After multiple attempts on her life, John's family tries to figure out who's after the woman he loves and stop them before it's too late.

Dangerous Abduction

Book 2

Widower James O'Connor has been fighting his growing attraction to his brother's sister-in-law for four long years, but when someone breaks into her home, destroying everything she owns, James takes her and her young son into his home. The break-in wasn't random. Marina and her son are in danger, and James swears to protect them, but can he keep them safe?

Marina Kelly dedicates her life to caring for her sweet little boy, Danny. Since she broke free from her abusive husband, she's sworn off men, but when James O'Connor keeps entering her thoughts and her dreams, it takes everything she has to keep her feelings hidden. Now, her sister and parents are out of the province, and she's in danger, Marina has no choice but to accept James's help and try to hide her attraction and growing feelings.

The attraction between them impossible to resist. Only her ex's family secret may tear it all apart. Can Marina and James unravel the family's hidden mystery without losing each other?

Dangerous Secrets

Book 3

Ian O'Connor has everything going for him. He's got the O'Connor drop dead good looks, an incredible body and to top it off he's a doctor. Why wouldn't anyone want the man but none of that was the reason Sandy Churchill was head over heels in love with the man. After he had stood her up for their first official date, she was weary of taking another chance. When she ends up in the hospital because she turned her back on a criminal determined to get away from her, Ian admits that he loves her and wants another chance. A secret from his past throws Sandy into a tailspin, but she has a secret that she's hiding from everyone.

Ian's on cloud nine when he finally takes a leap of faith and tells the woman he's loved for four years how he feels and wants a chance to make up for his screw up. They have two weeks of bliss, but a murder and secrets come back to haunt him. Sandy's reaction tells him there's another reason why she's avoiding him. She's hiding something, but he has no idea what and to make matters worse there's danger coming from her past that could hurt the people he loves the most.

Dangerous Beauty

Book 4

When you come from a privileged family, you're expected to follow a particular path in life. Unless you're Emily Bradshaw. Defying her father, Emily turned down a full scholarship to Dalhousie University. Instead, she followed her dream and opened her own salon in the small town of Hopedale with her friend. She's happy. Then her mother vanishes. Her father receives threatening messages and hires Newfoundland Security Services to protect his children. Emily doesn't like the idea, especially when the man that walks into her salon dressed in a black leather jacket makes her weak in the knees. Emily knows she's in danger but not the kind her father is worried about.

Keith O'Connor isn't expecting his newest security job to be anything out of the ordinary. Then he walks into Snippy Gals, a beauty salon in Hopedale. Keith gets the shock of his life when an auburn haired beauty turns to face him. Emily is defiant, sassy, and her sexy curves have him in a complete spin. Fighting his feelings for her becomes almost impossible, but when Emily's mother is found, a family secret is revealed turning Emily's life upside down. Can Keith help her cope and keep her out of the clutches of a vengeful stranger?

Dangerous Silence

Book 5

Mike O'Connor's reputation earned him the name Mr. Homerun, but after two hours with Billie, he's ready to change all that. There's one problem. She disappears before he can find out her last name.

Billie Carter had little choice but to leave when she received a desperate text from her friend. Peggy and her daughter have no family, both are deaf, and Billie wants to protect them from an abusive man.

When Peggy is brutally murdered, Billie is determined to protect Chloe. Like a dream come true, Mike walks through her door to help. They soon learn that the little girl is not the only one in danger, and it may take more than Mike to keep them safe.

Rhonda Brewer

Keep up to date on all things new.

Follow me on

Facebook

Twitter

Instagram

Sign up for my newsletter and never miss another release!

http://www.rhondabrewerauthor.com/talk-to-me

www.ingramcontent.com/pod-product-compliance
Lightning Source LLC
Chambersburg PA
CBHW070350260626
47161CB00001B/90